"WHAT IS

"While the nation slept, t................... a fortress down there."

"What are you talking about?"

Kurtzman flashed a photo of the complex onto the big-screen monitor. The aerial shot showed a main building built into a cliff overlooking the Pacific Ocean, with a harbor and breakwaters providing moorage for small ships. The landward side of the cliff had a heliport on top and several outbuildings on the flat, with a road leading inland. The faint trace of a fence could be seen enclosing it like a military base.

"Our man's peaceful little Sunflash research center isn't quite as peaceful as he wants us to believe. When I made the recon satellite run over Baja, I did it in the full spectra mode—EMR, MAD, radar."

"And?"

"And I came up with the same kind of reading I would have gotten cruising over a North Korean nuke plant."

DON PENDLETON'S

MACK BOLAN.

STONY MAN™

SUNFLASH

A GOLD EAGLE BOOK FROM

WORLDWIDE.

TORONTO • NEW YORK • LONDON
AMSTERDAM • PARIS • SYDNEY • HAMBURG
STOCKHOLM • ATHENS • TOKYO • MILAN
MADRID • WARSAW • BUDAPEST • AUCKLAND

If you purchased this book without a cover you should be aware that this book is stolen property. It was reported as "unsold and destroyed" to the publisher, and neither the author nor the publisher has received any payment for this "stripped book."

First edition May 1996

ISBN 0-373-61906-5

Special thanks and acknowledgment to
Michael Kasner for his contribution to this work.

SUNFLASH

Copyright © 1996 by Worldwide Library.

All rights reserved. Except for use in any review, the reproduction or utilization of this work in whole or in part in any form by any electronic, mechanical or other means, now known or hereafter invented, including xerography, photocopying and recording, or in any information storage or retrieval system, is forbidden without the written permission of the publisher, Worldwide Library, 225 Duncan Mill Road, Don Mills, Ontario, Canada M3B 3K9.

All characters in this book have no existence outside the imagination of the author and have no relation whatsoever to anyone bearing the same name or names. They are not even distantly inspired by any individual known or unknown to the author, and all incidents are pure invention.

® and TM are trademarks of Harlequin Enterprises Limited. Trademarks indicated with ® are registered in the United States Patent and Trademark Office, the Canadian Trade Marks Office and in other countries.

Printed in U.S.A.

SUNFLASH

CHAPTER ONE

San Luis Obispo, California

A bright flash winked into the California sunshine. The traffic had started to back up already along the freeways, but in a little while the southbound 101 freeway out of San Luis Obispo looked as if a giant mechanical serpent had taken it over. Even though the afternoon sun was still high in the unusually clear sky, the lead cars all had their lights turned on and were traveling at a high rate of speed, even for a Southern California highway.

Traffic reporter Greg Winters squirmed in his seat for a better look. Since the helicopter was flying against the flow of traffic, he couldn't tell exactly how fast the traffic was moving, but the lead cars looked as if they were doing at least a hundred miles per hour.

Winters had just finished delivering the latest update on traffic to commuters when both he and the pilot had noticed a bright flash that had seemed to come from the direction of the Diablo Canyon nuclear power plant to the north. Now he reached out to turn up the volume on the channel scanner he kept tuned to the police radio frequencies. An excited voice was saying something about an explosion right outside the power plant.

"You were right," Winters said to the pilot as he reached for the frequency knobs of his radio console. "There's been some kind of an explosion at Diablo Canyon."

"And look what's going on down there now!" the man added. "I can't believe it!"

Directly ahead of the pack of racing vehicles on this freeway version of the Indy 500, a battered old pickup with half a dozen Mexican laborers in the back and a hand-painted landscaping-service sign painted on the driver's door motored along as fast as its smoking engine could propel it, a little over fifty miles per hour. The lead cars were on it in an instant and the landscaping truck didn't have a chance. It was still traveling at about fifty miles per hour when the first car drove right into it at over a hundred.

From the air, it looked as if the pickup had been hit by an artillery shell. Bodies flew everywhere and the truck spun sideways before tipping over onto its right side. The car that had hit the pickup also spun out, blocking yet another of the three southbound lanes. Two of the following cars tried to swerve to evade the mess and sideswiped each other before T-boning the wreckage of the truck.

Ten seconds later a dozen more vehicles drove directly into the tangled carnage. By then the back markers had started slamming on their brakes, but it was too late. Winters watched in utter astonishment as car after car slammed into the tangle of twisted metal and bleeding bodies. When it was all over, more than a hundred cars, vans and light trucks were piled on top of one another in what had to be the world's biggest multimedia performance sculpture.

Then a trickle of gasoline from a ruptured fuel tank flowed past a hot exhaust pipe. At first the flame was almost invisible as it followed the trickle back to the fuel tank of a crumpled station wagon. In seconds the rear of the vehicle was ablaze.

Inside the station wagon, a woman frantically tried to get her three children out of their car seats. Once they were free, though, she found that she couldn't open any of the car's doors. Other vehicles had slammed against hers, blocking the doors. She had just started to scream when the fire finally heated the gas in the tank hot enough to create an explosive vapor. Her screams were lost in the booming detonation, and the fireball blew flaming scraps of the car over a wide area.

Since many of the crashed vehicles had damaged gas tanks, the flames found good homes. One after another, cars, vans and trucks started blowing up in a blazing chain reaction. Within seconds, an area the size of a suburban city block was an inferno.

Winters was shocked but kept his wits. Along with his traffic reporter job as the KSTZ Guy in the Sky, he also worked as a TV stringer dogging the police channels for fast-breaking stories to pass on to San Luis's Channel 2. He even carried a mini-cam with a microwave hookup in the chopper so he could transmit directly to their news studio.

Getting back on the radio to the TV station, Winters told them that he was onto one of the biggest stories of the decade and could provide film. When they gave their okay, he stayed over the scene of the spectacular freeway pileup. Alternately broadcasting the video scenes to the TV station and a description of the carnage to the radio station, he had a stunned audience all to himself until the major networks showed up an hour later.

THE CALIFORNIA Highway Patrol investigation of the San Luis Obispo freeway disaster quickly revealed that most of the drivers on the road that afternoon had been fleeing what they thought had been a catastrophic reactor accident at the Diablo Canyon nuclear power plant. Most of them had heard the news on local radio stations and had immediately phoned their friends and family. Quickly packing their valuables into their vehicles, they fled south to escape the nuclear nightmare.

When the investigators questioned the radio stations, they learned that anonymous calls had alerted them to the incident. Some of the stations had tried to act responsibly and had attempted to contact the power station for an official confirmation. But when there had been no answer, they had taken that for a confirmation and had sounded the alert to their listeners.

Since years of hysterical antinuclear power propaganda aimed at Diablo Canyon had preconditioned the residents of San Luis Obispo to panic, they did. After the southbound lanes of Highway 101 had been blocked by the pileup, they took their panic to the secondary roads and highways. It was estimated that more than a quarter of a million people fled San Luis, and all they had fled was a power outage caused by a transmission station fire.

There had been no reactor accident at the Diablo Canyon nuclear power plant, no radiation leak and no danger. The death toll from the freeway pileup and related road accidents, however, had been heavy. More than forty people died, many of them burned to death on the freeway, and hundreds more had been injured. It was the worst highway disaster in the history of the automobile.

Pasadena, California

In HIS TOWN HOUSE east of L.A., Benson Rondell watched the TV coverage of the San Luis Obispo freeway disaster with intense interest. Though he was into his mid-forties, Rondell had the firm body of a younger man and the even tan of a native Californian. The body and tan, however, were more the result of working out at his club than the sign of an athletic life-style. But in California, appearance was the only thing that mattered, particularly for a man who was running for governor on an independent ticket.

Benson Rondell, the owner and CEO of Sunflash, a high-tech solar engineering company, was a quickly rising gubernatorial hopeful and had been in the headlines a lot recently. Much of the coverage had been because of his pro-environment independent political campaign. Much more, though, had been written several months earlier when he had taken advantage of the North American Free Trade Agreement with Mexico and had relocated his solar-power research and manufacturing facilities from Pasadena to Baja California.

From there, he had announced that he intended to provide cheap solar-generated electrical power to a growing Mexican economy, and to Southern California, as well. His noble intentions had been lauded by antinuclear and environmental groups all over the nation, particularly by the Green Earth Movement, which his firm sponsored.

While Rondell's high-profile business activities were all out in the open, his activities within the radical environmental organization were more difficult to pin down. He was known to be a major contributor to the cause, but many corporations gave generously to the organization. It was both a legitimate tax write-off and even better PR for a firm to be seen supporting such a worthy cause. The fact that he had personally taken the organization from a nonentity and had turned it into the most well known, and vocal, organization of its kind was completely unknown.

Unlike most of the other environmental groups, the Green Earthers had sprung from infancy to adulthood in one big leap. And, since their formation a year and a half earlier, they had pushed the older, more established organizations off center stage of the environmental movement. Not since Earth First! had there been an environmental group that had raised so much controversy. With their green-shirt uniforms, military-style organization and high profile, the Green Earthers had quickly attracted an army of foot soldiers who were all too ready to take on all comers in the name of the holy crusade of saving the planet.

While a popular conservative talk-show host had labeled them eco-Nazi extremists and made accurate comparisons between the Green Shirts and the early Nazi Brown Shirts, the liberal establishment loved them. They were seen as pure warriors fighting the good fight against the evils of big business and entrenched special-interest groups who were bent on raping and pillaging a defenseless Mother Earth in the name of the capitalistic god of profit.

While Rondell's ties to the radical Green Earth Movement were shrouded in secrecy, so were his rumored ties to certain moneyed men in Mexico and Latin America who were connected to the drug trade.

Prior to the announcement of his move to Baja California, Sunflash had been a small company constantly fighting the battle of the bottom line and trying to survive on grants and handouts. This was the normal situation for any company in the alternative-technology business. Environmentalism didn't translate into business success. Somehow, though, he had been able to raise enough money to go into a joint venture with Mexican interests and build his new multimillion-dollar complex in Baja. Though it hadn't been established, the natural assumption was that drug money was behind his Mexican operations.

For a businessman and would-be politician who was always in the news, there were more questions than there were answers about Benson Rondell. But, try as they could, no investigative reporter had been able to come up with answers to those many questions. And those who tried too hard had had accidents.

Rondell turned to his private assistant, who was watching the news with him in his suite. "This kind of reminds me of the Hindenburg disaster, don't you think?"

"It sure does," the assistant replied, grinning. "But I think there'll be a bigger body count. Your plan worked beautifully. I would have never thought that a few phone calls would make such a difference."

Rondell allowed himself the pleasure of a wide grin. "It did work out rather well, didn't it?"

"What's next?"

"It's time to up the ante," Rondell replied. "Call downstairs and have them get the car ready. I need to fly south."

"Yes, sir."

As the assistant went to call his driver, Rondell grinned again as the TV cameras zoomed in on the still-burning twisted wreckage. It was all coming

together nicely. Before the year was out, he would
be one of the wealthiest men in the world, as well as
the governor of California. From there, it would be
only a short trip to the White House and ultimate
power for him and his backers.

CHAPTER TWO

San Francisco

Richard Jordan felt the sweat break out on his face as he waited in the air-conditioned lobby of the Pacific Coast Power building in the downtown San Francisco business district. This was a heck of a time to be having an antiperspirant failure. As the ads said, "Never let them see you sweat." But the adman who penned that copy had never had to face what he was facing today. Even with the double-paned glass panels in the lobby, he could hear the demonstrators chanting outside in the plaza in front of the PCP tower.

It was estimated that more than thirty thousand antinuclear demonstrators were out there, and they had been there for two days. If Jordan had had his way, he would have called the governor and requested the National Guard be moved in to clear the plaza. The Pacific Coast Power board of directors, however, had ordered him to go out and make a speech, answer their questions about the Diablo Canyon incident.

He would much rather have jabbed his eyes out with a sharp stick than say a single word to that clamoring crowd, but his job as PCP's president and CEO was on the line with both the directors and the stockholders. Their PCP stock had crashed to an all-time low, and they were looking for someone to blame it on. If he couldn't get this thing turned around fast, he'd be reaching for the rip cord of his golden parachute before the week was out.

"Gardener?" Jordan checked the time and looked around for his executive assistant.

"Sir?"

"Let's get this dog-and-pony show on the road."

"Yes, sir."

When Gardener unlocked the doors, the rage of the crowd was almost like a physical blow to Jordan's body. Steeling himself, the CEO calmly walked out to the podium that had been set up between the police barricades and the safety of the PCP tower. Since the podium was at the top of the steps leading up to the building, he had the high ground. But this time it didn't matter.

As Jordan stood there with the roar washing over him, he saw the Green Shirt agitators moving through the crowd, speaking to the men and women wearing the green arm bands of their organization.

After speaking to each one of them, a section of the crowd fell almost silent.

Spontaneous demonstration my ass, Jordan thought. If San Francisco's ultraliberal mayor hadn't caved in to the antinuclear radicals, the rally wouldn't be happening. It was one-hundred-percent organized and run by the Green Earth Movement. And from what he was seeing, they had taken a page from the organizational manual of Nazi Germany.

It took more than ten minutes before the crowd calmed down enough for him to be heard even with the PA set turned up full blast. "Ladies and gentlemen," he started, but he was forced to pause to let the jeering subside.

With the attention of the police focused on the mob in the streets, no one had given any thought to clearing the rooftops of the buildings surrounding the PCP plaza. These were peace-loving environmentalists, not political demonstrators, and no one had thought of snipers.

"He's about to start," one of the two men on the rooftop across from the plaza said in Spanish.

The other man didn't answer as he opened the long case at his side, revealing a custom-made 7.62 mm NATO bolt-action rifle with an eight-power scope mounted on it. Taking the rifle from the case, he worked the bolt to chamber a round and put the stock to his shoulder.

Focusing the scope on Jordan's upper left chest, he dialed in the range until he could almost see the weave of the man's dark suit. Then he took a deep breath and slowly exhaled. In the middle of letting his air out, he stroked the trigger of the sniper rifle. The sound of the rifle's report was lost in the noise of the crowd.

The 7.62 mm round took Jordan high in the left center of his chest and drilled clean through his heart. A look of total shock and amazement came over his face as he clawed at his chest. Pitching forward, he tumbled down the marble steps toward the police barricades. For a long moment, the crowd was stunned when they saw him fall. Then, with a roar like the breaking of a dam, they surged forward.

The police line was overwhelmed, and several policemen were trampled in the rush to be the first to reach the representative of the hated corporation. The winner started to kick Jordan's twitching body. He was soon joined by a woman who screamed as she aimed a kick at the dead man's crotch. In a flash, dozens more men and women swarmed over him. Pulling the decorative rocks from the flower beds, they hammered them down on the body in a frenzy of violence.

The CNN cameraman recording the scene went to his knees and started to vomit, his camera lying unattended at his side. This was one videotape that would never be seen on TV.

When police reinforcements were finally able to move the crowd back behind the smashed barricades, there was little left of Richard Jordan. A clear blood trail down the steps ended in a man-size red smear.

With Jordan a broken rag doll, the demonstrators no longer had a place to show their "rightful" concern for the environment. So they took their anger to the street. They smashed the windows of the cars parked around the plaza, then proceeded to the windows of the expensive storefronts, reaching in to help themselves. No one saw who started the first fire.

When it was all over, the rioters had caused more than fifty million dollars' worth of damage.

THAT NIGHT, the mayor of San Francisco, who had given her personal approval for the antinuclear demonstration held a news conference for all of the local television stations. Sandra Carlisle appeared to be shaken as she read from a prepared statement that a state of emergency had been proclaimed in the downtown district, and that a dawn-to-dusk curfew would be in effect until further notice.

When she ended her short announcement, she paused and looked directly into the cameras. "Effective immediately," she said, her voice quavering, "I am resigning my office as your mayor. I urge all San Franciscans to stay calm until order has been restored. Thank you."

A chorus of voices shouting questions followed the mayor as she stepped down from the podium and hurried for the exit. "Madam Mayor," one man shouted, "does this mean that you will not be running for the Senate?"

"What about the Green Earthers?" another shouted. "Do you still think that they are pointing out the path for the nation's future?"

The mayor shuddered at that question but didn't answer. For the rest of her life, the speech she had made not long ago at a huge outdoor rally of the Green Earth Movement would haunt her.

In that televised speech, she had lauded the group as the last hope for the preservation of the United States. She had praised them, saying that they were like angels sent to protect the earth from the ravages of greedy business interests.

Before Jordan's death, she had been a shoo-in for one of California's Senate seats in the upcoming election. And her name had been mentioned as a potential vice presidential running mate in the next national election. Now, however, she would be lucky to get elected dogcatcher in Death Valley. If, of course, she could stay out of prison.

Since she had personally approved the Green Earth Movement's demonstration permit over the objections of the city council, she was being held personally responsible for the riot, the deaths and the damage to the businesses in the city's center. The liability was in the tens of millions, and the city council had washed their hands of her.

Several lawsuits had already been filed against her, and several more were rumored to be in the works. The ex-mayor was beginning to see that divorcing her wealthy lawyer husband and embarking on a political career had been the worst mistake of her life.

Baja California

IN HIS STRATEGIC PLANNING room in the upper floor of the mountaintop Sunflash compound, Benson Rondell watched the TV news reports of the mayor's news conference. The existence of the room was known to only a select few of the Sunflash project, as was the true nature of Rondell's venture. To most of the employees of the corporation, the Baja complex was the solar-energy research project it appeared to be on the surface.

As was stated in the company's stock brochures, the people of the entire world would benefit from their ground-breaking researches into practical, nonpolluting, solar-power sources. This goal fit into the New Age, all-people-are-brothers view of the world most of the first- and second-level American employees of the corporation had. Those people would have been horrified to know the true purpose of Rondell's work.

The carefully selected Sunflash cadre, however, had personal goals other than those that might benefit humanity. They followed Rondell for their own gain. If the Sunflash project was even half as successful as Rondell and his backers planned, they would all be important and wealthy people in the new scheme of things.

In a *Fortune* article, Benson Rondell had once been touted as being *the* shaker and mover in the power industry. He was a brilliant engineer and designer, and eagerly sought after in the most prominent social circles. He also tried taking shortcuts when he ran low on cash to finance his dreams of practical solar-power generation. The opportunity presented itself for him to make a large cocaine buy at wholesale prices. By retailing it to his friends and social set, he had made enough to tide him over the rough spot.

However, he'd been nailed for running coke— though not by the DEA. It was the Cali cartel. He had inadvertently made the mistake of moving into one of their most lucrative territories without making the proper arrangements with them. As an amateur, it was an easy mistake to have made. The cartel, however, didn't usually give a man a break for ignorance. Unless, of course, it was a break across both knees.

BENSON RONDELL had been relaxing in his Pasadena town house when someone knocked on his door. When he opened it, two gunmen pushed their way in, weapons drawn, overpowered him and hustled him to the leather couch in his living room.

A man wearing an expensive pin-striped banker's suit entered the room and took a chair across the coffee table from Rondell. "My name is Hector Garcia, Mr. Rondell, and I represent certain business interests who are unhappy with your recent venture into, shall I say, wholesale activities. They see that as being their own monopoly and they do not like to see outsiders cutting into their profits."

Rondell knew that he was in deep trouble, but he also knew that the only possible way out was to keep his cool. "Is there anything I can do to make amends for my error?"

Looking around the town house, Garcia could see that Rondell had been born to what the Mexican had worked so long and so hard for the Cali cartel to acquire, but he wasn't envious. Garcia knew that Rondell had to be chastised for his indiscretion, but he didn't want to be hasty with this gringo businessman. It was true that he would make a good example of what happened to anyone who thought he could get away with moving in on Cali territory, but that lesson could be demonstrated with any of a number of street scum. He thought that Rondell would be more useful to the cartel alive.

Garcia had been at a planning session in Cali a few weeks earlier when the board of directors had been discussing new ways to invest the money that kept streaming into their coffers. They were talking about more money than the legitimate annual national budget of Colombia. If the right place could be found to invest this money the old-fashioned way, it could be put to work making even more. Particularly if the investment was in something that made the cartel even more powerful. Something like controlling the world's electrical power supply.

The cartel representative opened his briefcase, spread a stack of papers in front of him and chose a page. "It says here, Mr. Rondell, that your company, Sunflash, barely managed to keep from going into the red last year. It also says that you are planning an ambitious expansion program but do not have the capital to finance it."

He looked up from the page. "My principals have a proposal you might be interested in."

This was giving a new meaning to the term hostile takeover, but Rondell knew that he had no choice but to listen and go along with the proposal, whatever it was. The alternative was that Sunflash would go to his heirs.

WHEN THE FINAL arrangements had been made, Rondell had the financing he needed to expand his operation and the cartel had the beginning of a plan that would make them the virtual rulers of a good portion of the world. It was Rondell, however, who suggested bringing in an outside group to do the dirty work that would be necessary along the way.

A week before, he had been at a social function where he had been approached by a young woman soliciting corporate donations for a new environmental group that called itself the Green Earth Movement. She had been a good choice for a solicitor to approach him, as he had always been partial to well-endowed redheads with green eyes, and she was passionate about her topic. When she offered to come to his room and discuss the organization with him, he hadn't been able to refuse. And he had certainly not been able to refuse her blatant come-ons as soon as he had closed the door.

It was sometime later, while lying in the rumpled, sweaty sheets of his suite, that it came to him. Any group that was willing to send their women out to whore for corporate contributions was ripe for a takeover by someone who knew how to properly run an organization.

Plus, the kind of zeal and passion the woman had shown toward her cause could be put to much better use. If she was willing to prostitute herself in the name of saving the world, she would probably do anything she was told would further her cause.

"I want to meet your group's leaders," he told her. "I have an idea that might be beneficial to both of us."

CHAPTER THREE

Twelve hundred miles above Earth, a dull black satellite hung in a geosynchronous orbit over India. Since the vehicle was well within the zone set aside for a communications satellite, no one paid much attention to it. For all intents and purposes, it was just one of dozens of commercial communications satellites, which it was.

But it was a communications satellite with a difference. A shielded comm link connected the vehicle with its controllers on the ground at Rondell's complex in Baja. When orders from the strategic planning room were flashed to the satellite control center, the technicians activated their controls to bring the high-energy laser hidden inside the satellite to life.

Power from fully charged solar accumulators surged through the craft. Relays and solenoids came to life, and additional solar panels unfolded like the wings of a bat to soak up the power of the sun. More power went to onboard computers and steering controls. In just under ten minutes, the vehicle's microchips sent a signal to the ground that it was fully operational. When that signal arrived, the control center went into full operation and began putting the satellite to its intended use.

As per its instructions from the ground control station, the vehicle slowly swung its nose around until it was aimed at the Indian nuclear power plant serving the capital of New Delhi. Once the satellite was locked on to its target, a compartment in the rear slowly opened. When the clamshell doors were fully retracted, a device raised itself on controllable arms and extended over the nose of the craft like a finger pointing from a fist.

On command, relays tripped and solar-generated power surged through the device. The high-energy laser powered up and ran itself through a series of self-check programs. When the ready signal was sent back to the ground control station, a weapons operator took command of the laser. He had a console in front of him that displayed a map of the Indian subcontinent, and in front of the console was a joystick with a trigger built into the grip. The setup looked rather like a space-war game in a mall video arcade, but this game was for keeps.

Pulling the trigger back to its first position superimposed a glowing targeting ring on his map. Moving the control stick from side to side and back and forth moved the targeting ring over the map. His left hand controlled the magnification of the map as he quickly sought out his target, the New Delhi nuclear power plant. A keystroke brought the area around the plant into the targeting circle. Another keystroke magnified the map even further so that the individual buildings could be seen. Rolling his fist brought the cross hairs of the targeting circle to bear on the plant's reactor containment building.

After a final radar targeting pulse to achieve a positive lock on, the weapons operator pulled the trigger on the joystick with his right index finger and, deep in space, the laser fired.

The beam of ruby red coherent light flashed toward Earth at the speed of light. Even though the beam had to travel well over a thousand miles to reach its target, for all practical purposes it reached the earth instantaneously.

On the ground in India, a three foot area of the top of the concrete containment dome of the New Delhi nuclear power plant started to glow dull red.

UNLIKE IN MANY overgrown cities in the emerging nations, the lights in New Delhi burned by both night and day. This sufficiency of electrical energy was due in large part to the nuclear power generating plant that had been built by the Soviets back in the days when Moscow had been seriously courting the Indians. Along with the MiG-21 fighters and T-55 tanks they had supplied to the Indian armed forces, the Russians had been glad to give them a nuclear reactor or two, as well.

After the Chernobyl nuclear accident in the Ukraine showed the world the dangers of the old Soviet reactor designs, the Indians had looked at their "gift" more closely. They became even more careful about keeping up with the maintenance and repairs on their Russian-built facility. The reactor and containment room had been refitted with Western-made pumps and valves wherever it had been practicable. The control room had also been refitted with American instruments and controls. When they were finished with the overhaul, the Indian engineers considered their power plant to be as safe as any nuclear reactor in the world.

It was late at night when the first alarms sounded in the New Delhi plant. The engineer in charge of the night shift was in the control room in a flash and saw that there had been a dangerous rise in the coolant temperature. When increasing the coolant flow made no difference, he decided to do an emergency core dump to stop the reaction. The reactor core would have to be completely rebuilt before it could be operated again, but that was better than going up in a Chernobyl-style mushroom-shaped cloud.

Unlocking the door to the emergency core dump handle, he reached in and grasped the handle. Without hesitation, he pulled it down and locked it in the dump position. Deep inside the containment room, electrical motors whined as the uranium fuel rods were slammed home into their neutron-absorbing, carbon-fiber shields. To his horror, though, the engineer saw that the temperature in the heat exchange and coolant system was still climbing.

He was reaching for the emergency evacuation button when the containment room blew. A blast of superheated air smashed out the armored glass window of the control room and swept through the room. The control room crew died almost before anyone had time to notice that anything was wrong. The rest of the night shift fared little better when the containment building exploded.

Fortunately the New Delhi reactor was well outside the city. Nonetheless, over the years a sizable village of small houses and shops had grown up around the plant. The villagers made their living by supplying goods and services to the power-plant workers, and they died with them when the reactor exploded.

Even more fortunate was the fact that the wind was blowing away from New Delhi when the accident occurred. The engineer's emergency core dump saved the city from massive nuclear material contamination. The radiation that escaped came from the heat exchanger, not the reactor core.

Even though the casualties had been relatively light, thousands of demonstrators took to the streets in India's major cities to protest the dangers of nuclear power. India was a democracy, but that didn't mean that the government paid much attention to protestors of any kind. Someone was always protesting something in India, and if the nukes were shut down, India's economy would collapse.

Two DAYS LATER, a Japanese nuclear power plant on the island of Hokkaido had a catastrophic transmission network failure similar to the one that had knocked out the Diablo Canyon plant. As had happened in California, only the electrical transmission system went down—the reactor wasn't affected—but that didn't matter.

Early the next morning, the nuclear-phobic Japanese took to the streets of Tokyo in the thousands, demanding a complete shutdown of all the nuclear plants in Japan until the exact cause of the accident could be determined. Eighty percent of Japan's power was nuclear, and a shutdown would cripple the country. But, when you lived on an island, there was no place to run if a nuclear power plant went up like the one in New Delhi.

The Japanese government was more likely to be swayed by demonstrators than were the Indians, but even they couldn't afford to have the streets of the capital city paralyzed by a barely controlled mob. Calling out the experienced Tokyo riot-police units, they closed in on the demonstration from all sides. The Tokyo police didn't hold anything back, but neither did the demonstrators. For two days the streets of Tokyo ran with blood and the air was thick with tear gas, but little headway was made. The core of the city was closed down tightly, and business came to a standstill.

Finally the Diet called the Japanese Self-Defense Forces into action. With fixed bayonets, the army was finally able to break up the mob and bring order to the city. Though Tokyo was restored to normalcy, other antinuclear demonstrations continued throughout the country. And in the ranks of the demonstrators were seen the distinctive arm bands of the Green Earth Movement.

CHAPTER FOUR

Southern France

Half a world away, Yakov Katzenelenbogen touched the brakes of his rented BMW when he saw the brake lights of the traffic ahead of him come on. He was driving on what the map said was a major highway, but he knew that didn't mean much in the rural South of France. A herdsman was probably taking his time getting his flock of sheep across the road.

A wave of annoyance swept over him, but then he remembered that he was on vacation and was supposed to be enjoying himself instead of being in a hurry. Katzenelenbogen was also one of the Stony Man operatives, the leader of the top-secret paramilitary action team known as Phoenix Force. He was in France, taking a well-deserved break, but he was having a difficult time slipping back into civilian mode.

Minutes later Katz got closer to the obstruction and saw that it wasn't a flock of sheep that blocked the road, but a crowd of people. Most of them were

young, but he saw a few graybeards and middle-
aged women in the group, as well. Most of them
were carrying signs and he thought that he had encountered one of France's famous farmers' demonstrations until he got close enough to read what
was written on the placards.

The signs didn't urge crop price supports or de-
mands to pull out of the European Economic
Community. They demanded that a nuclear power
station be shut down immediately.

When he had turned onto the road, he vaguely
remembered having seen a signpost indicating that
there was a power station in the area. But that
wasn't surprising. More than seventy-five percent
of all electrical power used in France was gener-
ated from state-of-the-art nuclear power plants.
Unlike in the United States, where antinuclear hys-
teria had actually decreased the use of nuclear
power generation over the past few years, the Europeans were being far more realistic about the util-
ity of nuclear power.

Of all the European nations, France was the first
to realize that modern nuclear power plants were
the least environmentally harmful source of cheap
electrical power. And if France was to continue to
expand her growing economy, electricity was essential. Beyond a few diehards, though, there had

been little public concern about the plants. The French were a very practical people.

Looking beyond the crowd, Katz spotted the distinctive cooling tower of a nuclear plant behind a stand of trees roughly three hundred meters off the road. The French situated their power plants in the countryside away from population centers. That hadn't stopped this crowd, however, from coming to the countryside to protest.

Katzenelenbogen was astounded to see several green-shirted men and women in the crowd. The green shirts were the uniform of the Green Earth Movement, and he thought that particular form of hysterical environmental Nazism was confined to the United States. Europeans were usually too world wise to get caught up in the emotional crusades of the American left. To see that his homeland had fallen in with these people was disappointing. He had always thought that the French were much too smart for that.

When he saw the media vans, he realized that the French Green Shirts had taken another page from the American book of activism. There was no point in having a demonstration if the TV cameras weren't rolling. The purpose of the exercise wasn't so much to voice one's opinion as to get that opinion on the news in hopes of changing someone else's thoughts on the subject.

As he sat in the BMW, he saw several dark blue police vans approach from the other side of the demonstration. The vehicles parked in a line, and the rear doors opened to disgorge a large contingent of helmeted French National Police riot units. As calmly as if they were parading at their barracks, the police formed their line and started marching in step toward the demonstrators.

The protestors didn't give way, and Katz saw that the sign poles the demonstrators were carrying weren't wooden sticks. They were long metal batons that could reach past the clear shields of the police and rain blows on the officers.

He saw a policeman struck so hard on the helmet that the chin strap broke and the helmet was torn off the man's head. A second blow to the officer's unprotected head sent him crumpling to the ground. Katzenelenbogen knew killing blows, and he was sure that the officer had been severely injured if not killed outright.

Seeing one of their own go down, the cops surged forward, their riot batons slashing. Tear gas canisters arched over the crowd and burst into puffs of white smoke. The instant the gas appeared, most of the demonstrators took gas masks from their backpacks and tote bags and donned them for protection against the acrid fumes. Once they were protected, the combat resumed.

Throughout the riot, Katzenelenbogen noticed that the Green Shirts didn't personally strike a blow at the police. They were, however, everywhere behind the front line, directing the fighters. When a protestor went down, they directed someone else to take his place. Whoever these guys were, they were organized.

Even though the police had taken casualties, they were pushing the crowd back. As if the move had been rehearsed, the demonstrators suddenly turned and ran for the nuclear plant. Thinking they had them on the run, the riot police dashed after the protestors, breaking their own ordered ranks.

Again, as if it were planned, the rioters halted their flight and turned to face the cops. This time, with their ranks broken, the police were having a much harder time of it. Now it was the police who were giving ground until reinforcements arrived. The reinforcements brought out their rubber-bullet guns and turned the tide.

While the crowd's retreat and turn to attack maneuver had been successful in breaking the police line, their turning back from the plant had allowed three armored cars to come in behind them. Positioning themselves in front of the plant's entrance, the police unlimbered the machine guns on the vehicles and prepared to defend the power station.

Not even fanatic Green Shirts were willing to go up against armored cars with grim-faced National Police behind the guns, and the riot was contained.

It took several hours before the road was cleared, though. There were dead and injured to be transported, as well as debris from the gas canisters and the demonstration to be swept aside. Also, in the great French tradition, the police interrogated the drivers who had, through no fault of their own, been delayed by the afternoon's show.

When Katzenelenbogen was finally allowed to drive away, he decided that he would check in with Stony Man Farm when he arrived at his hotel. Seeing the Green Shirts in charge of the demonstration had made him uneasy. It was true that the news of the Diablo Canyon accident and ensuing traffic pileup had made the news even in Europe. But to find the American Green Earth movement protesting in France so soon after that incident was unsettling.

Vancouver, British Columbia

MACK BOLAN WAS ALSO taking a hard-earned rest. Even so, his reason for being in Canada was work related.

The Royal Canadian Mounted Police had recently intercepted several shipments of military arms and ammunition crossing into the country and were concerned. Canada had a British-style restrictive concept of a citizen's right to own firearms. Hunting weapons and handguns were allowed with the proper permits, but ownership of military assault weapons was closely regulated, which sat well with many Canadians.

The great influx of Asians into Vancouver over the past several years, however, had turned the city into a northern version of San Francisco. With the Asian immigrants had come the Asian gangs. First to set up shop had been the traditional Tongs and Triads, followed by the Southeast Asian drug lords and finally the Japanese Yakuza. They didn't abide by the firearms laws. To them, guns were a necessary tool for their business.

At first the Asian gangs had stayed within their own ethnic communities. Then, once every shopkeeper, flower seller and restaurant owner was plugged into the system, they moved farther afield. And when they did, they clashed with the other gangs.

Even with the turf wars, Canada's stringent gun laws had kept the gang violence to a minimum. Vancouver had a population of almost a million, but the murder rate was only a few percentage points of what it would have been had it been an American city of the same size.

The gun shipments had made the RCMP nervous. They knew that just because they had intercepted those two shipments, it didn't mean that others hadn't gotten through. And a flood of military-style weapons in the hands of the gangs would change life in Vancouver forever.

The Canadian Bolan was meeting in Vancouver was Staff Sergeant Ian Magruder of the Royal Canadian Mounted Police. Several years earlier, the Executioner had worked with the Mountie on a major drug case. The meet was set at the city's waterfront park, and the man was on time.

"You're looking fit," Magruder said as he took Bolan's proffered hand.

"It's the nature of the business. It keeps me on the run."

The Canadian shook his head. "I wish I could say the same. I've been stuck behind a desk trying to track down those damn guns."

"Tell me about them."

Magruder quickly recounted the interception of more than a hundred Chinese-made AK-47s and enough ammunition to start a small war. "In both cases, though, the smugglers weren't Asians, but Americans. Along with the guns, we've been getting some other unwelcome imports from the lower forty-eight lately."

Bolan waited for the Canadian to tell him that a new drug pipeline had opened up and was surprised when he didn't.

"The Green Earthers have opened up a chapter here in B.C.," Magruder continued. "As if we didn't have enough trouble with the tree huggers already, eh?"

"I don't know what to tell you about them," Bolan said. "I don't think that my contacts have come up with anything on them to be concerned about. As far as I know, the only difference between them and the rest of the environmental groups is that they're better organized and seem to have more money behind them."

Magruder shook his head. "That and the fact that they've been recruiting from our local skinhead gangs. I never thought that I would ever see the day when those punks were interested in anything other than making trouble in the ethnic neighborhoods."

The Mountie's pager beeped. "Excuse me," he said as he turned to walk to a nearby pay phone. When he returned, his face was grim.

"It's the tree huggers," Magruder said. "They're having some kind of demonstration at a dam construction site and it's gotten out of hand. I have to take a team up there to sort it out."

"Is there anything I can do to help?"

"I thought you were supposed to be on holiday."

A ghost of a smile tugged at Bolan's lips. "I can come along and watch."

Magruder grinned. "Why not?"

CHAPTER FIVE

Stony Man Farm

Barbara Price walked out to the camouflaged helicopter landing pad at Stony Man Farm and looked up at the speck in the sky approaching from the north. In her faded, tight blue jeans, cowboy boots and chambray shirt, she looked nothing at all like the mission controller for the country's most top-secret clandestine organization.

She was tall, honey-blond and slender, with the high cheekbones that fashion photographers had loved to caress with their cameras when she was a fashion model during her college years. She also had a steel-trap mind and the razor-edged ruthlessness that was required of someone who had to send men out to kill or die. It was a rare combination, but anyone who said that women were the weaker sex had never met Barbara Price.

When she had positively identified the approaching chopper, she spoke into the comm link clipped to her shirt collar. "He's inbound now."

"Roger," the comm center answered. "We have communication with him."

Price briefly turned her back to the rotorwash as the unmarked Bell JetRanger landed. When she turned back, she saw that Hal Brognola looked worried when he stepped from the aircraft. She hadn't received word that he was coming to the Farm until the chopper had requested landing clearance, and she had no idea what this visit was about. But, as she well knew, that usually meant that he was bearing bad news.

On paper, Brognola was a high-ranking official in the Justice Department and was assigned as a liaison officer to the White House. In the shadow world of covert operations, however, he was the director of the Sensitive Operations Group based at Stony Man Farm, and Price's boss. He was the man who passed the President's orders down to the people who would do the dirty work, and his visit could only mean another mission for the Farm's action teams.

"What's up, Hal?" she asked.

"I need to see you, Aaron and Wethers in the War Room ASAP."

They walked in silence to the front door of the farmhouse, and Price keyed the security lock to open the door. Once inside, Brognola still didn't speak, but headed directly for the elevator leading down into the basement War Room. Price stopped long enough to use the intercom to pass the word to Aaron Kurtzman and Huntington Wethers to join them.

When she reached the War Room, Wethers was already there. He was a tall, distinguished black man, and had been a professor of advanced cybernetics at Berkeley before Kurtzman contacted him about joining the Stony Man Farm team. He had jumped at the chance to work with one of the nation's most advanced artificial intelligence systems and made a good addition to the team. His years behind the lectern hadn't left him, though. He still looked and sounded like a college professor.

Brognola didn't say a word until Kurtzman wheeled his chair in and took his accustomed place at the conference table. Kurtzman hadn't always been confined to a wheelchair. During an attack on Stony Man Farm, a terrorist bullet in the spine had cut him down. But, though the wound had taken away the use of his legs, it hadn't diminished his usefulness to the Stony Man SOG mission.

"We have a situation here," Brognola began. "Someone has been blowing up nuclear power plants." He went on to brief them in detail on the Diablo Canyon, New Delhi and Hokkaido nuclear reactor incidents.

"As the Man so aptly put it," Brognola concluded, "once is an accident, twice is happenstance, but three times is enemy action. We have reason to believe that those accidents were deliberate sabotage."

"By whom?" Kurtzman asked bluntly.

"We have a possible candidate," the big Fed said, sidestepping the answer. "But the problem with the investigation is that it is very touchy politically."

"What's so different about that?" Kurtzman retorted. "The big problems are always political. If the nation's politicians ever get their heads out of their asses and take care of the nation's business the way they're supposed to, we'll be out of a job down here."

"It's worse than usual this time," Brognola said as he took a videocassette out of his briefcase. "I want you to watch this tape before I continue."

Walking over to the VCR at the end of the room, he inserted the cassette and hit the Play button. After a brief classified-material warning, the face of a smiling man in his early forties appeared on the big screen. A sea breeze ruffled his hair, and his eyes looked off into the distance as if he were seeing something that no one else could—a dream, a vision of the future.

As the music swelled in the background, a voice-over said, "As California approaches the millenium, one man stands ready to bring Californians into the future they deserve. Benson Rondell has seen the future, and it shines brightly in the Golden State. As the CEO of Sunflash, Benson Rondell has devoted his life to creating a better life for America, and he wants to start in California."

The scene faded to Rondell at an obviously staged political rally. The carefully selected crowd was exactly the right mix of politically correct ethnic diversity, with an emphasis on young professionals with their children and a sprinkling of blue-collar workers and retirees thrown in to pad it out. The candidate was moving through the crowd, pressing the flesh and answering their prepared questions about quality-of-living issues in their make-believe lives.

The scene then shifted to Rondell on a stage delivering a speech condemning nuclear power plants to a packed house. With all the sincerity in the world, he said that if he was elected governor he would outlaw all of the nuclear plants in California and replace them with solar-power generating systems. Flanking the stage were several green-shirted minions of the Green Earth Movement, holding signs calling for the complete abolition of nuclear facilities throughout the world.

With a last slogan designed to make the voter feel all warm and fuzzy about the candidate, the scene shifted back to the shot of Rondell on the beach.

"There he is," Brognola said as he hit the clicker to shut off the video. "The newest savior of the world and the founder of the next utopia, the state of California."

"He sure as hell knows how to make a video," Price said with honest admiration.

"He should," Brognola replied. "That little piece of work cost him a bundle, believe me. He's retained Tyler and Feldmann to do his campaign advertising, and they don't come cheap."

"But what does this guy running for governor have to do with those nuclear plant accidents?" Price asked. "I don't see the connection. Politicians say things like that all the time. Particularly in California. If he said that he was in favor of cheap, reliable nuclear power, he'd be stoned to death like that poor bastard in San Francisco."

"I know," the big Fed said. "And even though I don't have anything hard to back it up yet, I think that he's more than just another California political hopeful. Call it a hunch, a leap of faith if you like, but I think that he's the man behind the 'accidents.'"

"But why him and not some other antinuke candidate?"

Brognola quickly gave her a rundown on the history of Sunflash and Rondell's development of a practical solar-power generating system that he intended to use to replace nuclear-generated power.

"Even so," Price countered, "how could he have caused those accidents? I can maybe see him hiring some thugs to sabotage the Diablo Canyon transmission station to create a nuke scare, but the other two accidents occurred overseas. Does he have the foreign connections to handle something like that for him?"

"I don't know," he admitted. "And that's one of the things you're supposed to find out for me. Since this guy's running for governor on an independent ticket, both of the major parties have to handle him with kid gloves so it doesn't look like they're trying to torpedo his campaign. And since that precludes my using federal agencies to run background checks on him, I can't get a damned thing on him through the normal intelligence channels. Ever since the Perot campaign in 1992, using governmental agencies to check on political candidates is out.

"Also, since Rondell has the Green Earthers in his pocket, he has the support of every environmentalist on the planet. The President has to move very carefully against this guy, or he'll be accused of being antienvironmental and that will kill him at the polls.''

"To hell with the polls," Kurtzman retorted. "If you're right and this guy is behind this, we have to step on him."

"That's easy for you to say," Brognola said. "You're not the President. He lives and dies by the polls. But, due to the international scope of this crisis, he has to act quickly because this may be a plot by an American citizen to destroy the world's nuclear power business. And, I think, for his own benefit.''

"How's that?"

"Rondell recently took advantage of the North American Free Trade Agreement with Mexico and relocated his solar-power research complex and manufacturing facility to Baja California. From there, he says that he intends to provide electrical power to a growing Mexican economy, as well as sending it up to all of Southern California, which may soon be completely without nuclear power.

"Ever since the accident at the Chernobyl power plant, the world has been more aware of the dangers of nuclear power. And while the so-called environmentalists have forced us to cut back on our nuclear power generation here in the States, the rest of the world is relying on it more and more. Nuclear power plant construction is at an all-time high right now. China just recently announced that she wants to build five hundred new reactors by the year 2020.

"The environmentalists have renewed the cry for alternate energy sources. But, while the alternate power generating systems are high-tech engineering marvels, they have all proved to be less than satisfactory from a practical standpoint. The closest thing to a practical solution is the second-generation solar-power system developed by Rondell's firm. He's using a mercury vapor recirculation system that's several times more efficient than the earlier types. Even though his units seem to work well, the problem is that it's expensive, maybe too expensive to be economically feasible in the real world."

Price frowned. "I thought that the EPA had put severe restrictions on the manufacture of mercury vapor units because of the risk of mercury escaping and causing contamination?"

Brognola nodded. "That's another anomaly about Rondell's operation. In the past, the environmental extremists have gone ballistic about even the slightest danger of mercury contamination. And that includes the mercury used in solar-power systems. This time, though, since he has the Green Earth people in his pocket, they aren't saying diddly about his using it. This issue has a lot to do with his relocating his operation to Baja. Even with the blessing of the Green Shirts, the EPA environmental protection laws wouldn't let him build his facility in the States. But now that NAFTA's in effect, Rondell can operate in Mexico without our government being able to keep an eye on him."

Brognola started putting his papers back into his briefcase. "All I can say is that this has the highest priority. I need whatever information you can get together on this guy ASAP."

He closed his briefcase and stood. "And I'll need daily updates so I can pass them on to the President."

THE MINUTE BROGNOLA lifted off for his return flight to Washington, the Stony Man team went into action. Benson Rondell's political contacts might have made him immune from routine investigation, but that didn't mean that his secrets, if he had any, couldn't be found out. While the rest of the country was just learning about the so-called information superhighway, it was old news to Aaron Kurtzman, Hunt Wethers and the rest of the Farm's computer staff. In an age when everything imaginable was stored in a computer somewhere, there was nothing they couldn't ferret out if they kept at it long enough.

CHAPTER SIX

Vancouver, British Columbia

Mack Bolan followed Ian Magruder to the Vancouver barracks of the RCMP riot detail, where the Mounties were preparing to move out to the demonstration site. Out on the soccer field behind the barracks, a twin-rotor CH-47 Chinook helicopter bearing RCMP markings waited, its rotors turning, beside a smaller Bell JetRanger.

The Mounties who double-timed up the rear ramp of the Chinook wore black combat suits with Kevlar vests, helmets with face shields, mountain boots and assault harnesses. Their weapons, a mix of 12-gauge riot guns and Heckler & Koch automatic weapons, would be able to handle nearly any situation. They didn't want trouble, but if it came, the RCMP would be ready for it.

As soon as the Chinook was loaded, it lifted off for the construction site in the mountains to the north. Bolan and Magruder quickly boarded the JetRanger and followed them.

"THERE IT IS," Magruder said, pointing out the side window of the JetRanger. "The Big Elk Dam."

The dam construction site was high in a wooded valley cut by one of the most picturesque rivers Bolan had ever seen. Even in British Columbia, a land famous for its breathtaking natural beauty, this valley was exceptional. Bolan had to agree with the environmentalists that the raw earth and construction equipment looked decidedly out of place up here. But he also knew that cheap electrical power was essential for the British Columbia of the next century and that hydro power was better than burning coal to produce it.

As they got closer, Bolan could see two groups of people in front of the construction company's offices and equipment sheds, and it was easy to tell them apart. The construction crew wore hard hats, blue jeans and heavy jackets. They had iron bars, heavy wrenches and other tools of their trade in their hands. These union workers weren't about to let a bunch of college kids and professional malcontents keep them away from their high-paying jobs. They had their families to feed, bills to pay and, most of all, a reputation to uphold. Backing down from anyone who got in their face, particularly American tree huggers, wouldn't sit well.

The protestors facing them were obviously not working-class men and women. Their fashionable clothing and footwear had been designed for the college campus, not the realities of life in the north woods. Once again, the green shirts and arm bands of the Green Earth Movement were to be seen everywhere among the demonstrators.

Magruder wasn't wrong when he had said that the radical environmentalist organization had recently made serious inroads into British Columbia. Earlier American-based environmentalist groups had tried to take their acts north, but hadn't met with any great success. The Canadians were far more rational than Americans when it came to such things. This time, though, for whatever reason, it seemed to have worked.

Bolan also noticed that the news media was at the construction site in force. Like Katzenelenbogen, he knew that the only way this demonstration would be of any use to the Green Earth cause would be if it was widely publicized. A demonstration in the wilderness that didn't made the six-o'clock news might as well not have happened for all the good it would do them. The only questions were, why was it so important for them to have this amount of coverage, and what was it intended to accomplish?

After deploying on the ground, the Mounties started moving in to separate the demonstrators from the hard hats. As Bolan had expected, the demonstrators went on the attack as soon as the

RCMP moved in. The media circus they planned wouldn't work if there was no action. But, if the Green Shirts had wanted a serious confrontation with the RCMP, they had seriously underestimated the discipline of the Mounties.

Wielding their protest signs like clubs, the demonstrators charged. The Mounties stood their ground and absorbed the blows on their riot shields. Then, working in pairs, they started cutting individuals out of the pack, overwhelming them and binding their hands and feet with plastic riot restraints. Bolan wasn't surprised at the Mounties' professionalism as they quickly took command of the situation. They had long been a model for police forces all over the world, and their riot squads were no exception.

In a very short time the demonstration was over. A dozen protestors were in riot restraints, and the rest were leaving as quickly as they could. The media people looked slightly disappointed because there was so little blood and nothing to show except tapes of a professional police unit at work. And that wasn't news.

"WE'VE BEEN SUCKERED." Magruder sounded completely disgusted when he came back from taking a call on the helicopter's radio.

"How's that?"

"While we've been up here, the owner of the construction company and his wife have been kidnapped. We've just received a communiqué that he will be held until all work on the dam is permanently halted and the construction that has been accomplished has been dynamited and removed."

Bolan frowned. Kidnapping executives wasn't the usual procedure for environmental activists. They were more into flashy demonstrations and picketing that would make the lead story on the evening news. Kidnapping was more of a terrorist or a drug cartel tactic. "Are you sure that it's the same bunch you're dealing with here?"

"Why not?" Magruder replied. "I can't see two groups protesting the same dam construction site."

"You have a point there."

Bolan and the Canadian boarded the JetRanger and flew back to Vancouver to oversee the kidnapping investigation.

"YOU'RE WELCOME to come along," Magruder said as soon as he learned that they had a location for the kidnappers. "And since you're here as a consulting police official, I can provide you with a weapon."

Even though Bolan knew that the Mountie suspected that his "police" credentials were a fabrication, having access to a gun might be critical.

"You wouldn't happen to have an extra 9 mm Beretta, would you?"

"As a matter of fact, we do." Magruder smiled. "Tell the armorer at the end of the hall that I said he was to accommodate you."

An hour later they were airborne again with a crack RCMP Special Weapons Response Team following in another Chinook.

THE KIDNAPPERS' CABIN in the Canadian woods was situated on the top of a small hill with clear fields of fire all the way around it. No matter which way the Mounties approached, they would have to cross a hundred yards of cleared ground before they reached the house.

"We're going to need a diversion if we plan to storm that place," Magruder said as he lowered his field glasses. His men were in place all the way around the cabin, but the advantage wasn't with them.

"Even so," Bolan told him, "if you try that during daylight, someone's going to get killed."

"What do you recommend?"

"Wait until dark and let me go in there."

"I can't let you do that. You're here as an observer, not a participant."

"I've been through this more than once," Bolan reminded him, "and most of your men haven't."

"I'm not doubting your expertise," the Canadian replied. "But the higher-ups would sack me if I let you do that."

The door of the house opened and a woman appeared. Directly behind her stood a man in woodland-camouflage clothing, holding a pistol to her head.

"I want to talk to the man in charge," the kidnapper shouted to the Mounties in the tree line.

Magruder took the bullhorn and stepped out into the open. He hadn't gone two steps before a shot rang out and a rifle bullet took him high in the left chest. The shooter had been aiming for a heart shot, but only nicked the top of his lung. Nonetheless, the bullet shattered his shoulder blade when it exited his back.

Bolan ran out and dragged him back into the trees. "Don't try to talk," he said as he checked the wound. "Your lung's been hit and it'll collapse."

The RCMP medic quickly applied a field bandage to seal off the wound and Magruder was taken to the JetRanger for evacuation.

Once Magruder had been loaded on the chopper and flown out, Bolan went looking for the next senior man. Regardless of what Magruder had said about his not getting involved, this was personal now and the Executioner always took care of his personal business.

The sergeant in charge of the RCMP sniper team had his small unit well in hand, but was overdoing the tough NCO routine out of sheer nervousness.

"Is this your first real field operation?" Bolan asked.

"Yes, sir." The sergeant almost snapped to a position of attention.

"I've been on quite a few of these operations, and if I can offer a word of advice, you might want to lighten up on your men a little. They're under pressure already, and I'm going to need them at the top of their form tonight."

The sergeant frowned. "What's going to happen tonight?"

"I'm going in to rescue the hostages."

"No one told me anything about that," the sergeant said suspiciously.

"Staff Sergeant Magruder and I were working out the details before he was hit."

The sergeant had no reason to doubt what Bolan said. Now that Magruder was down, even though he was an American, Bolan was the highest ranking man on the scene. He had no idea why an American had been called in on this operation, but Magruder had brought him and that was good enough. Plus, it sounded like the guy had a plan which was more than anyone else had at the moment.

RATHER THAN WAITING until the dead of night, Bolan decided to make his move as soon as it was completely dark. Leaving the hostages in the hands of this particular gang a minute longer than was absolutely necessary was unthinkable. Their gunning down Magruder showed that they weren't likely to treat their hostages any better. As well, as soon as another senior RCMP arrived on the scene, the soldier wouldn't be able to carry out his plan.

Ian Magruder was a decent sort, and the Executioner owed him this one.

While Bolan waited for night to fall, he changed clothing with one of the Mounties who was close to his size. He passed on the man's Kevlar vest, however, just borrowing the assault harness with a pair of flash-bang grenades and his 9 mm H&K MP-5 submachine gun. The Beretta he had borrowed from the armory rode in a shoulder holster.

"Wait till I call that I'm in place," he told the sergeant, "then start shooting up the roof. They'll figure that you're planning to hit them with a frontal attack. That'll get their attention long enough for me to get inside. When you hear shots from inside, cease-fire and be ready to move in when I call."

"Good luck."

With his night-vision goggles to guide him, Bolan was able to quickly traverse the open ground and still keep to what little cover there was. When he reached the rear of the house, he saw that there was a large window that probably looked into the main room. That was easier than trying to go through a door.

"I'm in position," he transmitted. "Start the diversion."

"Roger sir."

Slipping the night-vision goggles over his eyes again, Bolan took a flash-bang grenade from his borrowed assault harness and waited.

From the other three sides of the clearing, the RCMP marksmen started shooting at the house. As Bolan had ordered, all of the shots were high, and as he had expected, the kidnappers quickly returned the fire. The distinctive clatter of AK-47s on full-auto rang out from inside the house. He could hear at least four of the assault rifles, and that gave him a little better idea of what he was facing.

The soldier pulled the pin on the grenade. Closing his eyes to preserve his night vision, he threw the bomb through the window and followed right behind it. The night-vision goggles showed him at least four figures with weapons in their hands, one of whom was facing him with a stunned look on his face and an AK in his hands. Bolan snapped two rounds at the first man as he cleared the window-frame.

Knowing the rounds were true, he rolled off to the side and fired two more shots. Another kidnapper screamed and went down. He was acquiring his next target when a shotgun roared and a load of 12-gauge buckshot sang past the side of his face.

Fortunately the gunner was using a pump gun, and while he worked the slide to chamber the next round, Bolan drilled him. Both rounds stabbed into his heart, and the pump gun clattered to the floor.

Suddenly there was silence. The soldier kept low and checked out the three bodies. All of them were wore camouflage, so he hadn't hit the hostage by mistake. But he had killed only three of them, and he had distinctly heard four AKs firing before he had made his move.

"Drop the gun," a man's voice said from the other side of the room, "or I'll kill him."

Bolan turned to see two figures moving toward the front door. The glowing green field of the night-vision goggles showed that the kidnapper was holding a man in front of him as a shield and had the muzzle of a pistol jammed against the side of his hostage's head.

The Executioner's response was automatic. The borrowed Beretta came up as fast as a striking snake and he fired, once.

The 9 mm round took the gunman right above the left eye, drove through his skull and exploded in his brain. He was dead before the muzzle-flash of Bolan's Beretta registered on his retina, with no time to order his finger to pull the trigger on his pistol.

"I'm clear," Bolan radioed to the RCMP sergeant. "You can come in now."

"Are you okay?" Bolan asked as he knelt beside the hostage who had fallen with the body of his kidnapper.

"You're an American!" the man said when he caught the accent.

"Yeah, I am," Bolan replied as he helped him to his feet.

A huge grin spread across the man's face, and he enveloped the Executioner in a bear hug. "Then I say God bless all Americans!"

It was all Bolan could do to get away from the man so he could go out and talk to the RCMP officers who had arrived a little too late to take command of the situation.

CHAPTER SEVEN

Sunflash Compound, Baja California

Benson Rondell wasn't the usual American political hopeful, not even for California. For one thing, he had never really wanted to go into politics. All he had wanted to do was make enough money to be a powerful man and live the good life. He now saw that trying to make this money by getting into the alternative-energy business had been a serious miscalculation, but all of that was behind him now.

The influx of money from the cartel had provided him with enough working capital that he could go ahead with his solar-power engineering plans. It had also made him one of the most high-profile businessmen in the country and had allowed him to bask in the glory of his image. He had expected that his repayment to the cartel would be taken from Sunflash's profits, but eventually they told him their plan to put him in the California statehouse.

At first he had flatly turned down the plan. He wanted power, but not power that was subject to the whims of the voters. But Hector Garcia had convinced him that the benefits that were to be gained from his seeking high office far outweighed the hassle. And he pointed out that it would give him protection against governmental interference with his operation.

Rondell had to admit that the Cali cartel didn't think small. Not only would they recoup their investment in Sunflash when nuclear power plants all over the world were shut down, having him in the California governor's house would make their main industry more profitable, as well.

The cartel saw his role as California's governor as being primarily aimed at eliminating their competition in the cocaine business. They had already been successful in erasing their biggest Colombian rivals from the South American drug scene, but that wasn't enough. If the Californian authorities could be focused on their other competitors, they too could be eliminated, leaving the international cocaine trade a Cali exclusive.

Nonetheless, going on the campaign trail wasn't one of Rondell's favorite things. The heat, the dust, the stench of closely packed humanity and having to make the same asinine speeches over and over again got old quickly. Then there were the polls and the media.

Even though the cartel had given him the best advisers and spin doctors that money could buy, the polls weren't running in his favor. Several influential California newspapers had started calling him "One Note Johnny" because his antinuclear power platform was thin. His opponents were beating him to death on crime, the homeless, the business drain from the greater L.A. area, drugs, illegal immigrants and a dozen other issues dear to the heart of every California voter.

In the beginning, he had told Garcia that he wasn't sure that the nuclear power issue would be enough by itself to get him elected. As an American, he was well aware that independent candidates usually didn't fare well at the polls because they usually ran single-issue campaigns. But since Garcia had convinced his cartel bosses to invest heavily in Sunflash, the only way for that money to be recovered was if the nuclear power plants were shut down. And that would best be done if a state, like California, outlawed their use. To do that, though, he had to get into the governor's house.

He was studying the latest poll results when his private line rang. "Rondell," he answered.

"This is Catherine. I need to talk to you."

Catherine Woodburn was a junior congresswoman from Southern California on the House Intelligence Committee and a Green Earth Movement groupie. She had built a strong pro-environmental voting record and always made sure that she was seen at trendy environmentalist gatherings. Her voting block of liberals liked their representative to publicly demonstrate her concern for the environment.

Rondell first met Woodburn at a Green Earth meeting right after he announced his candidacy, and she immediately offered her support for his campaign. It was always difficult for independent candidates to find friends in Washington, so he was happy to have her on board. Later, though, he learned that her devotion to environmental issues was more of a devotion to the idealistic young women who flocked to the green banner rather than to the environment itself. The congresswoman had always found good hunting in the ranks of the faithful.

Rondell had no problem with lesbians, even aggressive ones like Woodburn, as long as she came through for him when he needed her support. Not only did she give him the gloss of Capitol Hill backing, her position on the House Intelligence Committee was a definite plus for his campaign. From there, she fed him a steady stream of information about nuclear energy projects throughout the world.

"What's new in Washington, Catherine?"

"Are you sure that this line can't be tapped?"

"Take my word for it," Rondell said soothingly as he reached out to turn on his tape recorder. "It's completely secure."

"I just learned that you're being investigated."

Rondell's breath caught in his throat. This hadn't been in the cartel's plan. "About what?"

"About the nuclear accidents that have been happening all over the world."

"Go on."

"The chairman of our committee works out with the President in the Senate gym, and he learned that some kind of secret organization is looking into your company's operation and your campaign. No one has said that you had a direct hand in those incidents, but you're the man who has benefited the most from them and they want a closer look at what you're doing. What's going on here, Benson? You told me that you were completely legit."

"Nothing's 'going on,' Catherine," Rondell shot back. He had learned early on that to keep Woodburn from running roughshod over him, he had to assert himself. "Like I told you when we first met, I'm just trying to see that the world becomes a safer place by seeing that the nuclear power industry is put out of business before it puts all of us in a radioactive grave. Nothing more and nothing less."

"Save the bullshit for the campaign trail," she snapped. "I've heard it all before. I need to know if you had anything to do with those accidents."

"Don't be absurd. I'm a high-profile business-man and I'm running for governor of the state of California. How in the hell could I have done any-thing like that? Every step I take is covered by the media, and everything I do has to be open and aboveboard. I'd have to be a complete idiot to do anything like that. If anyone is investigating me, they are simply trying to take me out of the gover-nor's race. You ought to know how much Capitol Hill hates a successful independent candidate."

"If there is anything funny going on, Benson, I'll bail out on you in a heartbeat. I can't afford to have my name associated with scandal. Any kind of scandal."

The ultraliberal Catherine Woodburn had been more than eager to endorse his campaign without his having to ask for her support. She had also vol-unteered to pass on information from her commit-tee because it fit with her public persona as an ecogroupie who had zoomed in on the Green Earth Movement almost from the day it first started at-tracting widespread media attention. But he also knew that she would do as she threatened and would abandon him just as quickly if things turned sour.

"There's no scandal, Catherine, believe me. I'm as clean as rain."

"You'd better be," she snapped before abruptly terminating her call.

Rondell replaced the telephone receiver and stared out the window at the Pacific Ocean as he played back Woodburn's taped conversation. This was serious, but it wasn't the time to panic. According to what she had said, no one had suggested that he was in any way directly involved, just that he was the man who would benefit the most from a worldwide end to nuclear power plants. That element of doubt meant that they didn't have any hard information on him, but were only fishing.

He was aware that having his name kicking around the halls of Congress in that manner wasn't to his advantage. Coming to the attention of the House Intelligence Committee was like having your name mentioned to the IRS. Sooner or later someone would get bored and start snooping around. Even before he got hooked up with the cartel, Rondell had been careful to make sure that he kept his background clean. But, clean or not, there were always risks when you were the subject of a congressional investigation. And Woodburn's comment that some kind of spy agency was conducting the investigation was troubling, as well.

But this was where Hector Garcia and his bosses came in. The Cali cartel had one of the best counterintelligence agencies in the world. They should be able to counter this one way or the other.

He reached for the intercom button on his speaker phone. "Hector, can you come in here. We need to talk."

GARCIA WAS WEARING a yachting outfit, the kind that screamed old-money establishment. During the past two years, Rondell had never seen the Mexican wear anything casual like blue jeans or a golf shirt.

"What's up?"

"I have just received word that my name came up in the House Intelligence Committee in conjunction with the nuclear accidents."

"Your pet congresswoman came through again," the Mexican stated.

"She also threatened to bail out on me at the slightest hint of scandal, as she put it."

Garcia laughed. "You don't need to worry about her turning on you," he said. "A couple of her little environmentalist playmates were underage, and we have the photographic evidence to keep her in line if she tries to run out on us."

"That's not what I'm concerned about. I'm worried about what the committee will find when they start looking into Sunflash. Particularly into the financing of our Baja operation.''

Garcia smiled. ''That will not be a problem. Like I told you when we set this thing up, the financing is bulletproof. The money had been laundered so many times that it's whiter than white. And since we now have the blessing of the Mexican government, it is not an American affair. I can assure you that if they get too nosy, the Mexican government will put a stop to it. They are counting on us to provide the power they need to build their economy. But I will have to get this information to the board of directors immediately. This will have to be carefully considered and plans made to deal with it.''

''Maybe there is something I can do to stop this thing,'' Rondell said.

''What's that?''

''I can go public and say that I've learned that I'm being investigated by the federal government and claim that it's an effort by the major parties to derail my candidacy. The media will love that. In fact, if I work this right, I think I can gain a couple more points in the polls with it and, at the same time, put an end to the investigation itself. Using the federal government to torpedo an independent candidate is un-American.''

Garcia thought for a moment. "That's a good idea. Go ahead with it. But I'm still going to report this to Cali. They might want to take steps, as well."

"Just as long as it's subtle," Rondell warned. As he knew too well, the cartel often used a club when a flyswatter would do just as well.

"It will be," Garcia promised. "Things are going too well for us not to move carefully now."

"What about the polls?" Rondell brought up the other thing that was bothering him. "Did you see the forecast last night? I'm still lagging by fifteen percent."

Garcia's smile was all white teeth. "Just wait until the end of the week, Benson. You'll make all of that up and even jump ahead."

"What are you going to do?"

"I have discussed this with Cali and they think that we need another nuclear 'accident.'"

"Where?"

"That is what we are working on right now. Some of the board of directors want the accident to occur in the States. But others are talking about either Siberia or North Korea."

There was a side of Benson Rondell that deplored the fact that it was necessary to destroy the nuclear plants to achieve his goals. But he also thrilled to know that he commanded such power.

He had come a long way from the days when he had been an engineering school geek with a bad case of acne trying to find a date. Now he was the owner and CEO of a company that was about to become the most powerful organization in the world. And he was also about to become the governor of the most influential state in the country. From there, the White House couldn't be far away.

"Tell them that I'd like to hold off on the next strike until I can make my statement about the congressional investigation. I think it will be more effective that way. If the accident occurs after I have said that I know that I'm being closely watched, no one will think that I would dare to have anything to do with it."

Garcia thought for a moment. "You may have a point there. And if we organize another Green Earth demonstration, we can pick up even more support. I think another go at the Diablo Canyon plant would work nicely."

"Particularly if the police react badly," Rondell added. "We need to have the public completely on our side, and there's nothing that will do that like a little well-televised police brutality."

Rondell thought for a moment. "See if you can arrange for a girl to get hurt this time. The media always likes to exploit violence toward women.

We'll be able to get a lot of mileage out of hospital bedside interviews with her.''

Garcia smiled. ''I'm sure that can be arranged. The new shipment of AKs came in, and I have one of our specialists on hand. A well-aimed shot will do it.''

''She'll need to be a throwaway we can expend,'' Rondell said, ''rather than a Green Shirt officer. Just a concerned citizen who's willing to put her life on the line to save the planet from a nuclear holocaust.''

''That shouldn't be a problem,'' Garcia said. ''Gilmore says that he's been signing them up by the dozens in the last few weeks, and they're not all your typical ecofreaks.''

''Good. Tell him to find a solid-citizen type with a family, a job and the whole nine yards, not a dropout or a complete whacko. If this is going to work, we have to keep it as close to the mainstream as we can.''

''I'm sure that Derek can find someone for us. He's good at that sort of thing.''

Derek Gilmore was an enigma to Rondell. All he knew about the man was that he had come from the cartel highly recommended as an organizer and a leader of clandestine operations. Beyond that, he knew very little about him. He had to admit, however, that Gilmore had done a fantastic job of whipping the Green Earth Movement into shape as a force to be reckoned with on many levels. He was the one who had recommended using the award of the right to wear the green shirts as a way to reward those who were truly devoted to the cause. He was also the one who had organized the San Francisco demonstration at the PCP site. Whomever he was, he was good at what he did and would be an asset in the future.

"And," Rondell added, "try to have her get hit by a police bullet if possible."

Garcia smiled. "I'll try."

CHAPTER EIGHT

Stony Man Farm

When Aaron Kurtzman's computer team was finished with their preliminary electronic look into Benson Rondell, he called Barbara Price into the War Room for a briefing. She took her place at the table without a word and nodded at Hunt Wethers, who was waiting behind the podium with a thick stack of paper in front of him.

"Unfortunately everything about Benson Rondell and Sunflash checks out, more or less," Wethers began. "Everything except for the fact that he and his company haven't made enough money to be doing half the things he's been doing lately. Companies like his are notorious for loosing money, rather than making it. And, until recently, his Sunflash has been no exception."

"What kind of money are we talking about here?" Price asked. "Millions?"

"Tens of millions."

"That's not exactly chicken feed."

"It is when you see how much was put out to move his operation down to Mexico," Wethers said. "It's true that some of that expense was subsidized by the Mexican government, but he's built a very expensive facility down there and he didn't have the cash to do it. Nor, at first, the credit to do it. Now, though, it seems that he has more money on tap than he can spend."

Price was a firm believer in the old dictum of "Follow the money and everything else falls into place." Particularly this kind of money. "That's where we'll concentrate, then."

She turned to Kurtzman. "Can you get into the Mexican banking system?"

"No problem. Their computer security systems are years behind us."

"Get in there, then, and find out where all his money is coming from. And find out how the money got to the people who are giving it to him."

"Can do."

"Another interesting thing," Wethers continued, "is that Rondell had the Chinese launch a communications satellite for him a few months ago."

"Why the Chinese?"

"They'll do it cheaper than anyone else. Now that they've got their Red Dragon launcher working reliably, they've been taking business away from the other satellite launching services left and right. The French are even thinking of shutting down their own launch facility in French Guiana because of the revenue they've lost to them.

"What's most interesting about this, though," Wethers went on, "is that the satellite itself was built in South Korea before being shipped to Rondell's facility in Mexico for further modification."

"What kind of mods were done to it?"

"I don't have the slightest idea. And since all the work was done in-house, there's no easy way that we can find out. But according to the Sunflash company newsletter, it was modified so it could handle a new sophisticated communications security system."

"Is that likely?"

"Actually it is. Commercial communications and computer security is a real hot item in the business world right now. With the demise of the Soviet Union, all the spies are working for commercial interests, and a lot of companies are designing their own security systems, hoping to beat the hackers."

"What else do you have?"

"The one thing that we need to look into further is Rondell's connection with the Green Earth Movement. As you may know, they have been rather active on the antinuke front lately."

"That's an understatement."

Bolan's report of the protest and GEM's tie-in to the shootout in British Columbia had arrived right on the heels of Katz's brush with them in France. That, combined with the widely televised San Francisco and Tokyo riots, had moved the Green Earth Movement to the top of the suspect list. Rondell's connections to the radical environmentalists could be an important piece of the picture.

"While we don't know his exact tie to them, we do know that he's one of their major financial backers. We can also show that the Green Shirts became a force to be reckoned with in the environmentalist scene after he started making his contributions to the cause. But at this time we can't prove that he's actually calling the shots and directing the organization's activities."

"How much money is he giving them?"

"According to the IRS, it's within reason for a company the size of his. Plus, he lists additional personal contributions on his own itemized deductions. But again, they're also within the limits. If he's completely bankrolling them, it doesn't show up anywhere on paper. So far it looks like he's just one of the new 'concerned' businessmen trying to look 'greener than green' so he doesn't piss off the politically correct ecovoters."

"So it doesn't look like the Green Shirts are his private army?"

Hunt hesitated a moment before answering. "Not that we can prove at this time."

"Keep working on that angle, too," she said. "Hal has a feeling about those guys, and I completely agree with him. It's just too convenient that the world's biggest maker of solar-energy systems has the world's biggest bunch of antinuke protestors on his side. If he's not calling the shots, I'm going to be surprised."

"And," Wethers said, closing his folder, "I'm afraid that's all that we have at this time."

"So what do we really have here?" Price asked rhetorically. "We have a high-tech, would-be California political hopeful who spends more money than he seems to have on an expensive new facility in Mexico. He backs a radical environmental group and also has his own communications satellite that was built overseas and no one knows anything about it. And what does all this really mean?

"It doesn't mean jack, gentlemen," Price stated, answering her own question. "And none of it ties him into the nuclear accidents in any way. I can't go to Hal with this. He needs more."

"Exactly what do you want us to find?" Kurtzman asked.

Price leaned back in her chair, closed her eyes and stuck her long legs out straight in front of her. "I want a complete personality profile on this guy and his entire operation. And not just what you can glean from magazines. I want the goods on this guy. Everything from his jock size to his preference in women, or men, as the case might be.

"And, while you're doing that," she added, "I'm going to put Able Team to work on this, too. He might have moved his operation down to Mexico, but he was based in California for years. And if he's bad, he has to have left his fingerprints behind on something, somewhere."

"Has Lyons finished that gunrunning investigation yet?" Kurtzman asked.

"Not really," Price admitted. "But I'm pulling them off that for now. Hal has put a priority on Rondell, and I need to get something for him he can pass on to the President before he swallows his cigar."

Kurtzman smiled. "I can assume that he's been on the horn to you?"

Price grimaced. "He's been in contact every so often since he got back to his office. The President is facing a congressional inquiry into the aftermath of the Diablo Canyon incident, and he wants to know how and why it happened so he doesn't look like a complete idiot again."

"What do you want me to tell the Ironman when I give him the news? You know he doesn't like to be pulled off a case until it's finished."

"Just fax him everything you have on Rondell's California activities and tell him to get going on it ASAP. If he's got any questions, tell him to call me directly."

"Can do."

Price stood. "In the meantime, gentlemen, get to it."

"Does she mean *get to it,* as in all assholes and elbows?" Kurtzman grinned, then turned to Wethers. "It's old Army slang for troops who are busy policing up the area or digging holes in the ground. They're bent over at the waist and their arms are moving."

Wethers shook his head. "I sure didn't learn anything like that at Berkeley."

"I don't think you learned anything about an operation like this at Berkeley."

Wethers laughed. "You've got that right."

Kurtzman spun his chair around and headed for the door. Price had said that she wanted everything that there was to know about Rondell, so he would get it for her.

Near the California–Mexico Border

ABLE TEAM HAD BEEN investigating a cadre of Mexican gunrunners, but the play had gone sour. Beyond the fact that Lyons had made a small buy, they hadn't come up with anything they could use.

"Maybe we should just declare a Nixon-style victory and go home," Schwarz said. "This is a no-go for sure."

"I can't figure out what we're doing wrong, though," Blancanales said. "We've tried every contact we were given, but nothing has worked. We're obviously going at this the wrong way."

"There's sure as hell more to this than we've been able to come up with," Lyons agreed. "There were all those reports of Chinese AKs coming up from Mexico, and we haven't been able to tap into it at all."

"In case you didn't notice," Schwarz said, "those were M-16s you bought, not AKs."

"I know that," Lyons retorted. "The man said that he didn't have any AKs at the moment, but that he could make me a deal on half a dozen M-16s at the same price. Which, if you were up on costing weapons, was a hell of a deal. It would have looked odd if I hadn't gone for it."

"Maybe your seller isn't even connected with the Mexican gunrunners," Blancanales broke in. "Maybe he just wanted to unload some hot M-16s he happened to have had. Have you run the numbers on them yet?"

"No," Lyons admitted.

Schwarz got up out of his chair and headed for the laptop and modem he had set up on the desk in the room. A few minutes later he turned back to Lyons.

"Pol was right," he announced. "The M-16s you bought were ripped off from an Army National Guard depot in Utah last year. You were dealing with homegrown scumbags, not the imported variety."

"Shit!" Lyons said. "I'd better let Barbara know that we're at the end of the line."

"While you're at it," Blancanales said, "you might ask her if she has something else for us to do. We're not making much headway here."

"I know that, dammit!"

Vancouver, British Columbia

MACK BOLAN LOCATED Ian Magruder's hospital room by following the RCMP visitors going in to see him. The staff sergeant was hooked up to an IV drip and had an oxygen tube in his nose, but he was looking better than when Bolan had last seen him.

"I understand that you created somewhat of a sensation up there," Magruder said when he saw his visitor.

Bolan smiled thinly. "I guess you could say that. I don't think that the brass at CSIS were expecting to have a 'visiting fireman' take over in quite that manner, but a quick call to Washington got it all sorted out. They're not going to throw me in jail after all."

"You got them all, didn't you?"

Bolan nodded.

"And you got the hostages out safely?"

"Yeah."

"I'd like to thank you for saving my life and then saving the hostages."

"I'm glad to have been able to do it."

"I'm afraid that this will be my swan song," Magruder said, changing the subject. "My wife always gets mad when I go out in the field, and lately she's been after me to hand in my badge. This has fairly put the icing on the cake."

"It's a young man's game and you've done your part."

"You're not too much younger than I am, and I don't see you reading retirement-home brochures."

Bolan grinned. "I don't have a wife who's patiently waiting to spend the rest of her life with me. You'd better take her up on it before she decides that you're a lost cause and turns you in for a new one."

"Mr. Wilkenson, the man you rescued, has offered me a position as a security consultant for his company. It's a part-time desk job, and the pay's more than adequate."

"Take him up on it. It'll give you something to do in your retirement, but you won't have to get shot at. I'm sure it will make your wife a happier woman."

Magruder looked out the window for a moment. "I think you're right," he said. "It's gotten to the point that I need to look after number one, as you Americans say."

"I don't think you'll regret it."

"God, I hope not."

CHAPTER NINE

San Diego, California

"She wants us to do what?" Hermann Schwarz asked when Carl Lyons came back from the pay phone across the street. The three men of Able Team were still hanging around their motel suite waiting for something to develop, and Lyons had just checked in with Stony Man.

He grinned. "She wants us to do a background investigation on a high-profile businessman turned local politician named Benson Rondell."

Rosario Blancanales frowned. "You mean the guy whose face I've been seeing all over the place? The one who's running for governor?"

"That's the one."

"What's his scam?" Schwarz asked.

"That's what she wants us to find out."

"Why waste our time with this bullshit instead of letting Kurtzman run it up on his computers?"

"She wants the dirt, the real story."

"'Enquiring minds want to know,'" Schwarz quipped. "What's this guy accused of doing, other than skimming campaign funds and harassing the female volunteers, that is?''

"Blowing up nuclear power plants."

"Oh, that kind of dirt." Schwarz grinned. "That's okay then. I can handle that."

"I thought you might be able to. Particularly since it involves your going undercover."

"Why didn't she give me the undercover assignment?" Blancanales asked. Usually he did most of the team's undercover work because of his proven ability to work people to his advantage.

"She wants you free," Lyons replied, "to follow up on whatever Gadgets comes up with. You know, the office and club interviews."

"Where am I going undercover?" Schwarz asked.

"That's the best part of the deal, Bucko. You're going to sign on with an environmental group, the local chapter of the Green Earth Movement in Santa Barbara."

Schwarz was stunned. "You're kidding me, I hope."

"Nope."

"But aren't those the guys who smashed that power company president's body to shreds?"

Lyons nodded. "But don't worry. We'll keep track of you. The Bear's got a full legend worked up for you. All you have to do is go to a couple of meetings, ask a few questions and get a take on what's going on, that sort of thing."

"What kind of questions? I don't know diddly about trees and that kind of crap."

"Not questions about trees, dammit. They need to know if these nut cases have a special operations branch, a dirty-tricks department, and if they've been talking about knocking out nuke plants lately."

"Right. I walk in there and say, 'Hey guys! Anyone want to blow up a nuke plant?' and see who raises their hand. Piece of cake, nothing to it. Why don't I ever get any of the tough assignments instead of these weenie jobs?"

"I told Barbara you'd understand the mission."

"Thanks a lot."

Santa Barbara, California

HERMANN SCHWARZ LOOKED right at home in his stylish outfit when he walked into the community center for the Green Earth Movement meeting. With his hair fashionably long, but not too much so, he looked like a politically correct baby boomer doing his civic duty by showing his concern for the environment.

He had arrived early so he could scope out the place, but the meeting hall was almost empty. So, when the woman behind the mike started having trouble with the PA set, he walked up to the podium to make his first contact.

"Maybe I can help you fix that," he said, nodding at the PA amplifier. "I mess around with electronics a lot."

"Oh, would you please?" the woman said. "I don't have any idea what's wrong with it."

"I'm Alex Lord," Schwarz stated, offering his hand.

"I'm Sylvia Bowes," she said as she took his hand. "I don't think I've seen you here before."

He grinned sheepishly and shrugged. "No, I haven't been active in the movement in a long time. But with everything that's been going down lately, I thought that I should get involved again."

He stepped up onto the stage. "And the first thing I can do to get involved is to see if I can fix that amplifier for you."

He quickly discovered that the problem with the PA set was a corroded connector on one of the wires leading into the amp. Taking out his pocket-knife, he scraped it clean and plugged it back into the socket.

"There," he said as he straightened. "That should do it. Try it now."

She did and the microphone worked perfectly. "You're good at that."

"I should be, I'm an electrical engineer."

"Thank you, and I'm glad you came to the meeting."

"Me too."

After the meeting—a dull hour and a half of old business and back patting—Schwarz approached Bowes again. "I don't mean to be forward," he said, "but could I interest you in a latte? I don't know anyone else here, and there's a coffee shop right around the corner."

As he had expected, she took him up on his offer. He didn't have the smooth moves that Blancanales did, but he did all right for himself and he had picked up the right vibes from her.

After they got their coffee at the shop's counter and sat at a corner table, Schwarz launched into the "getting to know you" phase of the operation. If that went well, he'd go right into his "getting to know you even better" sequence. He didn't have much time, and he was willing to sacrifice himself for the cause. It didn't hurt that she wasn't all that bad to look at.

"I was with Earth First! in Oregon before they broke up," he said, starting in on his legend. Barbara Price and Kurtzman had faxed him an activist's bio that would stand up under a cursory inquiry. The Alex Lord of Earth First! had died in a Florida drug deal gone bad and had left no relatives behind. His name, though, would be on the

Earth First! roster if anyone wanted to verify his credentials.

"But," he said, shrugging, "I move around a lot with my work and I kind of dropped out of it, you know."

Bowes nodded sympathetically. "Sometimes it's so difficult."

Schwarz wasn't quite sure what it was that she thought was "so difficult," but whatever it was, it looked like he had her on his side so far.

"Anyway, I saw a flier for the meeting and thought I'd drop in and see what was going on down here."

"Oh, we're a real active chapter," she said. "We have six full-fledged Green Shirts and several more just about to make it into the ranks."

Schwarz was confused, and it had to have shown on his face because she quickly explained, "Only those who have proven their commitment to the organization are allowed to wear the green shirt. It's a real honor."

"How does one go about proving that?" he asked.

The woman's eyes took on a glow of excitement. "The regional office keeps track of the meetings and demonstrations you attend and the number of people that you recruit. Also, they count the contributions you make. And then, after you have proven yourself, they have a ceremony in the ancient forest and present you with your green shirt.''

She paused and looked down at her coffee. ''I know it sounds like the Boy Scouts, but they're really serious about saving the earth.''

Schwarz managed to keep his face straight. It sounded more like the Nazis to him, rather than the Boy Scouts. The Brown Shirts had gone to the woods, too, when they accepted another thug into their ranks. Their program, though, had been to save the earth for the German people by killing everyone else.

''Do you have your shirt yet?'' he asked.

She dropped her gaze again. ''No. I haven't been able to give it enough of my time. It's so hard to do what's right when you have to support other people. I love my daughter,'' she hastened to say. ''But if her father would take her on the weekends more often, I would be able to give more of my time to the movement.''

Schwarz made sympathetic sounds as she launched into a long and complicated account of her marriage to a man who didn't love the earth the way she did. His real sympathies, however, lay with her ex, who at least had had enough brains to dump this woman when she joined the eco-Nazis.

He was so tuned out, running on automatic pilot, that he almost missed her pickup line. ''Sure,'' he said when he realized that she had just asked him to come home with her for a nightcap. "I'd love that."

A couple hours later he was a bit put off when she moaned a name that sounded like Derek at the height of her passion. But, considering that he had known her for only six hours, it was understandable.

He would, however, have to find out who this Derek guy was. Her ex's name was Frank.

"SOMEONE HAS ALREADY run an employment and police record check on Alex Lord," Lyons said when Schwarz checked in with him the next day. With Stony Man's connections, his cover had been given a police record and an electronics company was carrying him on their books as a telecommuter employee. Theses records had also been flagged so that if anyone checked up on him, that fact would be passed on to the Farm.

"Geez," Schwarz said. "I've only been on the case a little over a day."

"Whatever you've been doing," Lyons said, "keep on doing it. It seems to be working."

Schwarz grinned, remembering the night before. "I don't think that will be a problem."

EARLY FRIDAY EVENING, Sylvia Bowes called to ask if Schwarz would like to go to a Green Earth

Movement rally. Her ex-husband had relented and was taking their daughter for the weekend, so she was free until Monday. Before he even had a chance to invite her over, she said that she would like to take him out to dinner and then asked if she could stay at his place afterward, so they could drive to the rally together in the morning.

Schwarz really liked modern women; they made his job so much easier.

AT THE RALLY the next morning, Schwarz didn't have to look far to find the Derek that Bowes had mentioned in bed. Derek Gilmore was the leader of the local chapter of the Green Earth Movement, and Bowes insisted that Schwarz meet him as soon as they arrived.

Gilmore didn't fit the mold of the typical environmental activist, though. For one thing, the brawny blonde looked more like an out-of-work commando. He wore the mandatory, well-washed plaid shirt with an outdoorsman's vest, but they were worn over a pair of camouflage battle dress uniform pants and a well-broken-in pair of Army-issue combat boots.

"Sylvia tells me that you're an electronics specialist?" Gilmore asked while he tried Schwarz's grip.

"That's right." Gadgets returned the pressure of the man's hand without flinching. Obviously he was intruding on what Gilmore saw as his territory.

"That's one thing we really need in the group, someone who can keep track of our equipment."

"What kind of gear are you talking about?"

Gilmore's faded blue eyes drilled into him. "Oh, just the usual organizational stuff. Sound equipment, tape and video recorders, that sort of thing."

"No sweat. I can handle it."

The featured speaker that afternoon was none other than California's most famous ecocandidate Benson Rondell. When the candidate's helicopter landed, he was almost mobbed by the faithful. Three other men got off the chopper with him. Two of them wore the green shirts of the movement's leadership, but looked like upper-level management types. The other one was a Hispanic male in his early thirties, wearing an expensive business suit. He looked for all the world like one of the drug cartel's polished front men, and Schwarz was instantly interested.

"Who's the guy in the suit with Rondell?" he asked Bowes.

"I don't know. I've seen him at several of Rondell's rallies and I think he's part of the campaign staff, but I don't know who he is."

"You go to a lot of the Rondell campaign functions?"

"Of course," she said. "I've been to every one that I could, and I've handed out his pamphlets and put up lawn signs all over town."

Rondell quickly mounted the stage and spoke about the horrors of the recent nuclear power accidents in India and Japan. It was preaching to the converted, but the crowd ate it up. Schwarz had to admit that the man could work a crowd. After a little less than an hour, he got back on the chopper and flew away to another appearance.

As they were leaving, Derek Gilmore approached them. "We're having a demonstration at Diablo Canyon tomorrow at noon," he said, looking straight at Bowes. "Can I count on your being there?"

"Yes," she answered, her eyes shining. "I'll be there."

"Me too," Schwarz hastened to add.

Gilmore smiled thinly. "Good, we need all the people we can get."

The man did an abrupt about-face and walked off.

"Do you know if Derek was ever in the Army?" Schwarz asked Bowes.

She frowned. "I don't know. Why?"

"Nothing. He just reminded me of someone I used to know."

All the way back to his apartment, Bowes kept up a running chatter about how proud she was that Derek Gilmore had asked her to go to the Diablo Canyon demonstration. It turned out that this was the first time she had been personally asked to show up, and she saw it as a sign that she was being considered as a Green Shirt candidate.

Schwarz wisely kept his own counsel and only murmured in the right places whenever she paused to take a breath. He didn't want to spoil their evening together.

CHAPTER TEN

Stony Man Farm

When Mack Bolan saw the verdant green hills of the Blue Ridge Mountains appear through the canopy of the Bell JetRanger helicopter, he was glad to be home again. Normally he didn't have much use for a home, not with the life he had lived for so many years. But Stony Man Farm was the closest thing to a home that he had. It was the place where he could get a home-cooked meal, have his laundry done and go to sleep without needing to wear his shoulder holster.

To most people, that wouldn't have been very much. But to a man in his line of work it meant a great deal.

What little he owned in the world was also stored at the Farm—not that he owned all that much: the personalized tools of his trade, a few mementos from the men and women who had been important to him and a couple changes of clothes were all that he could call his own. The life he led didn't lend itself to collecting the material goods that almost all other Americans considered to be absolutely essential to their lives. The things he valued most were his few enduring friendships, and Stony Man Farm was where his friends usually were.

One of his oldest friends was piloting the Bell JetRanger. Jack Grimaldi was Stony Man's resident hotshot pilot and aviation expert. He and Bolan went back more years than the Executioner liked to remember.

"Time to check in," Grimaldi said over the intercom. "I don't want Cowboy to get excited and warm up one of his Stingers."

Bolan smiled. Along with the ground defenses, the Farm had a full complement of ground-to-air weapons, as well. Aerial intruders were treated no better than any other kind. Fly too close to the Farm, and they would shoot first and ask questions later.

"Stony Base," Grimaldi called on the skip frequency scrambler used to secure all communications with the Farm, "this is Fly-boy. I'm inbound with my beeper beeping and requesting landing clearance."

"Roger, Fly-boy." The answer came as soon as his message cleared through the voiceprint analysis. "We've had you on the screen for the last fifteen mikes. Conditions are green, SOP in effect. You are cleared to land."

The last part of the message told him that the Farm wasn't under an alert and that he could set down the chopper without being tracked by John "Cowboy" Kissinger's antiaircraft defenses and blown out of the sky if he made a wrong move.

"Roger. We're on the way in."

The dirt landing strip that cut through the farmland looked like any other well-to-do farmer's landing strip and fit right in with the rest of the Stony Man facade. But, like everything else at the Farm, its looks were deceiving. Under the dirt, grass and camouflage was a concrete runway long enough to land a jet fighter if necessary. Grimaldi flared the chopper out in the middle of the runway and, as soon as the skids touched down, dumped his collective and reached out to cut the fuel to the turbines.

"I wonder what's hot today?" Bolan said.

"Damned if I know," the pilot replied. "You know how it is. No one tells me anything except fly here and fly there. I'm going to find me one of those mushroom patches we used to wear and sew it onto my flight suit."

Bolan grinned as he reached behind the seat for his kit bag. "Get me one of them too while you're at it."

Even though the Farm wasn't under an alert, a jeep full of blacksuits met the chopper anyway. As soon as Bolan and the pilot stepped down, they quickly went over the machine to ensure that it wasn't carrying any unwanted packages, particularly explosive or tracer-beacon packages. When the chopper was declared to be clean, it was towed over to the fuel tanks to be serviced and refueled.

When Bolan turned, he saw that Barbara Price had come to meet him, as well. "Hi, Barb." He smiled.

This was one of the other reasons he liked stopping by the Farm every now and then. Even in a life like his, there was still a place for beauty, and Barbara Price was one of the most beautiful women he had ever met. Even so, he had little personal time to spend with her.

"I'm glad you're back, Mack," she said in her business voice. "I'm calling in Phoenix force, and I'd like you to work with them on this one."

"What's up?"

"Hal thinks that there's a program underway to do away with the world's nuclear power plants."

"You mean the accidents at Diablo Canyon, India and Japan?"

"Yes."

"Who does he think is behind this?"

"A politician in California."

"You mean that guy who's running for governor?"

"Benson Rondell, yes."

"Other than being extremely vocal about the dangers of nuke plants, what's he done?"

"That's what I've got Able Team and Aaron's people working on finding out right now."

Even though it seemed unlikely to him, Bolan knew that if it had gone that far, there was probably something to it. Barbara and Hal didn't waste the Farm's resources on wild goose chases.

"I guess you'd better brief me on the situation."

Diablo Canyon

HERMANN SCHWARZ DIDN'T like the look of the situation at all. Whoever had planned the demonstration had created a recipe for disaster. There were far too many demonstrators and far too few police. There were also too many media vans with their video cameras and satcom links ready to record what happened and beam it to the networks.

He had read Bolan's report of the Green Earth confrontation at the dam site in British Columbia, and this looked like a rehash of that fiasco. The outnumbered San Luis Obispo County officers were in full riot gear with shields and batons, but they still looked nervous. All it would take would be one shot, from either side, and the place would explode.

"Don't you think that we ought to try to keep a low profile here?" he asked Sylvia Bowes as she tried to pull him through the crowd to get closer to the front line.

"Why?" she asked. Her face was flushed with excitement and her eyes glittered.

Why was it that people were so often turned on by the thought of danger, but usually didn't take the most simple precautions that would keep them from being nailed by it? "I think it's going to get nasty up there," he said cautiously. "Let's just hang back here so we don't get caught in the tear gas."

"But I want to be up there." She pointed toward the police lines in front of the barricaded entrance to the power plant.

Against his better judgment, Schwarz allowed himself to be pulled along after her. She was a bit naive, granted, but he didn't want to see her hurt. Maybe if he was with her he could get her out if things developed the way he thought they were going to.

He did manage to get her to stay in the third row. For all of her enthusiasm to get in on the "action," the sight of sweating cops behind their riot shields tempered her ardor somewhat.

No sooner were they in place than one of the Green Shirt coordinators walked by. "You there," he said, looking directly at Schwarz. "As soon as I give the sign, go for them. We want to force them back inside the gate."

The chanting grew louder, and Schwarz heard the police commander shout commands as the crowd surged forward. For a short time, it was bodies and protest signs against police batons. Many a demonstrator fell or turned back holding his or her head. But eventually the police lines were slowly forced back against the gate.

When Schwarz heard the first shot ring out, he grabbed for Bowes's arm to pull her down to safety. But he was too late. Her green eyes widened and she gasped, "My God!"

Schwarz saw a rapidly growing red stain appear on her lower back as her knees gave out and she crumpled to the ground. He scooped her up into his arms and spun around.

"Let me through!" he shouted as he shoved his way through the stunned protestors. "She's been shot!"

More shots rang out over the screams of the panicked demonstrators, but he didn't duck. He had to get her to the ambulances he had seen on their way in.

Pasadena, California

BENSON RONDELL and Hector Garcia were watching the live coverage of the demonstration on a news channel when the firing broke out and the tear gas erupted. Unlike the demonstrators in France, these protestors didn't have gas masks in their backpacks. They hadn't been ordered to carry masks because that would have tipped off the authorities that they had planned a violent confrontation. For this thing to play to Rondell's advantage on the six-o'clock news, it had to appear as if the police were the aggressors.

"Okay," Garcia said as he watched the protestors scatter, "we're set. You go down there tomorrow, visit the site of the confrontation and make an impassioned speech. Lay some flowers on the blood spots and the whole trip."

As good as Garcia's English was, he occasionally slipped into a slang expression that had long gone out of use. Every time Rondell noticed that trait, he was reminded that he had tied his fate to foreigners who didn't think exactly the same way that he did. But so far their thinking had been on the same track.

Rondell punched the intercom button to his secretary's office. "Yes, sir?"

"Get Jameson to write a short speech for me about the Diablo Canyon demonstration today," he said. "Nothing too dramatic, but have him tie this incident into the San Francisco riot. Tell him to emphasize that this is just one more indication of the will of the people to see an end to the nuclear terror in our backyards, that sort of thing. He'll know what spin to put on it."

"Right away, Mr. Rondell."

He turned back to Garcia. "This might be a good time for us to up the ante with that accident the board has been planning. Have they made a decision where they want it to occur yet?"

"They decided on Siberia," Garcia answered. "They want a real disaster this time that will completely panic the voters into seeing things your way. It's a Chernobyl-type plant, and it should go up quite nicely."

Considering that the Chernobyl incident had rendered several thousand square miles contaminated for centuries, a similar disaster, even in Siberia, would panic a lot of people no matter where they lived.

"It sounds good." Rondell smiled.

Diablo Canyon

SHOUTING AND CURSING, Schwarz forced his way through the panicked demonstrators with Bowes cradled protectively in his arms. At least someone had had the foresight to have a couple of ambulances on the scene. One of the paramedic crews saw him coming, opened the back of their vehicle and quickly got a gurney ready for the casualty.

"She's got a bullet wound in the back," he panted as he gently laid her on her unwounded side. "I don't know her blood type, so start a Ringer's IV, put a compress on it and give her oxygen."

"You a medic?" one of the ambulance crew asked.

Schwarz didn't want to get into a long-winded conversation about his qualifications to prescribe for a gunshot victim while she was bleeding to death. "Yeah."

As soon as the gurney was inside and locked down, Schwarz climbed into the back of the ambulance for the ride to the hospital. All the way there, he talked to her over the wail of the sirens, trying to keep her mind focused so she wouldn't go into deep shock and die before she could get to the emergency room.

Fortunately there was a hospital only a few miles away and the ambulance radioed ahead to put the trauma team on standby. Once she was in the hands of the ER crew, Schwarz ducked out a side entrance to wait out of sight until she came out of surgery.

Already the media vans were on the scene, and he didn't want some jerk to shove a microphone in his face and ask him how he felt. He couldn't afford to have his snarling face seen on the news while he was helping some reporter eat his microphone. He was supposed to be undercover, not the lead-in story.

CHAPTER ELEVEN

Stony Man Farm

Bolan was in the computer center, pouring himself a cup of coffee. Hal Brognola hadn't officially declared that a mission was on yet, but it was certain that one was shaping up. It was time for him to sit down and read himself into the situation so he could come up to speed as soon as possible.

Hunt Wethers handed him a folder. "You might want to familiarize yourself with what we've come up with so far on our man Benson Rondell."

Bolan took the folder, but laid it aside. "Just brief me, Hunt. Tell me who this guy is and why you think he's behind this."

Wethers quickly told the soldier as much as was known about Rondell, starting with his first degree, in electrical engineering with a physics minor, and his early design work for a company that built solar water-heating units.

"From there," Wethers said, "he patented the design for his solar-power generating system and started his own company with family money and a federal EPA grant. After struggling with his cash flow for several years, he apparently found a Mexican godfather, several actually, who have poured money into his company. From there, he has exploded all over the California scene. He keeps his corporate headquarters in Pasadena, but he's moved his manufacturing and research facility to Baja. And, of course, he's now running for governor."

The nice thing about working with Hunt Wethers, Bolan thought, was that his academic training gave him the ability to lay all the facts out in as brief a statement as possible. "What do we know about his personal life?"

"Not a lot," Wethers admitted. "He lives like a Boy Scout with no known vices except sponsoring environmentalist causes."

"How long has be been a megalomaniac?"

Wethers grinned. "As far as we know, he's been bent on saving the world since he was in engineering school. His big thing is to try to save the world from all uses of nuclear energy. I guess he was one of those kids who got scared to death by his grade-school Civil-Defense 'duck and cover' drills."

"But his company was failing before the Mexicans stepped in to prop him up, right?"

"That's about it," Wethers said. "None of the alternative-energy companies has ever made it on its own once it's run out of federal money."

Bolan turned to Kurtzman. "I know you've run his finances, so where did the Mexican money come from?"

Kurtzman frowned. "That's the weird thing. It's so clean that it squeaks. I looked for the cartel's fingerprints, but except for the fact that some of the money came from offshore banks, I wasn't able to tie them into it."

"That's too bad," Bolan said. "This has the smell of a cartel front job all over it. The fact that the money is so clean is almost a trademark."

"But why would drug lords want to blow up nuclear power plants?" Wethers asked.

"That's easy," Bolan replied. "If they've dumped a bundle of their money into a solar-energy company, they want a return on their investment. The problem is, of course, that no solar-power generating system can compete with cheap nuclear power. So, to recover their money, they have to create a market for their product, and blowing up nuke plants is a good way to start. Plus, once they're in and are controlling a nation's power supply, they control that nation."

"What can you come up with on the layout of Rondell's facility in Baja?" Bolan asked, changing the subject.

"Nothing yet," Kurtzman replied. "The main problem is that it was built in Mexico. If it had been built in the States, I'd have access to the blueprints, the material specifications, the environmental impact statements, the whole nine yards. As it is, though, the Mexican government isn't too concerned about bureaucratic crap like that. His Mexican backers probably greased a few palms in the right places, and he was allowed to build any damned thing he wanted, and to hell with the paperwork.

"But," he concluded, "I can at least guarantee you aerial recon shots of the place. One of the NRO birds is coming up over the Pacific any time now."

"That'll be a good start."

Kurtzman's fingers flew over his keyboard, bringing up a menu with red block letters across the top and bottom screaming NRO—Top Secret—Q Clearance Required. The National Reconnaissance Office was the little known and highly classified branch of the National Security Agency that supervised the operation of the Keyhole and other intelligence-gathering and missile-warning satellites. Until the recent flap in Congress about the incredible cost of their new top-secret headquarters building in the Washington area, not one in a hundred thousand Americans had ever heard of them.

In an age of ballistic nuclear missiles, the satellites the NRO controlled were America's front line of defense against an enemy sneak attack. With their twelve-inch resolution, real-time spy cameras and multisensor packages, the KH series spy birds could also be used to gather tactical intelligence.

The NRO also operated the highly classified Aurora space planes, the Pentagon's latest aviation ultrasecret. Designed as a successor to the aging SR-71 Blackbird high-speed spy planes, the Aurora was straight out of a science-fiction movie. It was a hybrid spy plane-spaceship capable of flying more than twice as fast as the old SR-71, which held the world's official speed record for an airbreathing aircraft. That record would instantly fall as soon as the Pentagon decided to declassify the Aurora project. Kurtzman wouldn't ask Brognola to clear an Aurora flight for this mission, though. The Keyhole birds would be able to get him what he needed.

"There," he said when he was finished keying in the program. "I should have some pictures for you in less than an hour."

"Give me a call when they come in," Bolan said. "I'll be upstairs."

AFTER GETTING HIS GEAR stashed in his room, Bolan was back down in the computer center. "We've got us a bit of a problem," Kurtzman said, the expression on his face indicating his concern.

"What is it?"

"While the nation slept, that bastard built himself a fortress down there."

"What are you talking about?"

Kurtzman flashed a photo of the complex onto the big-screen monitor. The aerial shot showed a main building built into a cliff overlooking the Pacific Ocean, with a harbor and breakwaters providing moorage for small ships. The landward side of the cliff had a heliport on top and several outbuildings on the flat, with a road leading inland. The faint trace of a fence could be seen enclosing it like a military base.

"Our man Rondell's peaceful little Sunflash research center isn't quite as peaceful as he wants us to believe. When I made the recon satellite run over Baja, I did it in the full spectra mode—EMR, IR, MAD, radar."

"And?"

"And I came up with the same kind of reading I would have gotten cruising over a North Korean nuke plant. That place is armed to the teeth. He's got threat radar. I picked up mine fields on the landward side. I got MAD returns that indicate heavy weapons emplacements. He's got—"

"I get the picture," Bolan said. "The question is, where did he get that stuff."

"And how did he pay for it," Kurtzman added. "First-class military hardware isn't cheap, not even if you buy it from the Russians."

Kurtzman moved his mouse to place the cursor below an antenna farm at the edge of the cliff. "Plus, there's one more thing that doesn't compute. He's got some kind of space communications system that seems a little excessive for pure commercial communications needs. From the number of antennas and data links he has, he could run a small launch facility all by himself."

"Or control space satellites?"

"No sweat."

"Give me the rundown on that communications satellite of his again."

Kurtzman's fingers raced over the keyboard and the image of a deep-space satellite appeared on the big-screen monitor. "It's a big one," he said. "Larger than you would expect he would need for straight communications use."

"Could he have hidden a weapon inside of it? A laser or a kinetic energy missile launcher?"

"It's possible," Kurtzman acknowledged. "The thing's big enough to hold a weapon and aiming radar, and it's got more than enough solar arrays to power them."

"The question, then, is could he have gotten a hidden weapon past the Chinese when they readied it for launch?"

"I don't see that as a problem at all. Even if they'd seen it, they might not have known what it was. Plus, the Chinese are so hungry for foreign currency, even if they had recognized it, they would have launched it anyway."

"Back to the Baja complex," Bolan said. "Where are his weak points?"

Kurtzman brought the aerial view of the Sunflash complex up on the monitor again. "That's the problem. As you can see, he built his operations building back into a mountain and the land side approaches aren't good. The fence is sure to be monitored, and I picked up a mine field inside. Right now, the sea looks like the most likely avenue of approach. There's the dock where his supply ships tie up and what looks like a storage facility built in the lower level. If you come in from the sea, it looks like you'll be able to bypass most of his defenses."

"That's the way we'll go, then," Bolan said. "Start planning for a seaborne attack."

"It's already started."

LEAVING KURTZMAN to his intelligence-gathering chores, Mack Bolan went down to the armory to check on the weapons he planned to use during the mission. John Kissinger, the Farm's weaponsmith, was in residence when he walked in.

"You guys are going in by sea this time, right?"

Bolan nodded. Even though Kissinger spent little time up in the computer room, very little got past him.

"Well, I've got some new underwater goodies you guys might want to consider taking along."

"What do you have?"

"You're not going to believe this, but I've got my hands on some of those new Russian underwater assault rifles and pistols."

Bolan believed it. There was little in the world of small arms that Kissinger couldn't get his hands on if he kept at it long enough. His years of working in weapons development and design for everyone from the U.S. Army to Colt had given him an automatic "in" with weapons people all over the world. And, for the prototype stuff, his CIA contacts had always proved helpful.

"Where in the hell did you get those?"

"I bought them last year in Abu Dhabi at the IDEX defense-industry show."

"I thought they only sold in bulk at those shows."

"I bought in bulk," Kissinger explained. "Brognola authorized me to get a dozen of both the APS assault rifles and the SPP-1 pistols, as well as ten thousand rounds of ammunition for them. We're just getting them in now because of the problem that came up with the end-user export certificates. The Russians wanted a bribe to speed things along the way, and I didn't feel like paying it. Anyway, they finally gave it up and shipped the goods to us."

"When do I get to see these new toys?"

"Right this way." If there was anything Kissinger liked more than talking about weapons, it was demonstrating them. "I just happen to have one of each cleaned and ready to go."

"This thing looks like a bastard AK with no stock," Bolan said when he spotted the Russian underwater rifle.

"It uses the AK's gas system," the weaponsmith confirmed. "But the bolt system's completely different and it only fires semiauto."

Kissinger picked up a strange-looking magazine. "The mag holds twenty-six rounds. Rather than firing conventional ammunition, though, both of these weapons use a special 5.66 mm cartridge designated the MPS."

He thumbed a round out of the magazine and held it out to Bolan. "As you can see, what makes these rounds different is that instead of being loaded with a conventional bullet, they're loaded with 120 mm steel darts.''

Bolan felt the needle point of the dart. "What's the range on them?''

"In the rifle, at a depth of five meters they can kill out to thirty meters. That range goes down, of course, as the depth increases. In the air, they're lethal out to a hundred meters. The pistol gets only half that range with the same dart because of the shorter barrel.''

Bolan reached for the strange-looking rifle. "Let's see how this thing shoots.''

While Kissinger hit the switch to send a target down to the end of the basement test range, Bolan extended the underwater rifle's collapsible stock and pulled back on the charging handle to chamber a round. Bringing the rifle to his shoulder, he flicked off the safety, sighted in on the target and squeezed the trigger. The report wasn't much louder than a .22-caliber rifle, and the recoil was only slightly more, as well. The dart had hit exactly where he had aimed.

"Not bad,'' he said before ripping off three shots in rapid fire. "Not bad at all. We'll take them. Now, what about that pistol?''

"The pistol is a bit more primitive,'' Kissinger said, handing it over. "As you can see, it has four single-shot barrels and fires like an old Sharps Derringer. The firing pin rotates to fire each barrel, and it loads manually. Considering how well the rifle works, I figure this to be a backup piece if you're in too big a hurry to change magazines on the rifle."

Bolan had used other underwater weapons before—spear guns and compressed-air guns—but none of them had really been effective. These Russian underwater weapons promised to be a real improvement. "We'll take them along, too."

After looking over the Russian guns, Bolan discussed the scuba gear they would need and arranged for it to be waiting for them in California. Since they wouldn't be working with the military this time, all of the logistics would have to be handled in-house.

Leaving the armory, Bolan went outside for a walk through the orchard. Now that a mission was being planned, he was anxious to get going on it. But he knew that Brognola wouldn't give them the go-ahead until the Man in the Oval Office had signed off on it.

CHAPTER TWELVE

Santa Barbara, California

"How's Sylvia?" Derek Gilmore asked Schwarz. The Green Earth leader had shown up at his door almost the minute that he returned from the hospital. Either Gilmore's timing was impeccable, or the apartment was being watched. Schwarz's vote was for the latter.

"She's hurt real bad," Schwarz told him, his voice shaking with anger. "The doctors aren't sure that she'll ever be able to walk again. The bullet nicked her spine."

Schwarz didn't have to feign anger to flavor his reply. He was upset, but not at the police. The bullet that had been taken out of Sylvia's back hadn't come from a police weapon; it had been fired from a ChiCom AK-47. And it had been fired from behind her. She'd either been hit by accident or she had been sacrificed for the cause. Either way, he was going to extract some big-time payback for this because she was in no condition to do it herself.

"By the way," Gilmore said, "I liked the way you handled getting her to the hospital so quickly. You're a man who doesn't lose his head."

Schwarz shrugged. "I saw the ambulances and knew she needed help quickly."

"How would you like to even the score with them?"

Schwarz noticed that Gilmore didn't say who "them" was, but he also knew that the Green Earther wasn't talking about the guy who had actually shot Sylvia Bowes.

"I'd love to," he said. "The bastards."

"I checked your record with Earth First!," the Green Shirt went on to say, "and I was impressed. You did some good work for them, and I need men like you to help me with some of our more sensitive projects. Like Benson Rondell says, we have to get that nuke plant shut down now. Every day that it remains in operation is one more day that we are all in danger."

Schwarz knew a line of bullshit when it was being fed to him, but again, he played along.

"What can I do to help?" he asked. "You name it and I'll do it."

"We've got something going and I'll get back to you right away," Gilmore promised.

"I'll be ready."

"I THINK I HAVE IT," Schwarz reported to Carl Lyons as soon as Gilmore left. "It looks like there's a definite tie-in between Rondell and the Green Earthers, and it sounds like they're planning some kind of operation at Diablo Canyon. Alex Lord's record with Earth First! got me invited to take part in it. That and the fact that I'm connected with Sylvia and I'm looking for a little payback."

"What's going down?"

"I don't know yet," Schwarz admitted. "But I was told it would be happening soon."

Lyons wasn't sorry to hear that Schwarz had come up with a lead, but he didn't like the way it felt to him. Gadgets hadn't been with the Green Earthers long enough for them to have accepted him for what had to be a criminal operation. It was going much too quickly, and Lyons didn't like it when things came too easily.

"I want you to come in. We need to go over our contingency plan."

"What do you mean?"

"I want to talk to you, dammit!"

"Okay, okay."

LYONS AND BLANCANALES had taken up residence on the ground floor of a midlevel motel on a quiet back street in Santa Barbara. Though the location was off the main drag, they had easy access to the highway and it was a good place to wait out Schwarz's operation. That didn't mean, however, that Lyons was going to let his teammate do it all his way.

"Dammit," Lyons said, his face right in Schwarz's, "I want you to wear one of those transponders of yours."

"But I don't need one. Gilmore thinks that I'm Alex Lord, and since Lord was a gunman for Earth First!, I'm cool with them."

"I don't give a damn if you're going to take your old Aunt Sally to a church bingo game. I want to be able to keep track of you. I don't like how this is going down."

"Okay, okay," Schwarz soothed, giving in. "I'll wear a transponder. Geez, you're acting like you're my mother or something."

"And you're acting like you haven't a brain in your head, man. This is too easy, and I think they're setting you up to take a fall. Just because that woman got hit, you don't have to go racing off on your white horse."

"I owe her one," Schwarz said, his voice low but firm. "I can't help but think that if I hadn't entered her life, she wouldn't have gotten shot."

"Gadgets," Blancanales said patiently. He had learned long ago that when Schwarz had his emotions involved, he had to go slowly. "Sylvia's a nice girl, but she's a twit or she never would have gotten involved with those assholes in the first place. You didn't invite her to that demonstration, she asked you to go with her, remember?''

"I still think that she was shot on purpose."

"Even if she was, you didn't have anything to do with it."

"And, if she was," Lyons broke in, "that's reason enough for you to go carefully around these guys. If they'll waste one of their own that way, they're not going to have a problem offing you."

"I'm not backing out," Schwarz said firmly. "I'm not going to let them get away with this."

"That's fine," Lyons told him. "Just wear that transponder so we can track you and keep your head out of your ass when you're with those guys. If something goes wrong, it'll take us a while to get to you."

Stony Man Farm

BARBARA PRICE WAS GLAD that Able Team had finally turned up something in California they could try to develop. Lyons and Blancanales had been working hard on the overt end of the investigation, but they'd had little results. As Kurtzman had said, it appeared that Rondell was clean. Maybe too clean, though.

She, too, had watched the news broadcasts of the Diablo Canyon demonstration and even though it had disintegrated into a mass panic as soon as the first shot had been fired, it had been a little too organized for her tastes. The demonstrations and protests she remembered from her younger years hadn't looked so much like Nazi Party rallies.

Plus, Schwarz wasn't the only one who thought that the Green Earthers had sacrificed the woman to get the headlines; she thought so, as well. Had it not been for Sylvia Bowes's being shot, the demonstration would have been dropped from the news on the second day. As it was now, though, the story would play as long as the media could milk it. The San Luis Obispo sheriff had already resigned and the county commissioner was under siege for not being able to control his officers.

She was glad that Schwarz had made the contact, but she was just as glad that Lyons and Blancanales were on hand to keep a close eye on Gadgets. Schwarz was levelheaded, but if his emotions were involved, it was possible that his judgment might become impaired.

Pasadena, California

THE HILTON'S auditorium was packed when Benson Rondell walked onto the stage. Having been alerted that he was going to make an important statement, the media was there in force, along with his faithful followers. Both groups would get more than what they came for this time.

After letting the thunderous applause sweep the hall for several minutes, Rondell signaled for silence and got it.

"One of the most difficult things about being an independent candidate for high office," he began, "is that one's background and private life become public entertainment in the media. For a person such as myself, who has been a productive businessman rather than a professional politician feeding at the public trough, this goes double. My business and my private life have become fodder for the media. While unfortunate, this is to be expected."

He paused and dramatically took a deep breath. "I have just learned that I am under investigation by the federal government because of my antinuclear stance. My company is also under investigation because I manufacture a solar power generating system that I hope will one day replace unsafe nuclear power—not only here in our own California, but all over the world."

Another thunderous round of applause and cheers broke out, and he let the crowd go on with it as long as it wanted.

"I don't say that I welcome this invasion of my privacy," he continued, "because I don't. I see it as a clumsy, underhanded attempt to derail my campaign by taking my time and energy away from my attempt to be elected to be your new governor."

Now the hall rang with people chanting his name. He stood for a long moment, soaking it in before raising his hands to silence the crowd.

"All I can say is that I will not let this investigation deter me from my goal of becoming the next governor of California. They can investigate all they like, they can do what they will to try to stop me, but I will not be stopped. I intend to be the next governor of the great state of California."

That should hold them, Rondell thought as he walked off the stage with the roar of the crowd echoing in his ears.

CONGRESSWOMAN CATHERINE Woodburn tried to keep her composure as she dialed Benson Rondell's private phone number, but her hand was shaking. How could he have done this to her? Going public with a statement that he had been informed that he was the subject of an Intelligence Committee investigation was stupid. It wouldn't take the proverbial rocket scientist to figure out which member of the committee had the closest ties to him.

If he had just kept his mouth shut, she could have worked to stop the investigation, but there was nothing she could do now. His news conference had made it impossible for her to help him.

"Benson, you bastard," she raged as soon as he picked up the phone. "What do you think you're doing?"

"I would recommend keeping a cool head, Catherine. This is no time to panic."

"What do you mean, 'keep a cool head'? You've used me and, if you go down, I'll go with you."

"If I may say so, Catherine, you used me as much as I have used you, as you say. The Green Earth Movement has been good to you." He paused. "Very good."

"I'm not talking about that, you cretin. I'm talking about you selling me out."

"But, Catherine, I want to talk about 'that,' as you put it. It just so happens that a couple of those sweet young things you picked out of your flock of fawning admirers for your private amusement were well under the legal age for the activities you were engaged in with them. And you weren't very subtle about it, which was a big mistake. My business associates became concerned with your activities and took steps to make sure that they were recorded on film. I've seen the photos and they are impressive, I must admit."

"You bastard," she said, her voice shaking with rage.

"That's not a wise thing to say to the man who holds your political future in his hands," he snapped. "I know that you have the 'politically correct' element in your district in your electoral pocket. But I think that child molesting charges, or should I more accurately say statutory lesbian rape, would give your seat to the first man who came along. I'll be glad to bankroll him, as well. Your only chance to ride this out is to hang tight and continue to let me know what's going on in Washington. If you bail out on me now, you're going to go down big time."

"If I go down, Rondell," she threatened, "I'll take you with me. I swear to God I will, and I don't care if I go to prison for it. You're not going to get away with this blackmail."

"Have it your way, bitch," he said as he replaced the receiver.

WHEN RONDELL CALLED Hector Garcia into his office to tell him about Congresswoman Woodburn's threat, the Mexican wasn't concerned. It wasn't the first time that an American politician had threatened the Cali cartel. The problem was that Congresswoman Woodburn didn't know that she was messing with the cartel, and that would cost her. But then, politics was always fraught with danger when you didn't know what game you were playing.

"This is a big problem with you Americans." Garcia sighed when Rondell finished playing the tape of Woodburn's call. "You should have never let women get into politics. Take us Mexicans. We have very few women in politics, and those few know their place. My associates never bother with them because they have no power. The men we work with stay bought because they are reasonable men and they know that a deal is a deal. Women, though, they are emotional. They forget that emotionalism has no place in a business agreement."

"Nonetheless," Rondell said, "what do we do about her? If she goes to the authorities and admits that she's been leaking classified committee information to me, I'll have a difficult time explaining that."

"There is no problem," Garcia said. "Like I said, women are ruled by emotion. She has made a mistake and now she must pay for it."

"You're going to have her killed?"

Garcia shrugged. "Accidents happen, you know, even to congresswomen. She can be at the wrong place at the wrong time. Or, even better, she can do something that she's done a hundred times before, only to discover that she's done it one too many times."

Rondell didn't like the sound of this. But this close to the election, he couldn't risk having her running her mouth. It was true that she had no hard information about his ultimate plans, and she knew nothing about his backers. But she knew the full extent of his involvement with the Green Earthers, and that could become a problem for him.

"I don't want to know anything about it until I read it in the newspaper."

Garcia laughed. "Not only will you read it in the newspaper, my friend, I can assure you that it will be on every news broadcast in the country. Congresswoman Woodburn is about to take a major fall. A woman of her...tastes leaves herself wide open."

Rondell shook his head and grinned at Garcia's pun. "Sometimes, Hector, I think that you've missed your true calling. You should get into stand-up comedy."

"She's not going to think it's funny. But then, it really won't matter because she won't be around to worry about what the papers will be saying about her. Catherine Woodburn is about to make one more mistake, a fatal one this time, but one easily explained, considering what she is."

Garcia stood. "I've got to make a few phone calls from my office. Like they say, the single's life is a real bitch."

With that cryptic comment, he left to take care of business.

CHAPTER THIRTEEN

Santa Barbara, California

Gadgets Schwarz didn't catch Benson Rondell's press conference when the candidate announced that he had been told that he was under investigation by the Feds. He missed it because Derek Gilmore had come by that morning to pick him up for the secret Green Earth mission. If he had heard the announcement, he certainly would have talked to Lyons about it and probably would have backed out because the opposition knew that they were being watched.

But he might not have, either.

He couldn't get the memory of Sylvia Bowes lying limp and bleeding in his arms out of his mind. Being a person who was overly worried about the future of the planet shouldn't be a ticket for an assassin's bullet in the back and a life in a wheelchair.

So when Gilmore showed up at his door, Schwarz walked out and got into the passenger seat of the Green Earth leader's Toyota sedan.

Gilmore said little as he drove south to the industrial district on the outskirts of Santa Barbara. As befitting a man with heavy thoughts of vengeance on his mind, Schwarz kept his silence, too.

"Here it is," Gilmore said as he parked the vehicle in front of a dilapidated warehouse a hundred meters away from a cement plant. "The other men are waiting inside for us."

Schwarz stepped out of the car and followed him in through the side door. Even though he had expected that the Green Earthers would have some kind of arsenal, he was surprised to see several open crates of Chinese-made AK-47 assault rifles lying on a table. There were enough of them to start a small war and, from the three-position selector switches on the sides of the receivers, he saw that they were the real full-auto military versions, not the recently banned semiauto, civilian look-alikes.

Whatever Gilmore was planning, it was going to be serious and, if they expected him to use one of the AKs, he would be in way over his head if it went bad.

He wasn't too surprised, however, to see a man unpacking what looked like plastic-wrapped one-kilo bricks of cocaine. The operations of the Green Earth Movement had to be financed somehow, and dealing drugs had become a traditional way for fringe groups to raise cash. There was no doubt that he had hit the jackpot this time, but he still had to get back with his information.

"Alex," Gilmore called from the other side of the room. "Can you come over here for a minute?"

"Sure."

Schwarz knew he was in trouble when he walked over and saw two of the Green Shirts swing around their AKs to cover him. He froze and held his arms at his sides. "What is this shit?"

Gilmore smiled, but it wasn't an attractive expression. "That's what I should be asking you, Mr. ATF man, or is it Mr. FBI?"

"What do you mean?" Schwarz sounded indignant. "I'm not with the government."

"Well, you're sure as hell not Alex Lord, either." Gilmore looked him up and down. "One of my regional officers just happens to be one of Lord's old drinking buddies from the Earth First! days, and when I mentioned your name, he told me in no uncertain terms that Lord was dead. He even attended the funeral and shacked up with his grieving old lady for a couple of months afterward.

"So," Gilmore concluded, "what is it, pal, ATF or FBI?"

"Neither," Schwarz replied, thinking fast. "But you're right about my not being Alex Lord. I'm a family friend of the Jordans, and I do a little P.I. work on the side. After Dick was killed, I told Mrs. Jordan that I'd look into his death."

That story didn't even begin to explain how he could have known about Alex Lord and why he had used his name to gain acceptance into the Green Earth Movement, but it was the best story he could come up with on short notice. He could only hope that Gilmore was more the physical rather than the cerebral type, and would buy it long enough for him to figure out a way to get the hell out of this mess.

Gilmore looked blank so Schwarz explained. "You remember Richard Jordan? He's the PCP guy your people killed in San Francisco, then smashed to bits."

"That poor bastard." Gilmore laughed. "But we didn't kill him. Someone else pulled the trigger on him."

"You had your people finish the job."

Gilmore shook his head. "No, not even that. That was, shall we say, a spontaneous eruption of the people's righteous indignation at the danger posed to them by the Diablo Canyon nuclear plant."

"Bullshit! It was a setup."

"It sounds good, though. The press ate it up. Did you see the coverage we got from that? It worked better than if we had planned it to go down that way."

"Sylvia was a setup, too, wasn't she?"

"Don't you read the papers? She was shot by a cop."

Schwarz didn't mention that the slug that had been taken from Sylvia's back had been IDed as a Chinese-manufactured 7.62 mm AK round. That was information the average P.I. wouldn't have.

"But enough of that," Gilmore said. "What's your real name?"

"William Vought," Schwarz answered. He had worked with a San Francisco P.I. named Bill Vought a long time ago, and he hoped that the man had kept his P.I. license up-to-date, because Gilmore was going to check.

"Okay, William Vought. I'm going to check your story out."

Motioning for his men to keep their AKs on him, Gilmore thoroughly patted Schwarz down for hardware and wires. When he found that he was clean, he took a set of plastic police restraints out of the side pocket of his BDU pants. "Put your hands behind your back."

"What are you going to do with me?"

"You're going to stay here where I can keep an eye on you until I hear from my boss."

"Benson Rondell?"

Gilmore looked at him strangely. "You're going to wish you hadn't said that, pal."

Schwarz didn't say anything more as he was marched over to the wall and dropped in a corner. With his hands tied behind his back and his ankles bound, as well, he was effectively immobilized. So effectively, in fact, that he didn't know how he was going to trip the transponder to let Lyons and Blancanales know that he was in trouble.

The transponder was serving as a pocket snap on his outdoorsman's vest. All he had to do was press it, and the signal it transmitted would change to indicate that there was an emergency. If his hands had been free, it would have taken a mere hundredth of a second. As it was, it took a half hour before he had a chance to wiggle around to where he could press his chest against one of the two-by-four studs and hope that it had activated the transponder.

"You trying to crawl through the wall?" one of the Green Shirts asked.

Schwarz worked his body around so his back was against the wall again. "I just had an itch."

"I KNEW IT!" Lyons growled when he saw the light on the transponder receiver start to blink. "He's been made. I told him that he'd been set up. Dammit! I wish he'd listened to me instead of getting his guts tied in a knot about that woman.''

''You want me to call this in to the Farm?'' Blancanales asked.

''No,'' Lyons said as he pulled his equipment bag from under the bed and unzipped it. ''I don't want to waste time. We're going in after him now and I'll talk to Barbara about it later.''

Blancanales knew that this would be sensitive because of Rondell's connections to the Green Earth people, and normally he would have wanted to check with the Farm. But with Schwarz in enemy hands, he could only agree with Lyons.

Since they were going in daylight, they didn't get into their combat blacksuits. The SWAT-team look would draw more attention than they needed. Instead, they put their assault harnesses with their magazine carriers, knives and grenades in a bag with their weapons, and they would suit up when they got to the location.

''You want me to take Gadgets's piece along, too?'' Blancanales asked as he laid his own Heckler & Koch MP-5 subgun in the bag.

''Yeah.'' Lyons glanced at the 5.56 mm Colt CAR-15 Schwarz favored. ''And a bandolier of magazines for it.''

Since Lyons's Dodge Ram pickup had a socket to plug in the GPS navigating system, he decided to take it instead of the van because it was faster. If they had to make a run for it, the Dodge would be the better vehicle.

"Damn," Blancanales muttered as he tried unsuccessfully to get the GPS system to show him their truck's location on the screen. "I know squat about this damned thing."

"Try turning on the base monitor." Lyons pointed to the switch.

"There. It's up!"

Lyons hit the ignition and the big Dodge V-10 rumbled to life. "Where do we go?"

"Head out of here south on Seaside. About four miles down, you'll turn right onto Industrial Way."

Lyons dropped the clutch and both of the sixty-series rear tires smoked as he powered out of the driveway and turned south onto Seaside Drive.

"Hold it down, Hot Rod," Blancanales snapped. "If we get stopped by one of the local yokels, we're going to need our Get Out of Jail Free cards, and I didn't bring mine."

"Just keep your nose in that GPS," Lyons growled, "and let me handle the driving."

Blancanales shrugged. It was going to be one of those days. "You got it."

"ACCORDING TO THIS," Blancanales said, pointing through the Dodge's windshield, "Gadgets's somewhere in that building over there."

Lyons pulled the pickup onto the gravel alongside the road that led past the industrial area, then killed the engine. This was a good place for them to recon the area before moving in. Both men quickly donned their assault harnesses and loaded magazines into their weapons.

While Blancanales kept watch, Lyons focused his field glasses on the building and saw what looked to be a small warehouse with a loading dock in front. A row of windows high up along the end wall indicated that it had a second floor. He could see only one door by the loading dock, but he knew there would be more, at least one in the back, if not a side door, too. They could get in there one way or the other, but since they didn't know the size of the opposition, it might be a little dicey to try one of the doors.

"How do you want to handle this?" Blancanales asked.

It was Sunday and there was little traffic in the small industrial park; even the cement plant was shut down for the weekend. But a gun battle in the area would still bring the police, though Lyons knew that it would take them a while to respond to this area on a Sunday. Most of the officers on duty would be working the residential areas, quelling domestic disputes and arresting streetwalkers and drug dealers.

The Able Team leader put his field glasses on the seat beside him and reached for his SPAS 12 assault shotgun. "We go in and get him out."

"Just like that?"

"I don't want to leave him in there too long, they might try to transfer him, and I don't want to get into a running gun battle chasing a vehicle."

"Heads up," Blancanales warned.

Lyons snapped up the field glasses and saw a tall, well-built blond man leave the building and walk to the tan Toyota sedan parked at the side of the warehouse. He was by himself and paid no attention to the two Able Team warriors parked in the Dodge Ram as he drove away.

"That's one less to deal with," Lyons said. "So we'd better get in there before he comes back with reinforcements."

"That's what I asked earlier, Carl. How do you want to work it?"

Lyons peered through the glasses again, sweeping them across the side of the aging warehouse. "Wood siding," he muttered. "Probably shiplap built on four-foot centers."

He grinned as he lowered the field glasses. "No sweat, Pol. We're simply going to drive in and see what they're doing."

"Oh no," Blancanales said, shaking his head. "You're not, are you?"

Lyons shrugged as he jacked a 12-gauge steel-buckshot round into the SPAS. "Why not?"

Hitting the key, the 488-cubic-inch, three-hundred-horse V-10 under the pickup's hood rumbled into life. Blancanales pulled the shoulder belt across his chest and snugged it tight. There were times when he really wished that he had chosen another profession. The Ironman was going to get him killed someday.

Lyons dropped the clutch and the Dodge leaped forward, its rear tires spewing a shower of gravel into the air. He backed off the throttle for a longer look as he drove past the front of the warehouse. The ground rose on the far side and it looked like the graveled parking area was only a few inches lower than the concrete foundation of the building. No problem.

Turning in front of the cement plant, Lyons lined up on the side of the warehouse. "Ready?" he asked as he slipped the truck's transfer case into four-wheel drive.

Blancanales gripped his H&K even tighter. "No."

Lyons nailed the throttle anyway.

SCHWARZ HEARD the wailing roar of the Dodge's big V-10 at full throttle a fraction of a second before anyone else and threw himself flat. Apparently the transponder had worked, and his friends were coming to the rescue. He just hoped that he wasn't sitting in the way.

CHAPTER FOURTEEN

The chromed bumper and brush guard on the front of the Dodge Ram was a quarter-inch thick and weighed more than forty pounds. Since it was bolted solidly to the pickup's frame, it made a perfect battering ram. The bumper came through the side of the warehouse at a little over fifty miles per hour, scattering jagged pieces of wooden siding and two-by-four studs in its wake.

The instant that Lyons felt both of his rear tires hit the concrete floor, he cranked the wheel all the way over to the right and locked the brakes. The rear end of the truck snapped around, killing its forward speed, and ended up almost pointed back the way it had come. Lyons was out the door before the Dodge stopped rolling, the SPAS assault gun in his hands blazing flame.

No one could fail to be stunned by a pickup truck coming through the wall at him at fifty miles per hour. The startled Green Shirts scattered to get out of its way, but they recovered quickly. Lyons got off only one 12-gauge blast before he heard the distinctive sound of an AK-47 on full-auto fire behind him.

Dropping behind one of the truck's tires for cover, he sent another load of steel double-aught buck downrange toward the sound of the AK and was rewarded by a scream of pain. A third blast took his adversary permanently out of play.

On the other side of the truck, Blancanales was working out with his H&K MP-5. The subgun's selector switch was set to 3-round-burst mode, so he wouldn't have to keep acquiring the target each time he fired. He had two gunmen on his side of the truck, and they were keeping him busy. Fortunately they were poor shots.

But with an AK shooting at you on full-auto, sooner or later one of the rounds would hit something that would hurt, and that didn't appeal to him.

Sighting in on the man closest to him—the one who had dropped behind the heavy wooden table against the wall—he loosed two 3-round bursts. The 9 mm slugs chewed into the plastic-wrapped packages on the top of the table, sending a fine white powder flying into the air. The gunman behind the table sneezed explosively and staggered out into open so he could breathe clean air.

He was trying to wipe the stinging powder from his eyes when Blancanales stitched him across the torso with a terminal burst of rounds. The gunman fell back into the plastic-wrapped packages of cocaine, then slowly slid to the floor.

Seeing his partner fall, Blancanales's other opponent gave a shout and rushed him, his AK blazing fire.

A burst of 7.62 mm AK slugs chipped concrete from the floor in front of Blancanales before whining away above his head. He appreciated the Chinese Norinco 7.62 mm ammo on the market today. It was steel core and bounced off hard surfaces instead of deforming and tumbling in all directions.

Snapping the selector switch to full-auto, Blancanales emptied the rest of the 32-round magazine in one long defensive burst. The solid stream of 9 mm fire lifted the charging gunman off his feet and dumped him, limp, on the concrete.

While Blancanales had been dispatching his two opponents, Lyons had briefly dueled with two more. Some people never learned that an AK on full auto wasn't a match for a well-aimed single shot from a 12-gauge. One of the Green Shirts hesitated when his AK magazine ran dry, and Lyons put a load of buckshot in the man's upper chest. The steel balls tore him open like a paper bag full of butcher's scraps.

The last gunman made the mistake of trying for the back door when he saw his partner's chest explode. He ran for it, his AK wildly blazing full-auto from the hip.

Lyons waited behind the truck until the gunman's magazine cycled dry. Then he stepped into the open, his Colt Python held in a two-handed grip with the hammer thumbed back for a smooth single-action first shot.

A part of him wanted to shout for the man to halt. But he knew that would be a waste of time, and he was in a hurry. He stroked the pistol's trigger instead, and the Python bucked in his hand. He pulled the big pistol back on target for a second shot, but saw that it wasn't necessary.

The .357 Magnum soft-nose slug took the running man under the left shoulder blade and punched through his rib cage to explode his heart. He tumbled forward under the impact, falling in a crumpled heap on the concrete, the AK clattering across the floor.

"Why don't you guys learn to knock?" Schwarz called out from the corner he had crawled into when the truck came crashing through the wall. "I was just about to take these guys into custody and you ruined it for me."

"YOU OKAY?" Blancanales knelt beside Schwarz while Lyons checked the five bodies for signs of life.

"Yeah, just get these damned restraints off me."

Two swipes of the razor edge of Blancanales's Cold Steel Tanto knife freed Schwarz, and he helped him to his feet.

"Damn!" Schwarz said after he checked the fifth Green Shirt body. "Gilmore must have bugged out before you guys showed up."

"Who's Gilmore?" Lyons asked.

"Derek Gilmore's the chief Green Shirt around here and the guy who set Sylvia up to get hit. And," he added as an afterthought, "he's the one who made me."

"What does he look like?"

"Tall, blond, well-built, looks like a merc instead of a tree hugger."

"That sounds like the guy we saw driving away in a Toyota sedan before we hit the door."

"Damn! From the way he was talking, I think he's the head storm trooper for this group."

"And it looks like he's been dabbling in the import business on the side." Blancanales mentally counted up at least half a million dollars' worth of packages of white powder scattered around the table.

"What do you want to do with all this?" Blancanales's eyes swept past the crates of AKs, the packages of cocaine and the bodies leaking red onto the floor.

"Leave it for the local cops," Lyons said. "With all the bullshit they've been taking recently, they can use a good drug bust."

"Speaking of the cops," Schwarz stated. "Shouldn't we get our asses out of here before someone shows up? You guys made quite a bit of noise, you know."

"It's Sunday afternoon," Lyons replied. "The local fuzz are out busting hookers and wife beaters. It'll take them a while to get their fingers out."

"I'm not doubting your expertise in this area," Blancanales said. "But I think we'd better get our battering ram out of here, anyway. I don't want to have to call Barbara to get us out of the local slam. I don't think Hal would like it very much."

"I guess you're right," Lyons answered.

None of the AK fire had hit anything vital on the Dodge, and Lyons simply drove it back out of the building the same way he had come in. With the bullet holes in the doors and fenders and the rear glass shot out, however, they would have to ditch the vehicle as soon as they could find a convenient place and report it stolen.

They could hear the sirens approaching as they turned onto Industrial Way. With the truck looking as it did, Lyons turned away from Santa Barbara when they hit Seaside Drive. It wouldn't hurt to take the long way back to the motel for a change.

CARL LYONS REPORTED Schwarz's kidnapping and rescue to Barbara Price. "Do I need to send in a cleanup crew to take care of the mess?" she asked.

"No," Lyons answered. "I think it's best to just leave it alone. The Santa Barbara police are going to think that it was a drug deal gone bad and will probably let it go at that. Rondell will have a pretty good idea what happened, of course, but if the cops don't come knocking on his door, he might think that he got away with it. With Schwarz's cover story of being a P.I. looking into the Jordan death, he might not know that we've tied him to the Green Shirts."

"You've got a point there."

"We did get another player for Kurtzman to try to tag," Lyons said. "Gadgets said that he was interrogated by a Derek Gilmore, who he thinks is a specialist from out of town, a merc instead of a tree hugger. You might want to run that name and see what you come up with."

"What're his vitals?"

Lyons passed on Schwarz's physical description of Gilmore and added that he seemed to favor BDU camouflage pants and combat boots.

"I'll have Aaron run this and see if he can come up with some photos for you to look at."

"What do you want us to do in the meantime?"

"I think our next action will be going down there in California, so I want you to stay there and be ready to assist Phoenix Force. And while you're waiting, you can finish up working the other leads you have on Rondell."

"What leads, Barb?" Lyons asked. "Like I said, his California operation's as smooth as a baby's butt. He even pays his suppliers on time. We can't get a handle on him at all. No one had anything to say about him except that he's too good to be true."

"We know that," she answered. "But keep hammering at it anyway."

"I'll do what I can."

AFTER CLEANING UP, Schwarz dressed in his regular clothing. The trendy environmental activist's uniform was rolled up and relegated to the trash can under the desk.

"I see that you've resigned from the Green Earth Movement," Lyons said, smiling.

"Where's the van keys?" Schwarz ignored the jab while his eyes scanned the desktop.

"Where you going?"

"To the hospital. I want to check in on Sylvia."

Lyons fished a key ring out of his pants pocket and tossed it to him. "Don't be too long. I'm expecting a call from the Farm."

"If you need me, I'll be at the hospital."

SCHWARZ FOUND Sylvia Bowes awake this time. She was still hooked up to a battery of machinery and tubes, but her color was better. "Hi," he said, holding out the bouquet of flowers he had picked up at the gift shop in the lobby. "I hope you like roses."

"Oh, Alex," she said, smiling wanly, "they're beautiful."

He pulled a bunch of faded posies out of the vase on her side table and replaced them with the roses, then took a seat beside her bed.

"My name isn't Alex," he said seriously. "It's Hermann Schwarz, but my friends call me Gadgets."

She looked confused. "But I don't understand. You told me that you were Alex Lord."

"It's a long story," he said as he quickly formulated a brief, censored version of who he was and what he did as part of Able Team. "I work for the government, and I went to the Green Earth meeting as part of an undercover assignment to gain information on a criminal investigation."

Bowes's eyes grew wide. She tried to move away from him, but the life support kept her in place. "It's true, then," she said. "Benson Rondell said that he was being investigated, and you're one of the federal agents who are investigating him, aren't you?"

"I am. Benson Rondell is a suspect in several serious incidents where people have been killed on his orders."

"I don't believe you," she snapped. "You're just trying to keep him from being elected so he won't shut down the nuclear power plants. He held a news conference and told us all about it."

"It's true that he's being investigated," Schwarz said. "But it's not to keep him from being elected. There's much more to it than that, but I can't really tell you about it right now."

The woman changed the subject. "You went to bed with me so you could get inside the Green Earth Movement, didn't you?"

"I needed to get inside the movement," he admitted. "But our going to bed wasn't part of any plan. That just happened, and I'm glad that it did."

"I'm not," she said. "And when I can get hold of Derek, I'm going to tell him who you are, so you won't be able to deceive anyone else in the movement."

"Look," he said, "Derek Gilmore set you up to be shot. It was no accident that you were wounded, and it wasn't the police who shot you."

"I've known Derek for as long as I've been with Green Earth," she said coldly. "And I have never seen anyone work harder to keep the planet from being destroyed. There is no way that he would have done anything to hurt me or anyone else."

"But he kidnapped me and—"

"Whatever your name is," she snapped, "get out of here now before I call for a nurse. You lied to me and I never want to see you again."

Schwarz got to his feet and turned for the door.

"And take your damned flowers with you."

Grabbing the vase from the nightstand, he slipped out into the hall and pulled the door closed behind him.

ON THE WAY down the corridor to the exit, Schwarz felt angry, helpless and wounded—all-around lousy. This was always the problem with trying to explain what he did for a living to a civilian. Particularly to a civilian who was predisposed to believe that the government was a heartless, capitalistic, evil empire bent on raping Mother Earth and killing all the small fuzzy creatures who lived in her warm bosom.

He didn't want to spend the rest of his life knowing that she thought he was some kind of scumbag who had used her and her equally gullible comrades to try to destroy their hero, Benson Rondell. But if she wouldn't listen to him, he didn't know how he was going to change her mind.

The only thing that would redeem him in her eyes would be for him to expose Benson Rondell for what he was. And that was exactly what he was going to do.

CHAPTER FIFTEEN

Pasadena, California

Benson Rondell's midmorning press release on the unfortunate death of Congresswoman Catherine Woodburn the night before was short and to the point. Keeping his voice solemn, as such an occasion called for, he admitted that Woodburn was the one who had told him about the federal investigation against him that he had spoken about earlier. But he was quick to explain that while he had welcomed the information from the congresswoman, he hadn't solicited it from her in any way. He explained her actions by saying that she had been outraged at what she saw as a blatant abuse of federal power and had acted upon that outrage.

He went on to say that while the congresswoman had been a welcome supporter of his campaign on environmental grounds, he hadn't known anything about her personal life. His relationship with her had been, as he put it, purely political, with no social contacts beyond their both being at Green Earth rallies and an occasional campaign appearance. He did, however, praise her as having been a true friend of the earth and said that his campaign would miss her valuable support.

He said nothing at all about the circumstances of Woodburn's death, nor about the seventeen-year-old girl who had been found dead with her. But he didn't have to. Both the television and the mainstream press were having a field day with that information already. It wasn't every day that a congresswoman was found naked and dead of a drug overdose in bed with an underage sex partner who had also ODed. The fact that the girl's naked body had been found with her wrists and ankles tied to the bed posts and surrounded with sex toys left little to the imagination about what they had been doing before they both died.

The furor over the congresswoman's death drove another piece of news onto the back pages. The shootout at the warehouse outside of Santa Barbara barely made a splash in the local papers. The fact that several of the dead gunmen were connected with the Green Earth Movement wasn't considered news. The cocaine that had been recovered was characterized as being one of the biggest hauls in recent years, and the DA's office hinted that they had been closing in on it before the shooting took place. The crime was summarized as being a drug-dealing and gunrunning operation gone bad.

And that was hardly news in California.

THE AFTERNOON after Rondell's press conference, his phone-poll ratings skyrocketed. The voters liked nothing more than a candidate who laid it all out on the table, particularly if he could claim to be a victim of a federal government conspiracy to prevent his being elected. And being associated with the Washington, D.C., sex scandal of the year apparently hadn't hurt him, either.

Even though he had claimed to have no knowledge about Woodburn's particular version of bedtime fun and games, there would always be those who would think that not only had he known about them, but that he had taken part in them, as well. And in Woodburn's district, those who thought that way wouldn't consider that enough to disqualify him from running for high office. In fact, if anything, it would only endear him to them all the more.

"You pulled it off beautifully." Garcia grinned broadly as he scanned the poll results in Rondell's office. "You've jumped way past the Republican candidate and are quickly closing in on the Democrat. A couple more weeks of this trend, and you'll be a shoo-in for the statehouse."

"It looks that way, doesn't it?" Rondell hadn't expected to get off this clean and was pleasantly surprised at the results. It was too bad that Woodburn had tried to cross him, but her usefulness had about come to an end anyway. And maybe it was better this way. She could have become an encumbrance.

"Now," the Mexican said, "we need to completely take the heat off you. The board of directors thinks that the Siberian strike will be enough to focus the public's mind on what your campaign is all about. The pollsters seem to think that one more nuclear accident should do it."

Rondell glanced at an orbital chart on the top of his desk. "The satellite will be in position in another eight hours," he said. "We can take care of that then."

"We do have another problem, though," Garcia said. "We have to deal with it ASAP."

"What's that?"

"Right after Woodburn warned you about the investigation, I put the word out for all of the upper-level Green Shirts to be on the lookout for infiltrators. Derek Gilmore caught one of them up in Santa Barbara."

"Someone from the government was investigating the Green Earth chapter there?" Rondell had believed Woodburn, but hadn't thought that the investigation had actually been started.

"He's not sure," Garcia replied. "Gilmore thinks that the guy's either FBI or ATF. When he interrogated him, though, the man said that he was a private investigator and a family friend of Richard Jordan, and he was looking into his death for his family."

"The Pacific Coast Power president?"

Garcia nodded.

"Why wasn't I told about this sooner?"

"It went down too fast," Garcia explained. "And I wanted you fresh for your press conferences. I didn't want you to have anything on your mind that might get in the way of your looking and sounding like a wronged man."

"I assume that you had Gilmore take him out?"

Garcia nodded again. "Derek snatched him yesterday and I'm meeting him in a few hours to decide what we're going to do with him."

"If he really is a Fed," Rondell said, "it might not be a good idea to kill him right now. Or if we have to, we'll need to have the body disappear completely."

"I think Derek can handle it."

Rondell had never inquired about Gilmore's credentials to be Garcia's right-hand man, and he really didn't want to know. There was something about Gilmore's faded blue eyes that made him think of a rabid dog. He had to admit, however, that he had done a good job of turning the Green Earth Movement into a paramilitary organization. He had a knack for knowing exactly which fanatical tree hugger could be turned into a bomb thrower or an assassin. He wondered, however, what he would be put up to after the election. He wasn't the sort of man he would want on his staff. But he could worry about that later.

"Just make sure that he does."

"He will," Garcia reassured him.

"LIKE I SAID," Derek Gilmore told Hector Garcia when the two met a few hours later in a beachfront park. "I don't know what went wrong. When I left the warehouse, this Vought guy, or whoever the hell he was, was securely tied up. Five guys were with him. When I went back this morning, the place was roped off and cops were swarming all over."

"Five men obviously weren't enough."

"That's the problem with trying to use these amateurs to do a man's work," Gilmore snapped. "If you'd let me have some of our own people, shit like this wouldn't have happened."

"You know what the board said about that," Garcia replied. "They want minimum exposure of our assets up here. There's too great a chance of one of them being IDed, and they don't want anyone making a connection between them and Rondell's operation—or the Green Earth Movement, for that matter."

"They're wrong, though," Gilmore stated flatly. "How in the hell can they expect me to do good work if I don't have the men to do it with?"

Garcia didn't like to hear Gilmore criticizing the board of directors. He owed everything he had to the Cali cartel, and had it not been for their picking him out of the gutter, more than likely he would be dead by now. As far as he was concerned, the drug lords of Cali were his personal gods and could do no wrong.

He also knew, though, that there was a lot of truth to what Gilmore was saying. Not only had their prisoner gotten away, the cops had policed up the shipment that had been stored there. There had been almost a million dollars' worth of Colombia's finest in the warehouse, and the board wasn't going to be happy about losing that, either.

"What do the cops think happened in the warehouse?" he asked. Along with organizing the Green Shirts, Gilmore ran a network of well-paid informers in high places in state and local government.

"They're calling it a drug deal gone bad, as they always do. And they're so busy patting themselves on the back for having made such a big cocaine bust that they're not looking into it any further than that."

"You'd better hope that it stays that way."

"It will," Gilmore said. "But if it doesn't, I'll be told as soon as they change their minds."

"I'm going to take Rondell down to the Baja complex for a couple of days in case this doesn't shake out the way we want it to. He'll be safe there and out of the public eye."

"How much longer until that damned election?"

"A month and a half."

"I'll be glad when this is over and I can get the hell out of here," Gilmore said. "I'm sick of these simple-minded bastards."

"It'll be over soon."

"Not soon enough for me."

Gilmore wasn't happy as he watched Garcia walk back down the beach to where he had parked his car. He didn't give a damn if that Mexican did speak perfect American. He was still a Spic just like his bosses in Colombia were. And in his experience, Spics had a bad habit of screwing up when the chips were down.

But he had known that when he had taken the job. Were it not for the fact that he was being paid enough money to finally be able to retire from the mercenary business for good, he would have turned them down flat when the job had been offered to him. But even the money they were paying him wouldn't be enough to protect him if he got sideways with the Feds and they were able to pin any of this on him.

The thing that no one seemed concerned about was who had rescued William Vought—or whoever—from the warehouse. If it had been an FBI or ATF raid, it would have been all over the papers and TV. As it was, there was nothing, and he knew that the man sure as hell hadn't freed himself. In fact, his police informant had said that they had found two sets of plastic restraints cut off, as if with a knife, so he had to have been helped.

This might be a good time for him to visit the Green Earth Movement's forest camp outside of Crescent City in Northern California. He had a complete change of ID documents stashed up there and could disappear into Oregon or Idaho on a moment's notice if things continued to go bad here.

Derek Gilmore didn't take a fall for anyone. Certainly not for a politician like Rondell or someone like Hector Garcia.

Stony Man Farm

"THERE'S BEEN another nuclear accident," Kurtzman's voice said over the intercom in Barbara

Price's office. "A power plant in Siberia just went into a Chernobyl-style meltdown."

"What's the damage?"

"It's too early to tell yet, but the satellite photos indicate that it's bad."

She dropped her head for a moment. "I'll be right down to take a look."

Though the two worst nuclear plant accidents hadn't occurred in the United States, Brognola was keeping the pressure on her to bring this worldwide threat to an end. They were closing in on Rondell as quickly as they could, but so far they didn't have anything they could make stick—such as just exactly how he was causing those "accidents."

In the computer room, Kurtzman switched the satellite videos onto the big-screen monitor. The real-time capability of the Keyhole recon birds meant that the video she was seeing was as live as it could be, with only a few seconds' delay from transmission from the deep reaches of space. Even though it was very early in the morning in Siberia, Price could clearly see the ruins of the power plant in the eerie blue glow from the collapsed containment dome.

Ten miles away, the city of Zorgin was completely blacked out. The Russians had never been good at providing backups for things like municipal electrical power plants. It would be weeks if not months before portable generators could be flown in to provide power for even the most essential things, such as hospitals. Winter was coming, and the population would suffer in the bitter cold.

When the reactor could no longer be seen, Kurtzman cleared his screen and, after bringing up a new menu, flashed an orbital chart showing the paths of commercial communications satellites onto his monitor.

"What're you doing?" Price asked.

"I want to check something out," he said without taking his eyes off the screen.

Price waited patiently. When Kurtzman was working a hunch, all you could do was wait. And while she was waiting, she went for a cup of coffee. Seeing that the pot was empty, she went about brewing a fresh pot.

Kurtzman was ready about the same time that the coffee was. "I was right," he said triumphantly. "We've got him now."

"What do you have?"

"Hal was right. Rondell is causing those reactor failures, and I can prove it."

"How?"

"His communications satellite was overhead each time that one of those accidents occurred. He has more than radio retrans gear in that thing. He has some kind of space weapon up there, as well.''

''What do you mean?''

''He has either a kinetic-energy launcher or a high-energy laser on board and is using it to bombard the reactors that have had the 'accidents.' ''

''The Chinese wouldn't have noticed something like that when they loaded his satellite onto the rocket to launch it?''

''Probably not,'' Kurtzman replied. ''I'll bet he delivered it to them sealed and ready for launching. The question now is which weapon he has. If it's a kinetic-energy launcher, we could be in real trouble.''

''You mean a laser isn't a problem?''

''Not really. All it can do is heat something like a containment dome and cause it to rupture. A kinetic-energy missile, however, can cause some real damage.''

''Okay,'' she said. ''I'll bite. What's a kinetic-energy missile?''

Kurtzman grinned broadly. ''Anything that falls out of the sky fast enough can be classified as a kinetic-energy missile. A brick, a rock.''

''You mean a meteorite?''

''That's the classic example, of course, but we're talking about something like a stainless-steel ball only a few inches in diameter. If it's fired from a linear accelerator, it can be moving at several thousand miles per hour when it hits the ground. The effect is something like a ten-thousand-pound HE bomb going off.

"However," he said, spinning in his chair and attacking his keyboard, "I don't think his satellite is big enough to hold a linear accelerator. It should have the power to run one, but I just don't think that it's big enough to contain it."

He went back to his menu and called up his data on the Chinese Red Dragon launch vehicle and zeroed in on its payload parameters, particularly the dimensions of the aerodynamic housing of the payload section. Then he plugged in an equation regarding the magnetic thrust of a classified, hypothetical linear accelerator designed for the Star Wars space defense program.

A moment later, he spun his chair. "You can tell Hal that Rondell's using a space laser. I'll bet the farm on that one."

Price smiled. "You are."

CHAPTER SIXTEEN

When Hal Brognola flew into Stony Man Farm this time, he alerted Barbara Price that he was coming in advance. In fact, he had ordered her to have the Stony Man War Room staff ready for a mission briefing as soon as he hit the ground. The President had finally given him the go-ahead, and he wanted Benson Rondell to be taken out of action immediately.

As Brognola had directed, the staff was waiting for him when he walked into the War Room, took his place at the end of the table and snapped open his briefcase. "The topic of today's discussion," he growled around the end of the overly chewed cigar stub clamped in his mouth, "is Benson Rondell."

This was no surprise to anyone, but exactly what angle the discussion would take was anyone's guess. What should have been a straightforward mission had taken so many bizarre twists that no one had a clue as to what the President had finally decided to do about it.

"After Congresswoman Woodburn's leak from the Intelligence Committee about your backgrounding Rondell, the evidence from Able Team's operation and the latest nuclear 'accident' in Siberia, the Man wants this guy to go down immediately. High-profile political candidate or not, we simply can't afford to screw around with him any longer.

"But," the big Fed cautioned, "now more than ever, it has to be done carefully. Even with the fallout from Woodburn's very convenient death, this guy still has a lot of clout on Capitol Hill. The President has been taking heat from both sides of the aisle since she made our investigation of him public. The Senate thinks that Rondell's this year's poster boy for NAFTA and the new economic order in the Western Hemisphere. And if that's not enough, we've just learned that he's in very good odor with the Mexican president. The Man got a call from Mexico City saying that it would be a shame if anything happened to delay the planned solar-power network Rondell has promised to build for Mexican industrial expansion."

He sat back in his chair and took a deep breath. "What all this means is that even though the President is convinced that Rondell has to take a fall, there can be no official involvement in this operation at all. That means no military backup and no headlines. It has to be done so that it looks like one of those unfortunate accidents that took out those nuke plants.''

''Are you sure that the Man hasn't been watching too many James Bond movies?'' Price asked. ''Rondell's complex in Baja is a little too big to just drop in a couple of blocks of C-4 and expect it all to go away in a spectacular fireball.''

''I know.'' Brognola rolled the stubby cigar in his mouth and bit down on it again. ''But it has to be done that way.''

Bolan had been sitting quietly at the end of the table. He agreed with Price's assessment of the situation, but there was more to it than just the Sunflash complex. ''Even if we take out his base in Mexico, Hal, what happens if we don't find Rondell there?''

''I want you to run him down and finish the job,'' Brognola growled.

''Isn't that setting a dangerous precedent?'' Bolan asked. ''Since Rondell's an independent candidate, this could look a lot like a political assassination, and we don't do that sort of thing in this country.''

''That's why you have to make it look good,'' Brognola said. ''And if possible, the Man would like to have proof that Rondell is linked to the Cali cartel and that they're actually the ones behind the reactor accidents. That will help him deal with the critics and will take the aftermath out of the dangerous realm of politics and put it into the criminal-activities category, where the courts can deal with it."

"What's the timetable on this?"

"Immediately, of course."

"Hal, unless you're authorizing us to use a nuke on the place," Bolan replied, "it's going to take us a little longer than that. Particularly since you said that we won't have any military assistance."

"I know. Just get it done as soon as humanly possible. Look, people, I know what you're facing and I know that without the usual military input, this is going to be even tougher than it really needs to be. But I hope you can understand why the Man has to have it done this way, and why he has to have it done as soon as you can do it."

Brognola looked up at the Eastern Standard Time clock in the row of clocks over the big screen at the end of the room. "Are there any more questions?" he asked. "I'm due back in Washington for a state dinner tonight. And, over brandy and cigars, I want to be able to tell the Man that everything is under control."

"I think we have everything we need right now," Price assured him. "And you can tell the President that we're doing everything we can to take care of it."

"That's all I ask," he said as he snapped his briefcase shut and got to his feet. "I'll be in touch."

"Hal's a bit more testy than usual," Bolan observed as he watched Brognola steam out of the War Room like a locomotive at full throttle. "When are the guys coming in?"

"Katz's due in sometime tonight and the rest of them should be following close behind him."

"Until they get here, I'll be down working with Aaron on getting the operation plan squared away."

"I'll let you know when they arrive."

YAKOV KATZENELENBOGEN was the first of the Phoenix Force warriors to arrive at the Farm. Since running into the Green Earth antinuclear demonstration in France, he had been keeping a close eye on the news and had actually cut his vacation plans short before Price's recall message reached him. As always, his well-honed instincts for trouble on the horizon were right on.

David McCarter and Rafael Encizo arrived together after a long drive up from Florida, where they had been fishing in the Gulf of Mexico. Encizo half wished he was still out in the boat hooking the big ones, but McCarter was ready to go back to work. Even fighting to land Gulf barracuda and swordfish got old after a while. He was ready for something a little more exciting than fish.

Gary Manning had been skiing in Canada. Since it was still early in the season, the skiing had been only fair and he hadn't been unhappy to get called back to the Farm. By the time the mission was over, there should be a little more base and he could go back.

The man last to arrive, Calvin James, had been reached at his brother's home in Chicago. Since his parents and other siblings were dead, his sole surviving brother was his only family, and it had been some time since he had last seen him. While it had been good to check in with the home base again, Chicago held too many bad memories for him to want to stay around too long.

Bolan met him at the front door. "Head on down to the War Room," he said. "Everyone else is waiting. And don't bother to unpack. You're moving out again tonight."

"Where we going?"

"Mexico."

IN THE WAR ROOM, Barbara Price and Hunt Wethers filled in Phoenix team on Benson Rondell, his Sunflash organization, his connection with the Green Earth Movement and the unproved suspicion that he was connected to the Cali cartel.

Then they recounted the nuclear power plant accidents that had occurred over the past few weeks and Kurtzman's theory that Rondell was causing them by employing a laser from a space weapon mounted in his communications satellite.

When they were finished, Bolan took the podium to go over the attack plan he and Kurtzman had roughed out. The plan wasn't finalized, but the details would have to wait until they were able to get a closer recon of the area. Satellite photos and computer constructs were good planning aids, but nothing could replace an old-fashioned recon of the target area by a man who was going to put his life on the line to try to destroy it.

"One of the first things I want to do," Bolan said, "is to send Calvin to Baja California to do a ground recon of Rondell's facility. The photos Aaron's gotten for us are good, but I want to have someone eyeball the place before we set everything in stone."

"Considering that I speak the language as my mother tongue," Encizo said, "shouldn't I be the one doing a recon in Mexico?"

"Normally I'd say yes, Rafael," Bolan said. "But this time I don't think it would work."

"What do you mean?"

"For one thing, Rondell's complex is set off by itself in the middle of Baja. It isn't a place where a

man of your age, and social station, would be likely
to go on a whim, and we don't have time to work up
a cover story for you. It is, however, on the road
that young American tourists take to find fun and
adventure in the sun. Calvin will be just one more
gringo tourist looking for cheap dope and tourist
girls to smoke it with. Plus he also speaks Spanish."

"Give me a break." The Cuban laughed as he
glanced over at a grinning Calvin James. "He
speaks Chicago Spanish, and that's not even the
same thing as real Español."

"It's good enough for what we need, and I need
you to get our transportation squared away in California. We're going in by sea this time."

That brought a smile to Encizo's face. There was
nothing he liked more than boats.

"While James is doing his recon," Bolan continued, "we're going to relocate to San Diego, link
up with Able Team and get our gear squared away."

It was a bare-bones briefing that Bolan laid out,
but his audience had been through so many that it
was all that was necessary. They had a job, they
knew where they were going to do it and that was
enough to get started. The rest of it would fall into
place when the time came.

"If there are no questions—" Bolan looked around the room when he was finished "—get settled in and we'll meet again after dinner."

WHILE THE OTHER Phoenix Force warriors were getting settled in, Bolan walked out to the Farm's helipad with Calvin James. Jack Grimaldi was waiting in the chopper to fly him to Washington's National Airport to catch a red-eye flight to Southern California.

"Carl will have everything set up for you when you get there," Bolan told him. "Your bike, your clothing and all the camping gear you'll need."

"No weapons this time?"

"Not in Mexico. Since you'll be on your own, I don't want you to carry anything that will give the local cops a reason to throw you in jail. It would take a couple weeks for us to get you out, and we don't have the time to waste. I need you in on this one."

He handed the ex-SEAL a small foam package. "The only thing extra I want you to take into Mexico are these two transponders. Make sure that you hide them on your bike so they can't be found unless they take it apart. They're passive transponders that only transmit when Kurtzman sends a signal, so they won't show up on antibugging detectors. Not that I think anyone will ever look that deep.''

''If they do,'' James said, ''I'm screwed no matter what they find.''

''That's why I don't want you to do anything to attract attention to yourself.''

James grinned. ''A black man in boots and biker leathers riding a Harley-Davidson isn't going to attract attention in Baja?''

''That's just the point. They'll be looking at what you appear to be and won't be able to see past that.''

''I hope you're right about that. Baja's a lonely place to be without friends.''

''You'll have the transponders, and if you spend longer than twelve hours in any one place, we'll assume that you've been made and we'll come looking for you.''

''I'd better not sleep in then. I'll have to kick the lovely señoritas out early so I can get back on the road.''

''If you two are done jacking your jaws,'' Grimaldi called from the open cockpit door of the JetRanger, ''we've got a flight to catch at National and the clock is running.''

Bolan extended his hand. ''Good luck, and check in from California before you head south.''

"Will do."

The Executioner watched Grimaldi and James fly out of sight before going back inside for the rest of the evening's activities. It would be a long night.

CHAPTER SEVENTEEN

San Diego, California

"This is starting to look like old-home week," Rosario Blancanales said with a grin when he saw the Stony Man team step off the plane at the San Diego airport. Led by Bolan's big frame, the commandos were all dressed in casual fall clothing, but the other passengers seemed to sense a sort of menace and gave them a wide berth as they deplaned together.

"Only if your home town's a suburb of hell," Schwarz said. "I sure don't want those guys living in my neighborhood."

After perfunctory greetings were exchanged in the terminal, Lyons led the Stony Man warriors out to the parking lot, where two vans were waiting. After dumping the bullet-riddled Dodge Ram pickup, Lyons had rented a second van to replace it so they could transport the men and equipment.

"What's wrong with Gadgets?" Bolan asked Lyons once they were alone on the road.

"He's got his ass in a knot because of that woman who got shot."

"The one who was with him at that Diablo Canyon demonstration when he was undercover?"

"Yeah." Lyons nodded. "He thinks that it was his fault that she got hit. He's been visiting her in the hospital, talking to her doctors, the whole nine yards."

"Is he up for the mission?" Bolan asked, concerned. He understood compassion for innocent victims, but not when it got in the way of the mission at hand.

"Oh, yeah. Once he has something useful to do, he'll snap out of it. I think he wants to get a little payback for her."

Missions of vengeance were something that the Executioner understood perhaps better than any living American. But he also knew that focusing on revenge could cloud a man's mind. "Keep an eye on him."

"I won't let him get in trouble," Lyons promised.

"Have you heard from Calvin yet?" Bolan asked the other question that was foremost in his mind. Having James off alone without backup was risky. He knew his way around the block, but even the best sometimes ran into trouble.

"No. We saw him off at the border, and that's the last we've heard from him. Unless there's an emergency, though, he won't be calling until he crosses back into the States.''

THE FORTY-TWO-FOOT charter fishing boat was tied up at the end of the dock, the name *High Roller* painted in big red letters on her stern. The paint was fresh, the wood trim varnished and she looked every inch a rich man's toy, which she was. But she was a toy for lease and had just signed on to work for Stony Man Farm.

"Not bad," Bolan said when he spotted the craft.

"I wanted something that could get us there in comfort—as well as speed—for a change," Lyons said. "She sleeps eight and is fully equipped, including a shower."

When they stepped out of the vans in the parking lot, Rafael Encizo clutched the nautical charts Lyons had picked up for him and pushed past the others to climb down inside the boat first. Nice paint and varnished wood didn't count for much with him; he wanted to see the mechanicals, the guts of the boat, before he would make his judgment.

While Encizo carefully went over the boat's engines and pumps, Schwarz installed the GPS system in the wheelhouse and checked over the loran and sonar systems, as well. Even though they would be using the GPS as their primary navigation system, if it went out, they could use the loran gear to navigate almost as well. Since they were going into barely charted waters, the sonar would keep them from going aground on an uncharted reef.

"The engines are in good shape," Encizo reported back topside.

Once their equipment and weapons had been loaded on board, the men settled in to wait until they heard from James. Since the *High Roller* was docked in plain sight of anyone who wanted to take a look, there was little they could do to prepare for their mission until they got underway.

Baja California

A DUSTY CALVIN JAMES pulled his Harley into the ramshackle gas station and killed the bike's engine. The only thing that indicated that this was a gas station and not another deserted shack along the side of the Baja Pacific Highway was the chipped enamel gas company sign and the solitary pump in front.

Putting down the kickstand, he leaned the bike over to rest on it and pushed his goggles onto his forehead. He had been on the road for only a day and a half, but it was already getting old. The Baja Pacific Highway wasn't a California freeway, and dodging overloaded Mexican vehicles on rutted two-lane roads was tiring.

He walked through the torn screen door and squinted in the dim light. The interior of the shack was no more impressive than the outside. Two plywood tables sat against one wall, and a bar was set up along the one opposite. A few fading girlie calendars shared the wall with dusty signs advertising Mexican beer and cigarettes. It didn't look too hopeful, but the muted hum of a generator out back made him think that he would at least be able to get a cold drink here, as well as a little information.

"Hello! Gringo!" said a voice behind him.

James turned back and saw a Mexican boy about twelve or thirteen years old rise from a chair hidden from sight behind the bar.

"You want gas?"

"No, I just want a beer if you have any."

"We got beer," the boy said, opening the door of a battered old refrigerator at the end of the bar, "and it's cold."

"Go for it."

"Twenty-five new pesos." He held the beer back until James reached into his pocket and came up with the cash.

"You get a lot of business out here?" James asked as he twisted the top off the long-neck bottle.

"We get mucho business now. The trucks drive through here all the time on the way to the gringo factory by the beach."

"What gringo factory?" James asked innocently.

"There is a big gringo factory up the road where the big mountain goes down to the sea."

James had gone over the satellite photos of the Sunflash facility in detail and knew that the boy had it right. Rondell's facility was built into the side of a sizable cliff overlooking the Pacific. He had memorized the photos, and he was here to check and make sure that the cameras hadn't missed anything important.

"What do they do at that factory?" he asked to keep the conversation going.

"I don't know. They say that they make electricity. That is why I have light and cold beer."

For most of the Mexicans living in Baja, that was what Rondell's ambitious plans would mean—cold beer and lights at night. The plans to power an emerging Mexican industry wouldn't mean much to most people in Baja.

"The trucks come through here all the time, you say?"

The boy shook his head. "Maybe the trucks come two, three times a week. But they always come, and the drivers are always thirsty when they come here, so I sell much beer. You want another one, señor?"

"Maybe one to go." He dug into his jeans pocket again.

The boy handed him another bottle and watched him walk out the door.

As soon as James started the Harley and drove off, the boy reached behind the bar and pulled out a portable radio. "Hello!" he almost shouted into the microphone. "Security! This is Ramon at the cantina. An American on a motorcycle—a black guy—stopped for a beer and he is heading in your direction."

As soon as the boy made his report, he sat down behind the bar, leaned his head against the wall and tried to go back to sleep. There wasn't much for him to do at the little gas station, but it sure was better than trying to scratch out a living on the streets and back alleys of Mexico City.

The highway led James out to the Pacific Coast, and ten miles down the road he saw the first of Rondell's solar panels gleaming in the sun. The flash of the sun from the polished mirrors was almost blinding. Several acres of desert were covered with the solar panels, and thick insulated cables connected them to what looked like a power transmission station. High-tension lines ran south from there to the horizon. Rondell's promise of providing electrical power to the Mexicans looked to have some substance to it. It was too bad that he was sponsored by the cartel.

There was no doubt that Mexico needed cheap electrical power if it was going to move into the modern world, but this wasn't the way for them to get it.

"WE HAVE an American riding a motorcycle toward the north beach," the duty officer in the Sunflash security center reported to Hector Garcia in his top-floor suite.

"Did he stop at the gas station?"

"He did, and the kid says that he's just a biker tourist, a black man."

"Keep him under close surveillance. If he gets too nosy, bring him in and we'll talk to him."

"Yes, sir."

WHEN HE REACHED the last of the solar panels, James turned his bike off the road and headed for the beach a few hundred yards away. Once on the sand, he drove slowly toward the cliff that held the Sunflash complex. He heeled the Harley over in a wide turn when he saw the chain-link fence cutting the beach off several hundred yards from the base of the cliff. Signs on the fence warned against trespassing on the property of the Sunflash Corporation in both English and Spanish.

A flash of movement at the edge of his vision told him that the fence was backed up with surveillance cameras hidden in the rocks, so he would obey the signs. As Bolan had said, he didn't want to draw any more attention to himself than was absolutely necessary. A little curiosity, however, would be completely in keeping with his role as a tourist.

Two hundred yards beyond the fence, the craggy rock mass abruptly ended in a sharp cliff going down into the surf. Looking closer, he saw that the cliff was more than just another rock looking out over the Pacific. A building had been built into its face. The concrete had been painted to match the color of the rock, and only the bronzed windows broke the illusion of the building actually being a part of the earth. The back side of the outcropping was rugged and bare except at the top, where he could see some kind of low structure had been built.

As Kurtzman's satellite recon shots had shown, this was going to be a tough nut to crack, and it didn't look any better up close. He could see the slender lines of fiber-optic strands along the top and bottom of the wire, and the sand beyond the fence showed regularly spaced, shallow depressions that usually meant land mines.

Bolan had been right about the beach. It was looking more and more like the only way to get into the place. What they did once they were inside was another matter, but that wasn't in his job description this day. He just had to find the best place for them to try to land. And to do that, he needed to take a small swim.

After eating a quick snack from the supplies in his saddlebags, he changed into his swim trunks and waded out into the rolling surf. As its name implied, the Pacific was peaceful, with only modest swells breaking over the sandy beach. If the Sunflash compound could be converted into a resort hotel, the beach would match anything on the Mexican Riviera from Mazatlán to Acapulco. When the water reached his chest, he struck out with swift strokes of his powerful arms.

Once he was past the breakers and half a mile into the swells, he turned and swam south, parallel to the shore, so he could get a look at the miniharbor behind the artificial breakwaters that extended from the cliffs under Sunflash. Even though whoever was behind those surveillance cameras had to have seen him go into the water, they would have a difficult time picking him out against the ocean waves.

As soon as he was past the breakwater on his side, he saw that the little harbor directly below the cliff was perfect for their purpose. There was a short pier in the center of the harbor to moor supply boats. A thirty-five-foot cabin cruiser was the only vessel tied up, and it looked like a company boat. From the wave patterns in the harbor, it looked as if the ocean floor between the breakwaters was gently sloping, perfect for a scuba assault.

Once James returned to his bike, he changed into his riding clothes. It was still light, and he wanted to be away from this place before night fell. He had seen what he needed to see and wanted to get back to California with the information as soon as he could.

"THE AMERICAN is leaving," the Sunflash guard watching the security camera monitors reported to his supervisor.

"Which way is he going?"

"South. You want me to send someone after him?"

"No. If he's leaving the area, he's not going to be any more trouble for us."

CHAPTER EIGHTEEN

San Diego, California

"Calvin's back," Carl Lyons announced as he looked up from the ship-to-shore phone in the *High Roller*'s wheelhouse, "and he's on the horn. He says everything's a go as planned from the sea."

"Tell him to get here as soon as he can," Bolan ordered. "We need to get this operation under way."

"Will do."

Barbara Price was waiting when Bolan called the Farm to report. "I just got off the phone with Hal," she said. "He wants to know when you're going to move out."

"Tell him that we just got back in contact with James," Bolan replied, "and he'll be joining us shortly. He says that it's a go as planned, so we'll be moving out immediately and hitting the target tomorrow night."

"I'll tell him."

"Is there anything new on the target area?"

"Aaron's been keeping a close eye on the place, but the photos don't show any changes from what you have. There has been some boat traffic in and out of the harbor, but he thinks that they've been carrying routine supplies. He did spot a thirty-five-foot-boat that seems to be used for patrolling the area directly around the complex, but it doesn't show any weapons above the deck."

"Has he been able to come up with anything on the internal layout of that place yet?"

"He's still working on it," she replied. "The problem is, Rondell used a Mexican architectural firm to design the structure. Apparently they didn't use a CAD computer to draw up the plans, so there's no way he can get at them. He hasn't given up yet, though. He's trying to find if any American electronic companies were used to install the electronic gear so he can try to talk to their workmen and build a floor plan from that."

"Tell him to keep working on that angle, and if he can come up with something, to fax it. But I'm not going to wait for it. We're going in as soon as we get there."

"I'll tell him."

WHEN JAMES RODE into the marina an hour later, Lyons and McCarter walked out to the parking lot to help him push his Harley into one of the vans for safekeeping until they got back. Grabbing his saddlebags, James followed them back to the dock.

"Let's do it." Bolan turned to Encizo as soon as the three were back on board. "Hal's waiting for us."

The Cuban hit the starter buttons for the twin Chrysler engines. The throaty sound of the big marine V-8s as they cranked up was music to his ears. "Cast off!" he shouted.

When Schwarz and Manning dropped the mooring lines, Encizo eased the boat away from the pier. Keeping his revs down, he slowly maneuvered his way through the traffic coming in and out of the marina and turned her nose toward the open sea. When they were clear of the pleasure craft, he reached out to advance both throttles and the *High Roller* surged forward.

Once they reached the open sea, Encizo kept his course due east until they reached the twelve mile limit and were in international waters. Only then did he alter his course to the south and Baja California.

WHEN THEY WERE in the shipping lanes, Encizo kept the vessel cruising along at full throttle, which translated to a little over twenty-eight knots in a calm sea. In the main cabin below, Bolan and Katzenelenbogen went over their assault plan one more time with Lyons, Blancanales and Schwarz. James's input hadn't forced them to make any major changes, so only fine-tuning was needed.

Six Stony Man warriors would swim in from at least a mile out, separate into three two-man teams and search for their primary target, the satellite control center. When they located that, they would rig it for demolition and withdraw. If they happened across Rondell in the process, they would grab him, but if they didn't, they wouldn't go hunting for him. Depending on the resistance they encountered when they got inside, they should be able to do the job and get clear within a half hour.

MISSION PREP WAS a little more complicated than merely going over the strike force's weapons and ammunition. Even though the military wasn't actively supporting this mission, Stony Man had been able to secure Navy SEAL rebreathing gear for the team to use.

Fitting the SEAL wet suits and scuba rebreathing gear for each man took some time. Calvin James had David McCarter to help him with this chore, though, and the outfitting went as quickly as possible. After each man had been outfitted, James took a short test dive off the stern of the boat to make sure that his rebreathing gear was working.

"I wish we'd been able to get one more scuba rig," Lyons said. "I'd love to go in on this one."

"I'd like to have you with us," James admitted. "Since we still don't know how many gunmen Rondell has in there, we could sure use the extra firepower."

Bolan's plan to have Able Team stay with the boat to be their backup and their ride home was sound. If anything went wrong at Sunflash, Lyons would pilot the boat to the dock and Able Team would fight their way inside. But if the Stony Man warriors were able to handle it on their own, they would have to sit this one out. And if there was anything that Carl Lyons hated, it was sitting out a dance when everyone else was out on the floor having fun.

"But," James said, "it's nice to know that you guys will be ready to come in and lend a hand if we get in over our heads."

"We'll be ready," Lyons promised. "You can bet your sweet ass on that one."

"We will be," James said with a grin.

WHILE JAMES AND MCCARTER were going over the scuba gear, Manning kept himself busy making up the demolition packages they would need. They had received five standard SEAL demo packs with the diving equipment, so he had everything he needed

to work with. The problem was that they didn't
know exactly what they were going to encounter
once they were inside the complex. To be prepared
for all contingencies, he had to make up multipur-
pose explosive charges that could be effectively used
against anything they came across that needed to be
blown to pieces.

The explosive material he had been supplied with
was Octol, an ultrafast chemical explosive origi-
nally designed to initiate nuclear explosions. It was
one of the newest military explosives and was a lot
easier to work with than C-4 plastique. C-4 still had
its uses, not the least of which was heating rations
in the field. But Octol was an overall improvement, particularly if you needed to cut through
things like concrete or steel.

He fused two dozen one-pound explosive blocks
with the new multifunction detonators to the built-
in antitampering devices, then affixed peel-away
adhesive strips to all of the blocks.

The SEAL demo packs also contained twenty-
five-foot rolls of linear cutting charges, which
worked like a cross between standard detonation
cord and a shaped charge. One rolled out a section
of the V-shaped cord and placed the arms of the V
against the target, where an adhesive strip held it in
place. When it was detonated, the cutting charge
cord could slice through a half inch of armor plate

like a cutting torch going through plastic wrap. He had no idea what they would encounter inside the complex, but this was one of the best things a dynamiter could have in his ruck. He made five short rolls of the explosive material and affixed variable time detonators to them.

After making up all the charges, Manning separated the explosives into five piles and loaded them into five matt black mesh bags designed to be clipped to the divers' harnesses. Since the explosives and detonators were SEAL issue, they were waterproof.

WHEN THE SCUBA GEAR and demo charges were ready to go, it was time for the team to go over the Russian underwater weapons one more time. They had all had a chance to familiarize themselves with the guns back at the Farm, but since the men had never used them in combat, they had to be more than just familiar with them. Bolan planned to arm only a couple of the team members with the new weapons, but everyone would need to know how to use them. In combat, you either knew your weapon cold or you died.

While the rest of the team practiced firing their new weapons, Katzenelenbogen broke down his silenced Uzi and cleaned it. He and his Uzi went back a long way, and it was the perfect weapon for a man who had to fire one-handed. Even with the silencer fitted over the barrel, it was light and balanced well in one hand. Also, the Uzi could be fired underwater in an emergency.

As he reassembled the Israeli-made submachine gun, the veteran Israeli warrior thought it ironic that the best-known product of his people was one of the world's most effective killing machines. But, as a man who had fought in most of his adopted nations' wars, he knew that had it not been for the Israelis' building effective weapons, his people would have been pushed into the sea.

When everything was ready and every item had been double-checked, the Stony Man commandos relaxed. After all, they were at sea on a cruise and it would be a shame to waste the waves and the weather.

BY MIDMORNING the following day they were close enough to their target area to go to battle stations. In the back of the boat, James and McCarter were stripped to the waist and had their deep-sea fishing rigs deployed. They were actually trailing bait, hoping to catch something to eat on the way back. The *High Roller* was registered as a charter fishing boat, and it would look suspicious if no one was fishing from the stern.

"There it is," Encizo said as he turned the boat's wheel a few points to starboard.

Bolan looked out the windscreen of the wheelhouse and saw the cliff jutting out into the Pacific. As James had said, the Sunflash building was impressive. But as long as there was a way inside, the complex could be taken.

Through his field glasses, Bolan could clearly see the dock and the loading doors of the lowest level. He expected that they would find the satellite control center on the upper levels, but going in from the land and climbing the back of the cliff was too difficult and too risky. It would be much easier to go in from the dock and work their way up once they were inside.

After slowly motoring past Sunflash, Encizo continued south for another half hour. Making a slow, wide turn back to the north, he kept the *High Roller* over the horizon to keep them off any radar as they moved into position directly out to sea from the complex. When Bolan gave the word, it would take only an hour to get in close enough to launch the divers.

BOLAN CHECKED IN with Stony Man Farm at 1800 hours local time for a final go-ahead.

"Hal wants you to go in tonight if at all possible," Barbara Price said over the satcom link.

"Aaron says that Rondell's killer satellite is coming into range of another nuclear power plant in the morning and he doesn't want to risk having another incident."

"We're ready," Bolan replied. "Our resident nautical expert assures me that the tide's with us and the moon won't come up till 0342, so we'll launch at midnight. That'll give us over three hours to swim in, do what we're going to do and swim back out to the pickup point."

"Be careful," she said. "I don't like the fact that we don't know anything about the layout of the inside of that place or the size of his security force."

"They don't have any reason to think that we're coming, so we have the element of surprise working for us. Plus, I don't think that we'll be going up against trained troops. He'll have hired local gunmen, not specialists."

"You take care anyway."

CHAPTER NINETEEN

Stony Man Farm

As soon as she got off the radio to Bolan, Price headed down to the computer center. Hal Brognola wasn't at the Farm while the mission was going down, and that didn't happen all that often. She wondered if he was working away at something behind the scenes.

"I've got the Keyhole bird coming on-line in ninety seconds," Aaron Kurtzman announced when she approached his workstation.

With their computers hooked into the NRO, Stony Man made almost as much use of the spy satellites as the secret government spy agency did. When the recon bird was over Baja, they would be able to follow as much of the action as could be seen from above ground. The problem was that most of the mission would be carried out inside the Sunflash complex, where not even the Keyhole cameras could gain access. Nonetheless, having an overwatch on high might come in handy before the mission was over.

"It's on-line and the pictures are coming in."

"Where's their boat?" Price asked when she wasn't able to pick out the craft among the wave tops.

Kurtzman's fingers tapped out a command for the computer to locate the *High Roller* in the dark, midnight Pacific Ocean below. The computer took the signal from the satellite, electronically erased the darkness and gave the scene a greenish cast. Then it searched for the right shape on the water, IDed it and enhanced the image of the small boat so it stood out against the background.

"There they are," he said, glancing up at the mission time clock in the upper left corner of the screen. "And it looks like they've started moving in."

Price poured a cup of coffee and sat on the chair beside Kurtzman to watch as the fishing boat edged in closer to the shore. Being an electronic voyeur to combat bothered her more than usual this time. As many times as she had watched a scene like this from space, she still marveled at the technology that made it possible. But even in this age of technological marvels, it was still men of flesh and blood who had to go in and do the dirty work.

Part of her uneasiness in relation to this mission came from the fact that they hadn't been able to determine the inside layout of Rondell's fortress.

Making it to the shore was dangerous enough, but they could help watch out for them from space. The real danger wouldn't come until they breached the complex and got inside, where she couldn't help them in any way.

And that bothered her.

Off the Baja Coast

CARL LYONS HAD THE HELM and his eyes were on the GPS screen as he brought the boat to within a mile and a half of the breakwater on the south side of the Sunflash complex. The tide was with them, so they could afford to launch farther out than they had initially planned. They were still within radar range if anyone was looking for them, but the sound of their engines couldn't be heard on shore. Since they were sailing parallel to the beach, from north to south, if they were caught on radar they might be taken for night fishermen on their way down to Cabo San Lucas.

The boat was completely blacked out now, only small red battle lights illuminating the engine instruments and navigation equipment. This was both to hide them from observers on the shore and to preserve the commandos' night vision for the long swim into the harbor.

"We're coming up on the launch point," he called back to the rear of the boat.

On the boat's fantail, Bolan and the other Stony Man warriors were in their wet suits and rebreathing gear, with their weapons and demolition packs strapped to their harnesses. Schwarz and Blancanales used red-lensed flashlights to help them check over their gear one last time.

"Everyone ready?" Bolan asked.

When he got five thumbs up, he called up to Lyons, "Give us the mark, Carl."

"Get ready."

The men lowered their masks and turned to sit backward on the boat's gunwale, their weapons and demo bags clutched to their chests.

"Five," Lyons called out from the wheelhouse. "Four, three, two, one. Go!"

One by one, the Stony team tumbled backward off the boat's side into the water and were lost from sight in the wake of its passage.

Once the swimmers were away, Lyons continued his course to the southeast to get out of sight of Sunflash before turning back toward the position where he would wait until the team called for the extraction. For the pickup itself, he would bring the boat in just out of range of small-arms fire so the swimmers wouldn't have to fight the tide to reach him.

As soon as the *High Roller* had swept completely past them, Calvin James gathered up the swimmers and headed for the Baja shore a mile and a half away. As the team's most experienced underwater navigator, he led the commandos in a tight follow-the-leader formation through the crystal-clear water. Even though the water was clear, it was still a moonless midnight and the Pacific was a big ocean. This was no time to be losing anyone in the dark.

They were about a quarter of a mile out when they heard Rondell's patrol boat approaching. The whine of its engine and the beating pulse of its prop cutting through the water sounded loud. The latest satellite photos that had been faxed to them on the fishing boat had shown that the patrol boat wasn't moored at its usual slip at Rondell's dock.

They had hoped that it would stay at sea all night, but wherever it had been, it was back now and that added another dimension to the situation that would have to be taken into account. The problem was that James didn't know how far away the boat was or where it was going. Sound traveled five times as fast in water as it did in the air, and it sounded like the boat was coming on fast and directly toward them.

Jerking his thumb at the sea bottom, James led the team into a dive. Following like a school of fish, the other swimmers trailed James to the sandy bottom. At his signal, they halted and waited for the boat to cut through the water some fifty feet above their heads. They were close enough to Rondell's dock that the light reflecting off the boat's churning wake looked phosphorescent against the dark sea.

In a second the boat was past them and turning into the harbor. As the beating of the prop faded, James gave the signal to move out again. Keeping close to the seaweed and debris that littered the sandy bottom of the harbor, the Stony Man team continued on to its target.

WHEN JAMES REACHED the end of the south breakwater, he stopped. As he had hoped, the water in the man-made harbor was clear enough that the reflection of the dockside lights alone was enough for them to see their targets clearly. However, the clarity of the water also made them more visible, as well, if anyone wanted to look into the water. Nonetheless, he had to make a close-in recon.

Motioning for the others to remain where they were, he unslung his underwater assault rifle and chambered the first dart in the magazine. Keeping to the breakwater, he swam up to the corner where the loading dock met the breakwater. Staying in the shadows thrown by the lights, he rose until his diving mask just cleared the water.

They were in luck; only two sentries were walking their posts along the loading platform, at opposite ends of the dock. As the satellite photos had shown, it didn't look as if there were any weapon emplacements covering the harbor. This was supposed to be a peaceful research facility, but since the sensor runs had indicated that the landward side was defended, this was a lucky break.

The patrol boat that had passed them was tied up to the pier in the center of the little harbor. But there was no one on deck and no lights were showing through the portholes. The crew had to have left the craft and disappeared into the complex. It looked like things were going their way.

After making his recon, James ducked back down and swam to the end of the breakwater, where he had left the others. Using his underwater slate, he quickly drew a diagram of the dock area and marked the positions of the two guards and the patrol boat. Since he and Bolan were carrying the Russian underwater rifles, he sketched a plan to take out the guards from under the water. When Bolan gave him a thumbs-up, the swimmers moved out along the breakwater toward the dock.

James and Bolan left the others and swam along the front of the dock. James stopped a couple of yards short of the sentry and allowed himself to sink to the bottom of the harbor. The Executioner swam closer to the dock and turned facedown in the water. Filling his lungs with air, he dropped his weight belt and rose to the surface right in front of the guard. To make sure that the man saw him, he released a big bubble of air.

The guard heard the noise and walked to the edge of the pier to look at what was floating in the harbor. Lying on his back on the bottom, James sighted in on him as he leaned over the edge, taking care to compensate for the refraction difference between the air and the saltwater, and triggered a single round. Fired underwater, the Russian assault rifle made no noise. Trailing a thin line of bubbles, the 120 mm steel dart drilled through the water before breaking the surface of the swells.

James's aim had been true, and the dart took the guard in the side of his head, directly behind his right eye, penetrating the thin bone at his temple and driving into his brain. Since he was already bent over at the waist trying to look under the water, the reflex of the dart slamming into his brain and shutting off his neuronal synapses snapped his upper torso forward. He went headfirst over the edge of the dock into the water.

"Hey, Juan!" the other guard shouted when he heard the splash. "What are you doing, man?"

Leaving his AK slung over his shoulder, he walked to the edge of the dock. "If the chief catches you drinking, man, you'll be sorry."

When he saw his partner's body lying motionless on the bottom, he reached around for his AK. The assault rifle didn't clear his shoulder before Bolan abruptly rose from the water and triggered a short burst from his Russian dart rifle. The darts stitched him up the left side, one of them tearing through his carotid artery.

Clawing at his throat and giving a strangled cry, the guard crumpled to the dock, the crash of his AK against the concrete sounding loud over the gentle slap of the waves.

After waiting to see if the noise had attracted anyone's attention, Bolan climbed onto the dock and took the magnetic coded entry card from the chain on the dead guard's belt. It was convenient that Rondell had placed his trust in electronic gadgets; it would ensure that they could get inside quickly without having to blow the door.

He motioned to McCarter and James to ease the body of the second guard into the water. Once he had been disposed of, the Stony Man warriors removed their scuba gear and fins and left them on the bottom of the harbor. It wouldn't do to have anyone find them on the deck.

The six men did leave their black wet suits on as they dashed across the dock and pressed themselves against the wall. Bolan slid the security card into the electronic lock and heard the click as the lock released and the green light came on over the alphanumeric keypad.

Dropping his night-vision goggles over his eyes, he opened the door a crack and slid through, the Russian assault weapon at the ready. When the goggles showed that the darkened room was empty, he keyed the throat mike to his comm link. "We're inside."

"Roger," Lyons radioed back.

WHEN THE OTHER Stony Man warriors joined Bolan inside the lower floor, they spread out to sweep through it and make sure that they were alone. As Kurtzman and Bolan had expected, the lower floor of the complex was a cargo storage area for the supply ships. Crates and boxes of supplies were stacked in neat rows. A propane-powered forklift was waiting to move them as soon as the day shift started.

At the south side of the huge room, a concrete ramp led up to the next floor, and a bank of elevators stood along the wall, as well. Not knowing what the elevators would open onto, Bolan signaled for the team to take the ramp.

Katzenelenbogen led the way up with the barrel of his silenced Uzi resting across his prosthesis and his left hand around the pistol grip. It had been a cakewalk so far, but the gruff Israeli had been in the business far too long to expect that it would remain that way very much longer.

CHAPTER TWENTY

The second floor of the cliffside complex housed the environmental control equipment for the building. All the electrical power, water, heating and air conditioning supplied to the structure was controlled from there. No matter what else the Stony team could get to, destroying the machinery would set Rondell's plans back for months. If this floor was properly taken out, the complex wouldn't be habitable until it was repaired.

Bolan signaled for James and Manning to remain there and fix their demo charges to the vital equipment while he took the others to look for their primary target, the satellite control center. Manning and James quickly secured the second level while the other four commandos raced up the stairwell on the other side of the room.

"What's in that tank?" James asked, pointing to a huge white cylinder lying flat against the wall at the far end of the room.

Manning glanced over and saw that the cylinder was stenciled with the international warning for liquified gas. "It's either propane or natural gas," he said, walking over to get a closer look.

"Bingo!" He grinned when he got closer to the cylinder.

"We've found our demo target," he immediately radioed up to Bolan.

"The satellite control center?"

"No, something even better. I've found a five-thousand-liter liquid-propane tank. It looks like they're using the gas to power some of their machinery. I can rig this thing to go off like a fuel-air explosive bomb without too much trouble, and, when it goes off, it should take out the entire building."

While their mission orders were to take out Rondell's link to his private killer satellite, eradicating the building itself would solve the problem just as well. And, as Bolan well knew, an FAE explosion would do exactly that. "Do it," he ordered.

Fuel-air explosive bombs had first been dreamed up during the Vietnam War as a way to instantly create helicopter landing zones in the jungle, but the basic principle went back much further than that. Every gasoline engine that had ever been built worked on the fuel-air explosive principle.

In Vietnam, C-130 Hercules transports would fly over the triple-canopy jungle with the rear ramp doors open. Over the target, the loadmaster would pop a LAPES parachute like the ones that were used to snatch cargo pallets out in a Low Altitude Parachute Extraction Supply drop. This time, though, the chute pulled a ten-thousand-pound liquid-propane tank out of the cargo hold. The tank was fitted with additional parachutes to slow the fall and give the Hercules's crew time to get the hell out of the area as fast as their four thundering turboprops could take them.

A thousand feet above the ground, an explosive charge would burst the propane tank. Freed from the pressure that had kept the gas liquified, the propane flashed into its gaseous form. But, since propane was heavier than air, the gas quickly settled to the ground in the shape of an inverted bowl. A few seconds after the initial charge went off, a second charge, a flash charge, detonated the propane and hell visited the jungle below.

With the typical military flair for sarcastic understatement, the Hercules crews called their huge fuel-air bombs "daisy cutters." In reality they would blow a four-hundred-foot clear spot, even triple-canopy jungle, down to bedrock. The only problem was that the tons of trees and brush that had once filled this space was now shoved into a ring around the opening like a fortress wall.

The grunts who were airlifted into these instant landing zones always had to use chain saws to cut

their way through the twisted debris before they
could go on about their mission. But they wouldn't
have to worry about any NVA who might have been
in the area. Along with clearing a nice hole in the
jungle, a daisy cutter could kill every living thing
within a quarter-mile radius of the blast. Even those
as far as half a mile away were often permanently
deafened.

A similar FAE system had been used in the Gulf
War on some of Saddam's Republican Guard tank
units with equally devastating results. Exactly what
an FAE explosion would do in an enclosed area that
would funnel the blast upward, Manning didn't
exactly know. But he was certain that it would more
than destroy the complex and everyone in it.

Telling James to stand guard, Manning opened
his demo bag, took out the tools of his trade and
went to work. Had he not been in enemy territory,
he would have whistled while he worked. It had
been a long time since he had had a chance like this.

EVEN THOUGH MANNING had discovered the secret to putting the Sunflash complex permanently
out of business, Bolan and the other three Stony
Man warriors continued their search for the satellite control room. If possible, Brognola wanted
them to get photographic proof of what Rondell

had been doing to substantiate his decision to make the strike.

Even though most of the doors on each floor were labeled in both English and Spanish, it was slow going. Since there was a good chance that most of the Sunflash employees had no idea what Rondell was up to, they didn't expect to find a sign directing them to the target they sought. They made it halfway through their search of the fourth floor before their luck ran out.

They had just gotten into the corridor, and, after taking out the surveillance camera, were working their way down the hall, when a door opened behind them and a man in a khaki Sunflash security uniform stepped out. He drew his side arm and shouted *"¡Hola!"* when he saw the four figures in their black wet suits.

Katz spun in a crouch and caressed the trigger of his Uzi. The only sound that could be heard from the silenced weapon was a metallic clicking as the bolt moved back and forth in the subgun's receiver. The floor was carpeted so not even the tinkle of falling 9 mm brass could be heard.

The guard gave a strangled cry as the 9 mm slugs stitched him across the chest and sent him crashing back against the wall.

Now Katz could see the sign on the door the guard had come out of and it read Hombre. The man had been caught leaving the men's room. No sooner had he read the sign than he heard another man's footsteps on the tile floor inside.

He lunged for the door, but the man inside beat him to it and he heard the lock snap shut. Leveling the Uzi, Katz fired a burst through the door at chest height, but he heard the man speaking on a radio just before he fired.

"WE HAVE INTRUDERS in the complex." The Spanish-speaking voice on the intercom in Benson Rondell's room brought him out of a sound sleep. It took a long, groggy moment before he was able to translate the words into English, but when he did, he leaped out of bed and hurriedly dressed.

Garcia had promised him that there was no way he could be touched if he was in Baja, and he had believed him. He didn't know all the details of the complex's defenses—that was supposed to be Garcia's job—but what he did know of them was impressive. But if someone was attacking them, they weren't as impressive as he had thought.

As he raced down the hall to the elevator that would take him to the security control room, he didn't take the time to even try to translate the rest of the words the voice on the intercom was saying. There were intruders in his building and that was all he needed to know.

"What's going on?" Rondell shouted as he burst into the security control center and saw that Garcia was there ahead of him. "What's this about someone attacking us?"

Hector Garcia had his hands full at the moment. From his monitor in the tenth-floor security command center, he was too busy deploying his forces to have time to calm a frightened American, no matter who he was.

"Later, dammit," he snapped. "I'm busy."

Even though Sunflash's remote Baja location made it an unlikely target, Garcia's Cali bosses had insisted that he have a full platoon of guards on hand to secure the huge facility and the surrounding area. That had meant that he'd had to bring in extra supplies, including women, for their off-duty hours. But now he was glad for the board's paranoia, because it meant that he had the men to deal with this.

From what he could make of the reports that were coming in, it looked like there were less than a dozen or so of the attackers, and it looked like they were all confined below the fifth floor. With the forces he had on hand, it shouldn't be too difficult to see that they stayed, and died, down there. Barking orders in Spanish, he directed his security squads to converge on them and wipe them out.

A little overwhelmed, Rondell took an empty chair in front of one of the security monitors and watched the screen. All he could see, though, were the Sunflash guards buckling on their equipment belts as they ran to their stations. None of the screens showed the intruders. Then he noticed that several of the screens were blank. It didn't occur to him that they had been disabled by the intruders.

So far, Garcia hadn't wasted any time trying to figure out who these men were or where they had come from. That would come later when the bodies were laid out for his inspection on the loading dock. Right now he needed to concentrate on seeing that they died quickly before they did any damage to the facility.

He did, however, remember the fishing boat that had been reported offshore earlier that day. But since the Sunflash complex was located in a favorite area for American sports fishermen on their way down from California to the famous fishing grounds of Cabo San Lucas and Mazatlán to the south, he had given it no thought. At sunup tomorrow, however, he would launch the helicopter and look for this boat and make sure that its occupants were fishermen and not commandos.

WHILE JAMES GUARDED the doors of the second floor, Manning took out his roll of linear shaped charge and quickly wrapped a length of it around each end of the five-thousand-liter propane tank. To make sure that the liquid gas got into the air fast enough when the tank burst, he placed two more lines of the shaped charge along both the top and the bottom. When the linear charges went off, the tank would open up like an upside-down soup can with a fire cracker inside and a brick on top. There would be nothing to prevent the liquid propane from pouring out into the air, flashing into its gaseous form and mixing with oxygen to create the explosive mixture.

Once the linear charges were all tied together with det cord and fused, he put a detonator at both ends of the tank with the timers set two seconds apart.

He placed the first ignition charge a few feet from the tank and fused it separately and set the timer for thirty seconds after the main charges. That would give the liquid propane enough time to flash into gas so it could mix with the air and become an explosive mixture. A backup ignition charge was placed on the other side of the room, set for five seconds after the main charge.

When the last charge was set, Manning quickly went over each one of them again and set the anti-tampering switches on each of the detonators. Now they could be activated, but they couldn't be disarmed. No matter what happened to them, one way or the other, the place was going to go up.

"We're done down here," Manning radioed up to Bolan. "Everything's rigged and ready to go."

"Roger. We're coming back down," Bolan said over the rattle of automatic fire. "We've run into resistance and I'm calling it off. Keep your level secure and don't set the timers until we get down there."

"Got you covered," Manning said confidently.

No sooner had he said that, however, than he heard James shout a warning from the other side of the room and trigger a long burst from his Russian dart rifle. Spinning, he saw a khaki-clad security squad burst out of the elevator.

Swinging around his slung H&K, he fired a short burst before ducking for cover and reaching for his comm link. "Striker," he radioed, "we've been outflanked by about half a dozen of them. They came down the elevator."

That wasn't what Bolan wanted to hear at the moment. He had been about to radio Manning and James to have them join him to provide fire support while they pulled back. As it was, it looked like both of them were going to be on their own for a while.

Just then, James cut in. "We're really in trouble down here, Striker. Manning just took a hit."

"Hang on, we're coming down."

FROM THEIR POSITION half a mile offshore, Able Team had been monitoring the Stony team's comm link chatter and knew that things weren't going well for them inside the complex. So far, no one had been hit, but that could change at any minute. Even so, Bolan's instructions had been specific. They were to stand offshore until he called them in. Lyons wasn't one to shirk a fight, but he also knew how to follow orders whether he liked them or not.

He had the boat's helm while Schwarz watched the shore through powerful field glasses. Even though the offshore breeze brought them the muffled sounds of firing, so far all the fighting was taking place inside the building. Then he heard James call, saying that Manning had been hit.

"There's a squad of goons making their way around to the loading dock," Schwarz shouted. "If they get in there, they'll cut our guys off."

Lyons didn't hesitate for a moment. With Manning wounded, they would have trouble fighting their way past the guards blocking their exit. "Striker," he radioed, "this is Ironman. You have a squad coming in from the dock level to cut you off. We're going in to take care of them for you."

"Roger," Bolan sent back. "We're on our way down to the second level to get Manning and

James. As soon as we link up with them, we'll be on our way out, so keep the dock clear for us.''

"Roger."

Slamming the boat's throttles all the way forward, he cut the wheel sharply to the left and headed directly for the docks. The engines screamed on the red line as Able Team roared to the rescue.

CHAPTER TWENTY-ONE

Bolan knew what was going down, but he was having a difficult time doing anything about it. Now that the complex was alerted, their lack of knowledge of its layout, beyond the route they had taken, was definitely working against them. Every time they beat back a threat, another one appeared from a different direction. So far the guards had been coming at them in twos and threes, and they had been able to handle them.

This time they heard the ping of the elevator bell behind them in time to turn and deliver a deadly barrage right as the doors opened. When the last body fell half outside the car, blocking the door, McCarter raced forward to see if they had missed anyone.

"Shoot up the elevator controls," Bolan shouted.

McCarter complied, with spectacular results as the wiring shorted out. But that was only one of at least three elevator shafts and several stairwells in the complex. They might not be so lucky the next time.

Bolan motioned toward the stairwell at the end of the hall, and they ran for it.

ON THE OCEAN, Lyons had his situation a little better under control. The Sunflash guards sprinting to the end of the dock heard the *High Roller*'s twin engines screaming toward them at full RPM. Skidding to a halt, they turned to deal with it instead of moving to safety behind the concrete walls of the lower level.

Blancanales had the M-60 light machine gun set up on the boat's foredeck, and he opened fire on the guards as soon as they came within range. Even with Lyons skipping the boat from one wave top to the next at full throttle, he was still able to fire effectively. A couple of the guards went down while the others scattered or threw themselves flat to get out of the line of fire.

When Blancanales paused to load a fresh ammo belt into the M-60, three of the guards picked themselves up and raced for the Sunflash patrol boat tied to the pier. Firing the boat's engines, they cut the mooring lines, slammed the throttle forward and headed straight out of the harbor toward the *High Roller*. The patrol boat didn't have any heavy guns mounted on her decks, but AKs firing from the foredeck were dangerous enough. The

High Roller wasn't built to withstand small-arms fire.

The Sunflash boat, however, was a different matter. When Blancanales didn't seem to be able to make any progress against it with the M-60, Schwarz dived for the M-16, which had an M-203 grenade launcher mounted under the barrel. A couple of 40 mm HE grenades in the right place should take care of the problem.

Throwing the weapon to his shoulder, he tried to compensate for the motion of the boat when he sighted in and fired. The characteristic thump of the grenade launcher sent the 40 mm round arching over the water. The grenade hit a few feet to the side of the patrol boat, sending a harmless geyser of water into the air.

"Ironman!" Schwarz shouted as he slid the M-203's breech forward to chamber the next round. "Keep a steady course so I can hit the bastards!"

Lyons immediately chopped the throttles to the engines to give Schwarz his shot. As soon as the *High Roller* settled in the water, Schwarz had the over-and-under M-16 to his shoulder again, with the grenade launcher's sights centered on the craft.

This time the 40 mm round impacted on the side of the open wheelhouse, sending razor-sharp shrapnel slashing into the guard at the helm. The boat keeled over sharply, turning her side to the

High Roller and presenting a perfect target for Schwarz to finish the job. The next grenade had to have detonated near a fuel tank, because the patrol boat suddenly erupted into a boiling ball of fire.

One of the guards leaped from the fantail, his uniform aflame. Schwarz didn't see either of the other two get off before a second explosion shredded the hull. A moment later, all that was left of the Sunflash boat was a burning fuel slick on the water.

Carefully maneuvering the *High Roller* to keep clear of the fuel, Lyons entered the harbor.

RONDELL AND GARCIA closely followed the progress of the battle from the security control center. So far, things weren't going their way, but the security troops had at least forced the commandos to retreat. The problem was that every time he sent a new squad up against them, or tried to get in behind them, they were immediately chewed to pieces. Whoever these guys were, they were good.

Garcia hadn't given up yet, but Rondell was frantic. The spectacular destruction of the patrol boat was the last straw for him. If these people were well enough equipped to take it out, Garcia's Colombians might not be able to handle them after all.

"I want to get out of here, Hector," he said, being careful to keep his voice under control. "I'm not going to die because your men can't do their jobs."

"I'm busy, dammit!" Garcia snapped. "Just stay the hell out of the way and let me do my job."

"Your job is to protect me," Rondell snapped back. "If your men are as good as you say they are, they will take care of the intruders and we can come back when they're all dead. Right now, I want to get the hell out of here. I didn't sign on with you people to become a target. I'm not going to be any damned good to your board of directors if I'm dead."

Garcia had to admit that Rondell had a good point. Risking Rondell's life unnecessarily might not be a good move. The complex itself had cost the cartel millions and had to be protected. But without Rondell to run it, all the money they had spent would be wasted. More importantly, having Rondell in the California statehouse was even more essential to the cartel's long-range plans. Either way, being responsible for his death wasn't in Garcia's best interests.

"Okay," the Mexican decided. "I'll get the pilot out to the landing pad."

Rondell was out the door and running for the elevator that led up to the helipad before Garcia was even out of his chair. The man might be a good politician, the Mexican thought, but he sure lacked balls. But then, in his opinion, all politicians lacked balls. That's why they were politicians.

Stony Man Farm

"SOMEONE'S TRYING to get away in the Sunflash chopper," Kurtzman announced as he zoomed in on the computer-enhanced image of the Sunflash helicopter on the helipad. "The rotors are turning. It's got to be Rondell."

Price keyed her mike to warn Lyons of this development. "Ironman, this is Stony Man control. Be advised that your principal is escaping in a helicopter."

"Roger," was Lyons's curt reply. "We don't have anything that will reach him right now, so we're going to have to let him go. See if the Bear can track him when he takes off. Ironman out."

Kurtzman shook his head. "I don't have anything to track him with. If I tilt the satellite's cameras to try to follow the chopper, I won't be able to watch the complex. It's one or the other. I can't do both."

"Keep watching Sunflash," Price instructed. "We'll track him down later."

Baja California

LYONS SAW the helicopter when it lifted off the pad and appeared above the side of the mountain. He would have fired on it if he'd had any heavy weapons that could have reached it, but the aircraft was too far away for their light weapons to have any effect. Their prey was getting away, but their primary mission was to destroy the compound, not kill Rondell.

"Striker," he radioed, "Ironman. Your back door is secure for now at least. Get your asses out of there ASAP so we can go home."

"Roger, we'll be linking up with James and Manning in a minute, and we'll be coming out shortly."

"We'll be waiting, out."

No sooner had Lyons spoken than a heavy machine gun opened up on him from a bunker hidden in the rocky face of the cliff. From the familiar deep-throated chunk-chunking sound, it could only be a U.S.-made .50-caliber M-2.

Lyons slammed the throttles all the way forward and spun the boat's wheel hard over. He had no choice but to get out of range of that gun. The *High Roller* was a well-built boat, but that Ma Deuce would cut through her like the proverbial hot knife through butter.

As Lyons zigzagged to present a more difficult target, Blancanales returned fire with his lighter M-60, the two lines of tracers cutting across each other. It looked like he was getting some hits in the right area when another M-2 opened up from the other side of the cliff. There was nothing they could do now but run for the open sea.

"Striker, Ironman."

"Striker here, go."

"We came under fire from a couple of hidden .50-cal bunkers and had to pull back out of range."

"Where are they?"

"There's one of them in the cliffs right above each of the breakwaters. Their fields of fire criss-cross the harbor and I don't have anything to take them out."

"Roger, Ironman. Get yourself clear. We'll take care of them on our way out. Striker out."

JAMES AND THE WOUNDED Manning were holding their own on the second floor. They hadn't been able to make much headway against the four guards who were left of the six who had come down the elevator. With the explosives in place, they had to keep control of the floor. Since the antitampering switches had been set, if they backed out and left them and the guards tried to disarm them, they would detonate.

"Cal," Bolan's voice said in his ear, "we're in place on the landing at the top of the stairs and ready to come down. What's the situation?"

James quickly gave him the location of the Sun-flash guards.

"Lay down a base of fire. We're coming in."

James's Russian assault dart rifle and Manning's H&K kept the guards' heads down as Bolan and the others broke through the door and stormed down the stairs. Caught between the two groups of Stony Man warriors, the Sunflash guards had no choice but to fight or die. It was over in less than sixty seconds.

"Can you walk?" Bolan knelt beside Manning.

"I'm okay," the Canadian replied as he got to his feet.

"What do you have the detonators set for?"

"Twenty minutes. Is that enough?"

"It'll have to be," Bolan said. "We don't have time to reset them all."

THE MINUTE THEY BROKE OUT onto the dock, the .50-caliber machine gun opened up. It wasn't able to depress its muzzle enough to hit them, though it was keeping them where they were. If they tried to get back into the water, they'd be cut to pieces.

Bolan hadn't paid much attention to the cliffs overlooking the breakwaters on the way in, but one look at them now was all it took for him to understand why Lyons had been forced to withdraw. The two machine guns were set up so that each one covered its own side of the breakwater and half of the dock. But their fields of fire could also converge on the mouth of the small harbor. If Lyons tried to come in to pick them up, the *High Roller* would be obliterated.

They were going to have to take care of at least one of the guns themselves, then swim back out to the boat. And they didn't have long to do it.

"Have you got any demo blocks left?" McCarter yelled to Encizo when he found that he couldn't get a clear shot at the bunker's aperture.

The Cuban dug into his demo bag and came up with two.

"Set the timers to ten seconds."

"Got it."

"When I tell you, activate the timer and toss it over to me."

McCarter held his hands out to catch the explosive package. "Now!"

Encizo tossed it over, and, with a single motion, McCarter caught it in his right hand and threw it up toward the bunker. The one-pound demo block sailed through the air like a plastic brick.

He had thrown it high, hoping that it would lodge in the rocks above the bunker's aperture and bring them down on it when it exploded. Instead, it bounced off and was on its way back down when it exploded harmlessly in the air.

"Throw me another one," he yelled to Encizo, "and cut it back to five seconds this time."

Encizo set the timer and tossed it over. This time the demo block sailed through the air and detonated directly in front of the bunker's aperture. Even though it didn't have the fragmentation effect of a real hand grenade, the blast effect alone was enough to blind the man behind the gun and stun his loader.

When the second explosion silenced the weapon, the other machine-gun crew decided it didn't want to continue the battle and abandoned the bunker.

THOUGH THE SUNFLASH security force seemed to have had enough for the moment, Bolan and the rest of the Stony Man warriors kept guard while James put Manning's rebreathing gear and tanks on him along with his fins.

"Get him going fast," Bolan ordered as soon as Manning was suited up. "We don't have much time."

Encizo helped James ease the wounded man into the warm water at the end of the dock. James made sure that his rebreathing gear was working properly before taking him any deeper. Keeping to the bottom of the harbor in case the second .50-caliber machine gun tried to reach them, James pulled Manning along with him with powerful strokes of his arms. The clock was counting, and they had to be clear of this place before it went up.

As soon as James and Manning had cleared the end of the harbor, the other four commandos quickly donned their diving gear and followed them. While Encizo, McCarter and Katz swam ahead, Bolan stayed back with James to help him tow Manning. The timers were running.

CHAPTER TWENTY-TWO

In the Pacific

"Get us as far out to sea as you can!" Manning gasped as Schwarz dragged him inside the *High Roller*. "Quick!"

When Schwarz didn't immediately run for the wheelhouse, Manning yelled, "The propane bomb, dammit! It's about to go off! Get us the hell out of here!"

This time Schwarz didn't hesitate. He had caught the comm link chatter about the propane tank, and he knew what a fuel-air explosive could do.

"Ironman!" he yelled. "The bomb's about to go off!"

Lyons slammed the throttles of both engines up against the stops and wrenched the wheel around to turn the boat's bow toward the open sea. Even with both of the big marine V-8 engines screaming at the red line, though, it seemed to take forever before the boat was moving fast enough for his tastes.

"It should be right about—" Manning started to say when the mountain exploded.

A blinding white flash lit up the night sky over Baja, and it was followed a split second later by an ear-shattering roar as all five thousand liters of liquid propane, now a highly volatile gas well mixed with oxygen, detonated. The Sunflash complex and much of the mountain it was built into simply disappeared in the blast. The concrete and structural steel of modern buildings was strong, but it wasn't strong enough to withstand the force of that kind of explosion.

The stern of the vessel was to the shore, which was the only thing that saved them when the shock wave hit. Had the fishing boat had her side to the shore, the blast of hot compressed air would have capsized her. As it was, it lifted the stern of the boat far enough out of the water for her twin props to beat dry air for a few seconds before they slammed back down.

A few seconds later a shower of rock and debris rained around them. One of the larger chunks smashed through the roof of the wheelhouse and crashed against the loran and sonar cabinet shattering both instruments. Another rock smashed through the foredeck and ended up in one of the berths below.

"Geez!" Schwarz said, awed, as he picked himself up off the deck. "What did you guys do to that place?"

Manning grinned through his pain. "Just a little propane and air. It works every time."

NOW THAT THEY WERE in the clear, Calvin James had the medic bag out and was carefully cutting Manning's wet suit away from the wound in his side. It looked like the bullet had bounced off his ribs instead of penetrating into his body cavity and tearing up his internal organs.

"Easy," Manning said through clenched teeth. "That hurts like hell."

"How is he?" Bolan asked.

"It looks like he's got a broken rib," James replied. "But I don't think the bullet hit anything vital."

"Does he need an airlift?"

"I don't think so," James said. "I can patch him up well enough here to get him back to San Diego safely. That way we won't have to involve civilians or the Coast Guard."

They could radio ahead and arrange for a Stony Man-cleared doctor to meet them at the pier so they wouldn't have to answer a doctor's questions at a local hospital.

"I'll set things up when I call the Farm," Bolan told him.

"If you two are done discussing my case over my head like you think I'm a child," Manning groused, "maybe I can have someone put a dressing on this before I bleed to death."

"Sorry," James said.

As the *High Roller* fled north at full throttle, the mountain glowed behind them like a volcano.

IN THE FLEEING helicopter, Rondell couldn't believe his eyes when his sight returned. The entire Sunflash complex had disappeared as if it had been nuked. Much of the mountain it had been built into had disappeared, as well. He started shaking when it sunk home that he could have been destroyed along with it. Had he not insisted that Garcia get him out of there, he would be dead right now.

So much for the Cali bosses always knowing what was going on in the federal government. The narcodollars they had paid to their informants had been wasted this time. And he would never again place his life in their hands. The fact that they might hold him responsible for the destruction and demand his life in return hadn't occurred to him yet.

Hector Garcia was also stunned. It had to have been the American military that had attacked them. But the board of directors had told him that they had ironclad assurances that the military wouldn't be involved in any action against Rondell. Apparently their well-paid informants in Washington had dropped the ball on this one. It would, however, be the last time that these people dropped the ball. The Cali cartel didn't allow their informants to make two mistakes. They paid their informants well, and they expected good information for their money. If they didn't produce, they were held accountable with predictable results.

He also knew that he would be held accountable for this disaster. The Cali leadership had given this project to him and had made him responsible for its success. Millions of narcodollars had been invested in the Sunflash project, and all they had to show for it now was a smoking hole in the ground. Someone's head was going on the block for this, and he knew that it would be his.

The cartel handsomely rewarded good work, but it also severely punished any failure. The more disastrous the failure, the more severe the punishment. He had witnessed Cali-style punishment before and knew that if he was punished for this his death wouldn't come easy.

Like all men, he knew that he would die one day, but he wanted to die quick and easy and not have it dragged out over several pain-racked days. And he wanted to be buried with his body intact and not have it hacked to bits with machetes and fed to the pigs. The only way that he would die peacefully in bed would be if he made sure that the cartel didn't get their hands on him. That, however, wasn't going to be easy.

There was no way that he would be safe anywhere in Latin America now. Fortunately, though, he had most of his substantial fortune in an offshore bank account that he could access from anywhere on the planet. If he could find a place to hide, he would eventually be able to start over. He didn't know where he would go yet, but he would have time to figure that out later. Right now, he had to disappear completely.

He turned to Rondell, who was still in a state of shock at how close he had come to dying. "That forest camp in Northern California, how far away is it from the nearest town?"

"What?"

"Gilmore's Green Earth training camp," Garcia said. "How far away from the town is it?"

"It's an hour and a half's drive out of Crescent City," Rondell answered. "Why?"

That should do it for now, Garcia thought. After hiding out in the deep woods for a few days, he would make his way to Canada and get his money transferred to him before disappearing completely.

"If it hasn't occurred to you yet," Garcia said, "you and I have just made the Cali Most Wanted list."

"What do you mean?"

"It's simple." He shrugged expressively. "As soon as the board catches up with us, they are going to kill us."

"But I didn't do anything wrong! If they're pissed at anyone, they should take it out on the people who told them that the federal government wouldn't move against my facility."

"Oh," Garcia said, smiling thinly, "they will. But they're also going to take it out on you."

"But what about my campaign? They said that they needed me in the statehouse so they could—"

Garcia cut him off in midsentence. "All of that is out the window now. You and I cost them a great deal of money, and they don't like that."

"But I didn't go to them, they came to me. You're the one who thought this whole thing up in the first place."

"That's why I asked about the forest camp. I'm going there to keep out of sight until I can work out my disappearing act. If you have any brains at all, you'll forget about being governor of California and come with me. If you go back to Pasadena, you won't last a day."

Rondell sat back against the seat and stared out the window. This wasn't the way it was supposed to have worked. With the power he had at his command at Sunflash and the backing of the cartel, he was supposed to become one of the greatest men of the century. Now, if what Garcia said was correct, he would be a hunted man for the rest of his life. He would go with Garcia for now, but he intended to check with the cartel before he gave up on his plans.

Since Garcia had been proved wrong about Sunflash, he could be wrong about this, as well.

When Rondell kept silent, Garcia picked up the spare headset, keyed the mike and told the pilot to head for the secluded forest camp in Northern California.

"I will have to stop for fuel, Señor Garcia," the pilot replied, his voice not quite under control. Rondell wasn't the only one who was shook up at having barely missed going up in a ball of flame. "We don't have the range to get there with what I have on board."

Garcia thought for a moment. There was no way to know whether the attack force had noticed the chopper leaving. But if they had and had reported it, the police could be looking for them. But it was still worth the risk, because the chopper would get him where he wanted to go faster than any car.

"Find some out-of-the-way airfield to land," he said. "And remember to pay cash for the fuel."

"Yes, sir."

Stony Man Farm

EVEN THOUGH THE MISSION had left a few loose ends hanging—including one named Benson Rondell—Hal Brognola didn't look unhappy when he walked into the Stony Man War Room the next morning. If anything, he looked happier than he had in a long time. Rondell's secret satellite control facility was a jagged smoking hole in a Mexican mountain and would never threaten anyone again. And if the man who was responsible had escaped and was on the run, it didn't seem to be bothering him at all.

The press was having a field day with the Baja explosion. The liberal newspapers were screaming that the destruction was a government plot designed to protect the nuclear power industry. The radical leftists were saying that it had been an attack by the capitalists against a man who was trying to bring a new era of justice to California politics.

Everyone was blaming the military and demanding an investigation. But when no one was able to tie any movement of American military forces into the incident, that theory fell flat. Then Pemex, the Mexican national oil and gas company, admitted that the Sunflash compound had had a five-thousand-liter liquid-propane tank in the building. That seemed to settle the question.

Everyone, of course, assumed that Benson Rondell had perished in the blast along with everyone else. Stony Man Farm wasn't about to say otherwise until they were told to do so by Hal Brognola. For whatever reason, the President wanted the knowledge of Rondell's having escaped to remain a secret for now, so it would.

"The problem," Brognola tried to explain to Barbara Price, "is that we still don't have anything to directly tie Rondell to the nuclear accidents, and we're sure as hell not going to find it now. The team did too good a job in Baja. There's not enough left down there to even sift through for evidence to prove that he ever had anything like a satellite control system."

"But how about the photos we have of the antennas and the evidence of the radar satellite tracking plots?" she asked. "That's how we got onto his killer satellite in the first place."

"That's not good enough for the arena of public scrutiny and the media," he said. "It's too open to interpretation."

Price didn't believe what she was hearing. Everything was "open to interpretation," but that had never stopped anyone before.

"Anyway," Brognola concluded, "the President is satisfied that the crisis is over, and he wants you to stand down on this mission."

"He doesn't want us to track down Rondell?"

Brognola shook his head. "No. He wants the DEA or the California authorities to locate him and pick him up."

"On what charges?"

"They're going to try to link him to the cocaine shipment that was found in the warehouse that Able

Team raided. Even though the local cops were willing to go with their initial impression that it had just been a local drug-gang battle, I put the DEA to working on it, and they're following up some leads between the Green Shirt bodies Lyons left in the warehouse and Rondell.''

"But that's not going to fly worth a damn in court, Hal," Price protested. "You know how those things go. Rondell will play his fiddle about a federal conspiracy against him and he'll walk. You know that."

He stood abruptly and snapped shut his brief-case. "Nonetheless," he said, "we've done our part and it's out of our hands now."

CHAPTER TWENTY-THREE

Santa Barbara, California

Barbara Price wasn't the only one who was unhappy with the results of the Stony Man team's raid on Rondell's Baja Sunflash complex. The fact that Benson Rondell had escaped didn't sit well with Hermann Schwarz at all. In fact, to say that he was angry would have been a serious understatement. But unlike Brognola and the President, he wasn't about to let someone else take care of that problem for him. In fact, he insisted that he scratch that itch himself.

Since he didn't want to upset the recovering Sylvia Bowes again, he didn't even try to visit her. But he had been able to bribe one of the nurses on her floor into giving him a daily update on her condition. The latest report was that she had taken a turn for the worse, and the surgeons were going in again to try to repair more of the damage to her internal organs now that the bullet wound had started to heal. There was, however, little hope that she would ever be able to use her legs again.

When he learned that, Schwarz doubled his resolve to take vengeance. "I'm not standing down yet," he suddenly announced when Lyons and Blancanales started packing their gear.

"What do you mean?" Blancanales asked, frowning.

"Take the banana out of your ear, Pol. I said that I'm not finished with that bastard yet. I still owe him, and I'm going to see that he gets what he's owed."

"But Barb said that Hal has called off the operation now that Rondell's out of business. It's up to the FBI or the DEA to run him down. We're officially out of it."

Schwarz had no quarrel with either the FBI or the DEA. But, as far as he was concerned, they'd better stand back and keep the hell out of his way on this one. If they didn't, he would simply run roughshod over them. Benson Rondell still had a lot to answer for, and Schwarz was going to see that he did exactly that.

"On top of that," Blancanales added, "we don't have the slightest idea where he is. Kurtzman said that he wasn't able to track him when he flew out."

"For God's sake, Pol," Schwarz said, sounding thoroughly disgusted, "that's never stopped us before, has it? If you'll remember, we're supposed to be the experts at tracking people."

"Look," Blancanales stated, not about to give up trying to talk sense into his partner, "use your head, man. This guy's on the run and he's got enough money to run anywhere he wants to. Hell, he's probably not even in the country now. I know I sure as hell wouldn't be if I was him."

"I'll be able to find him." Schwarz sounded confident. "The first thing I'll do is find Derek Gilmore, then he and I are going to have a little chat before I break his skull wide open. He'll sure as hell know where Rondell is, you can bet your ass on that."

"And just where the hell do you think that you're going to find this Gilmore guy? I have a hundred bucks that says he's hit the bricks, too, by now. If he's the professional that you said he was, he isn't going to stick around any more than Rondell did."

"I'll find him with the Green Shirt tree huggers," Schwarz stated. "They all think that he's the boss, and I don't think that he's going to give that up. He likes the feeling of power too much. He'll just go underground with them and continue to play his stupid games until he thinks it's safe for him to surface again."

"For the sake of argument," Blancanales said patiently, "let's say you're right and he's hiding with the Green Shirts. How are you going to smoke him out?".

"That's easy." Schwarz grinned. "I'm simply going to order up another environmentalist uniform from the catalog, then I'll join the Green Earth Movement again."

"You've got to be out of your rabbit-assed mind, Gadgets!" Blancanales finally exploded. He was supposed to be the people expert, the man who could talk his way into Fort Knox and back out. But talking to Schwarz sometimes was like talking to a space alien.

"What the hell's wrong with you, man? Do you have a death wish or something? If I remember correctly, the last time that you got involved with those tree hugging Nazis, Lyons and I had to drive through a wall to rescue your ass and got a perfectly good Dodge pickup shot all to hell in the process."

"Think about it," Schwarz replied calmly. "Most of the Green Earthers have no idea what Rondell and Gilmore were doing on the side. Because of that, the rank and file won't know anything about my Alex Lord cover having been blown. I'll try to get Aaron to ship me another set of ID documents under another name, though, just to make sure. But I'll just show up at their next demonstration, join the fun and games and start trying to get a lead on him."

"But how about—"

"But nothing, Pol. I'm going after him."

Blancanales took a deep breath and started over. "What I started to say, before I was so rudely interrupted by a man who's completely out of his mind, is, why don't you let the Ironman and me come in on this with you? The three of us can cover more ground than you can by yourself."

Schwarz shook his head slowly. "I appreciate the offer, I really do. But I've got to do this by myself. If you join me, there's too great a chance of you getting in trouble if I run into a problem."

"That's exactly why you need us working with you."

"No."

Lyons had purposefully stayed out of the conversation. With Schwarz's mind made up, there was little he could do to stop him. He would, however, take some steps to make sure that Gadgets didn't get stepped on while he was chasing Rondell and Gilmore.

"Leave it, Pol," Lyons said. "The man says he doesn't want our help, so we don't help him. It's as simple as that."

Blancanales turned toward him, a confused look on his face as he slowly shook his head. "God! You've lost your mind, too."

Stony Man Farm

NOW THAT BROGNOLA had declared that the Sunflash operation was officially over, Barbara Price went about closing the mission down. At the Farm, no one paid any attention to the last mission unless it had been a failure. Everyone's efforts were always focused on preparing for the next mission, and the one after that.

The first step in the process was to deal with the men. Stony Man Farm was a citadel of modern high technology, but without the men of Phoenix Force and Able Team, it might as well not even exist. All the high-tech whizbang served only one purpose, and that purpose was to support the men who did the in-trench work.

The first of the men she checked in on was Gary Manning. His wound had proved not to be serious, and he was returning to the Farm to recuperate. He would be on the walking-wounded list for at least four weeks and would also have to take a couple more weeks off before he was back at the top of his form. But that was to be expected. No one else had been hurt, so she wouldn't have to deal with doctors, hospitals or physical therapists.

After checking on Manning, she contacted the rest of Phoenix Force to learn their plans. There was nothing on the threat board, and Brognola hadn't mentioned any presidential concerns, so things should be slow for a while. But she still needed to keep track of her human resources. After talking to her, the Phoenix Force warriors would go on about their other lives until they were called to action again. All of them that was, except for Mack Bolan.

The Executioner had only one life, and since it was always lived "on duty," there was no telling where his sense of duty would take him next. But like the men of the action teams, he would keep her informed about where he was and what he was doing.

After logging on with each of the Phoenix Force warriors, she checked in with Carl Lyons to see what Able Team would be doing in the next few days. He said that he and Blancanales were going back to their old haunts, but he didn't mention what Schwarz had in mind.

"Has Gadgets mentioned where he's going to be?" she asked.

There was a slight pause before Lyons answered. "I don't know. I think he plans to take it easy for a couple of weeks. He needs a vacation, and I think it'll do him good."

Price frowned. Gadgets Schwarz wasn't known for taking long vacations. Usually more than a couple of days off had him climbing the walls from sheer boredom. But he had apparently gotten emotionally involved with a woman this time, so maybe that had something to do with his taking time off. If that was the case, she also thought it would do him good to relax for a while.

"Tell him to have fun," she said, "and to give me a call when he can."

"Will do," Lyons promised.

Santa Barbara, California

IF GADGETS SCHWARZ was taking a vacation, Santa was a punk and sold dope to school kids. As far as Lyons and Blancanales were concerned, though, the only vacation he was taking was a vacation from his senses. After both of them had tried their best to talk him out of going after Rondell and anyone else who had been involved with the would-be politician's schemes, he insisted on returning to Santa Barbara. They didn't want him to go, but short of cuffing him and throwing him into a jail cell, there was no holding him back.

Lyons also didn't like having to tell Price a lie, but this time it was necessary. Gadgets needed the time to work this out, and he didn't need to have

Barb ragging his ass any more than he needed him and Blancanales on his case. But the Able Team leader wasn't just going to let it drop and keep his nose out of it, either. In fact, he was so concerned about his partner that he got hold of Mack Bolan to talk to him about the situation.

"The worst thing," Lyons said after he explained what Schwarz was planning to do, "is that Pol and I offered to go in with him on this, but he told us in no uncertain terms to butt out. He knows that he's going to go down in flames if this goes wrong, and he doesn't want to take us down with him. I appreciate the thought, but I don't want him out there on his own."

"I'm not doing anything right at the moment," the Executioner said. "Why don't I see if I can lend him a hand?"

Schwarz wasn't the only one who thought that Benson Rondell needed to pay for his sins. Bolan also believed that the man had stepped over the line into the world of barbarism. And since he had single-mindedly devoted his life to making the world safe from the barbarians, Rondell was now a target. Even if Schwarz wasn't involved, Bolan would have gladly undertaken the task himself.

"Someone needs to," Lyons said, sounding relieved. "The guy's really in over his head this time, and he's going to get it cut off if he's not careful."

The ex-LAPD sergeant shook his head. "Women. Man, I never thought I'd see him do something like this. I mean bystanders are always getting caught up in this shit. This isn't the first time that we've had someone get hit on one of these operations. And, sadly, I'm sure that it won't be the last."

"I'll take care of it," Bolan said.

"Do you want Pol and me to stand by in case you need a backup, someone to clean up after you?"

"That might be a good idea. I have a feeling that Gadgets's program is going to get complicated before it's over."

"So do I."

DEREK GILMORE WAS on the run, but that didn't mean that he had left the country or even California. Now that Benson Rondell was history, Gilmore's employment with him had ended. His activities with the Green Earth Movement hadn't, however.

Since the average member of the organization had no idea of what had been going on behind the scenes, they would have no reason not to still see him as their leader. He could hide out with them until he was ready to move on.

Along with the paychecks he had received from the cartel via Garcia, Gilmore had been making even more money on the side running a cocaine network, using the Green Shirts as his distribution mules.

The cartel would have killed him in a heartbeat had they known about his sideline. But as the leader of the Green Shirts, he had been able to cut out several of them who didn't mind making a little on the side themselves. The raid on the warehouse had cost him several of his best men, but there were more where they came from, and there was more product to move, as well.

Garcia had disappeared with Rondell, but he had left the key to Gilmore's financial independence behind—several keys, in fact. Two hundred and fifty kilos, a little over five hundred pounds, of Cali's best was in another Santa Barbara warehouse, waiting to enter the California cocaine distribution network. Even if he discounted the powder for a quick sale, he should still see at least a million dollars from the deal, even after paying off his help. That, with what he already had stashed away, would let him live very comfortably for the rest of his life.

Like Garcia, he had worked for the cartel long enough to know what their response was going to be to the Rondell disaster. He knew that he had only a few days, a week at the most, before he would have to run himself. But he intended to make as much money from his enterprise as he could before he was forced to disappear.

CHAPTER TWENTY-FOUR

Cali, Colombia

The Cali drug lords also wanted to find Benson Rondell, along with Hector Garcia, and they weren't buying the theory that the two men had been vaporized in the explosion. They knew that Rondell and Garcia had flown to Baja earlier, and they had learned that no wreckage of the Sunflash helicopter had been found in the devastation. Until they found Rondell's and Garcia's bodies, or the pieces thereof, they would continue to assume that the two men had flown out before the explosion and were alive somewhere.

The Baja disaster had precipitated a major crisis among the Cali drug lords. Their famous cocaine cartel wasn't a monolithic organization, a dictatorship with all the orders coming from one man at the top. Instead, the cartel was a loose confederation of independent cocaine-producing gang leaders who had banded together for their mutual benefit. Forming the cartel meant that they could spend more of their time taking care of business and less of it competing with one another. Each of the major producers had a seat on the so-called "board of directors," and their decisions were more or less made democratically by majority vote.

That didn't mean, however, that the cartel's board of directors was without internal friction—far from it. Turf battles and arguments about how to expand their business were all too common. And there were never-ending discussions about how they were going to spend their billions of dollars.

While this wrangling was unproductive, the reason for the dissent was simple—the cartel had two factions within it. One of the factions was made up of the hard-liners who wanted only to be drug gang leaders and live in their mountaintop fortresses like feudal kings lording it over the local peasantry. The other faction took a more modern view of the world and wanted to use their money to buy into legitimate businesses so they could live in civilized, big-city comfort, like capitalist tycoons. And with goals that far apart, there wasn't much room for compromise.

In fact, it had been the modernist faction that had pushed so hard for the cartel's investment in Rondell's project, on Garcia's advice. Even though the investment was huge, the hard-liners finally agreed to go along with it as an experiment in how modernization would work. Now that the experiment had gone bad, though, the hard-liners were back in the driver's seat on the board, and they wanted old-fashioned vengeance. They knew that they couldn't get their money back, but they could ensure that nothing like this would ever happen again. The example they would make of the men who had been responsible for this debacle would see to that.

Over the protests of the modernists, who warned of the dangers of sending an assassination team into the United States, the board voted to dispatch a three-man hit team to the north with orders to find and kill Rondell.

They were also ordered to kidnap Hector Garcia and bring him back to Cali alive. Since he was one of their own, he wouldn't get to pay for his mistake as easily as the American would. He would have to stand trial in person in front of the board of directors and try to explain himself. If he was found to be guilty, he would be a long time in dying. He was a cartel man, and that was the Cali way.

Stony Man Farm

ALONG WITH SCHWARZ and the Cali hit team, one other man was also searching for the Sunflash fugitives, but he was doing it from a wheelchair. Even though Brognola had terminated the mission,

Aaron Kurtzman had taken it upon himself to assist Schwarz in his search for Rondell and Gilmore.

When the Stony Man cybernetics team wasn't actively working on a mission, its members kept themselves busy by tracking all kinds of information that might come in handy someday. Everything from satellite photos to interesting Internet exchanges and foreign press articles flowed into Stony Man Farm on a daily basis. They were all cybernetically cataloged and stored away for possible future use.

While that kept most of the crew fairly busy during these off-mission times, Kurtzman still had a lot of time on his hands. And, as the saying went, "Idle hands are the devil's workshop." In this case, though, it was idle electronic hands. Most of his off-mission time was spent in his personal interests of the moment, whatever they might be. This time, the personal interest was to help Schwarz exorcise the demon that was haunting him. He knew all about demons and knew that the best way to deal with them was with action.

The first thing Kurtzman tried to track down was the location of the helicopter Rondell had used to make his escape. It took only a few minutes for him to get the aircraft's model and tail number from the FAA registration files. Another few minutes got him the range, fuel-tank capacity and gallons-per-hour rating for the ship's turbine.

The Bell 230 had a fuel tank that gave it a cruising range of approximately four hundred miles at two hundred miles per hour. Like most choppers, it was short-legged, which meant that it would have to stop for fuel often if Rondell wanted to put any distance between himself and the smoking hole in the Baja mountain. And, had he fled at top speed, the range would have been even less.

A click of his mouse brought a map of North America onto the screen, and Kurtzman quickly superimposed a circle over the Baja site, representing the chopper's maximum range on its internal fuel supply. Now all he had to do was to work his way through every aviation-fuel dealer within that circle to see who had filled the tanks on a Bell 230 helicopter that night or the following morning.

He was assuming, of course, that Rondell hadn't set up a secret air base and fuel supply. But the chances were that he hadn't, because there had been no reason for him to do so. Things had been going his way for quite some time, and a man who had things all his way wouldn't think of setting up secret bases.

He started by checking the airports in the northern half of the circle first. If Brognola's assumption that Rondell had been financed by the cartel was correct, he was unlikely to have fled south. The Cali bosses didn't like failures that cost them money, and since Rondell had failed, they would be looking for him. In Latin America he would be a gringo, and there would be no place for him to hide. His only hope was to get to the States or maybe Canada and fade into the background.

Baja California

KURTZMAN WASN'T the only one who figured out that following the missing Sunflash chopper would bring them to Rondell. On their way north, the Cali hit team stopped by the Baja location of the defunct Sunflash complex and talked with everyone who had witnessed the explosion. Even in a desolate area like that part of Baja, there were always people around and some of them had been awake that night.

The boy at the gas-station security outpost had been the most helpful. He had been in his narrow bunk in the back room dreaming of the women in the skin magazine he had just gotten from one of the truck drivers when he felt the need to go to the outhouse. He had just opened the back door when he heard the sound of the helicopter's rotors and looked up into the moonless night sky.

He had thought it strange that the Sunflash helicopter had taken off in complete darkness, as the lights were usually turned on for night flights. The aircraft had also stayed low to the ground and had flown inland for a mile or so before climbing for altitude and turning to the north. He stood and watched the chopper fly out of sight toward the United States a moment before the mountain exploded.

The shock wave of the detonation had almost deafened him, and even though he had not been looking directly at it, the flash had blinded him for a long time. When he could see again, the mountain had lost most of its top, and it was glowing as if it was a volcano. He started to run for his life, but realized that a big explosion had occurred and that it wasn't dangerous to him now.

At first light the next morning, he had gone with everyone else who lived for miles around to see what had happened. When he came across his first body part, an arm still clad in Sunflash security force khaki, he turned back and hadn't returned.

After hearing him out, Rico, the leader of the hit team, studied the boy for a long moment. "I appreciate the information. If anyone asks," Rico said, "you haven't seen us or talked to us. Understand?"

The boy gulped hard, glad to have gotten off so lightly. "Yes, sir." He was smart enough to know that this slick, round-faced fat man was a boss and deserved respect. "I understand completely."

The hit man reached down and ruffled the boy's dark hair. "You remember to do that and you will go far. You forget and your mother will cry."

"I will remember.

"But what am I to do now?" the boy asked as the three Colombians turned to go back out to their car. "Now that the factory is gone, no one will come through here anymore and I will have no business."

"Someone will come later and tell you what to do," Rico said. "Until then, you wait here."

He pulled several large-denomination new peso bills from the roll in his pocket and handed them over. "This will pay for what you need until then."

"Thank you, sir," the boy said, almost bursting into tears. "Thank you."

"You're welcome," the round-faced man told him.

"DO YOU THINK the kid's telling the truth?" the number-two man on the hit team asked when they were back in their air-conditioned Buick and were heading north.

Rico smiled. "Of course he is. He's too young to lie. And too dumb. It's only when they get a little older that they get smart enough to think that they can lie to me. But they never get smart enough to keep me from knowing when they are lying."

This was the first time that the number two man on the team, Jose Simon, had worked with Rico, the killer with only one name. Some of the cartel's other hitters had warned him that he had to be very careful when working with Rico. He looked like a fat-cat businessman, but he had the soul of a snake, a mean snake. So far, though, he had seen none of this himself and wondered if Rico was living on a past reputation.

"How far is it to the border?" Jose asked.

"About three hours," the driver said. He had worked as a wheelman for Rico before, and he knew better than to try to make idle chitchat with the assassin. Jose would learn, too, or he would remain in the north when they returned to Colombia.

"What's our move when we get there?" Jose purposefully asked Rico.

The hitter shrugged expressively as if any idiot knew what was to be done next. "We find Gilmore and ask him where Rondell and Garcia are. Then we go where they are and kill them."

Something about the way Rico said that made Jose sit back and keep quiet. Maybe there was something to this fat man after all.

Santa Barbara, California

THE WORD ON THE STREETS of Santa Barbara was that a major cocaine sale was going down. Rumor had it that you could get high grade Cali product wholesale for seventy-five cents on the dollar. Schwarz picked up on that rumor right away. And since he had been in the warehouse where Gilmore and his confederates had been packaging coke for resale, he immediately tied it to the Green Shirt leader. He was waiting for a cash transfer to come in, however, before he made his move.

Schwarz had his Beretta in his hand behind his back when he answered the knock on the door of his rented apartment. Even though Lyons and Blancanales were supposed to know where he was staying, no one else did and he wasn't about to take any chances.

He was stunned to see Mack Bolan standing there, his hands held open at his sides. "What are you doing here?"

A dozen scenarios flashed through his mind as he waited for the answer to his question. Had Brognola decided that he had stepped too far over the line and sent the Executioner after him?

"The Ironman thought you could use some help," Bolan said casually. "And since I'm on vacation right now myself, why don't I join you? The two of us working together can cover a lot more ground than either one of us can working alone."

Schwarz relaxed. There would have been a problem had Bolan been sent to bring him back under control. There was no way that he could go head-to-head with the Executioner and win. That just wasn't in the cards. Working with him, however, would make his task that much easier. Few men had escaped when the Executioner had taken it upon himself to see that they paid for their crimes. Benson Rondell and Derek Gilmore would soon join the long list of those who hadn't.

"Great," he said. "Come on in and I'll get you a cup of coffee."

After accepting a cup of coffee from Schwarz, Bolan got right to the point. "What have you come up with so far on Gilmore?"

"Well, nothing I can tie his name to directly. But it seems that someone in town's holding a fire sale on Cali cocaine."

"Are they now?"

"That's the word on the streets."

"Is the word good?"

"I haven't tried it myself yet," Schwarz admitted. "I've had trouble getting enough flash money together for a wholesale buy."

"That's not a problem," Bolan said. "I can front you ten grand or so."

"That should do it. Now all I have to do is to get into my drug-dealer outfit and go downtown to make the buy."

"Don't get too flashy," Bolan cautioned him. "Dress casual and I'll go along as your bodyguard."

"How about my doing a politically correct yuppie-pond-scum imitation. I can rent a minivan and pretend that I'm picking up adult party favors for the country-club set."

"In Santa Barbara," Bolan said, "that's about right."

CHAPTER TWENTY-FIVE

Stony Man Farm

For the past day or two, Barbara Price had known that something odd was going on in the computer center. When she walked into Kurtzman's cybernetic sanctum, she noticed that his computer screen was blank, as were the screens of Hunt Wethers and Akira Tokaido. As long as she was in the room, not much would be going on and the conversation was forced. At first she had dismissed her suspicions as being a figment of an overactive imagination, but it was the same every time she went down there, and it was starting to bother her.

She didn't have the slightest idea what they were doing, but as the mission controller, she should have. If there was anything in the world she hated, it was not knowing what was going on right under her nose. But now that the mission closure tasks had been taken care of, she was going to find out what was going on.

She strolled into the computer room, her coffee mug in her hand, and poured herself a cup of

Kurtzman's infamous brew. It seemed a little puny today, and she wondered what had happened. Maybe their food supplier had switched coffee brands on them again.

Sipping her weak coffee, she walked up behind Kurtzman. "What're you working on?" she asked casually.

He clicked a key and a complex math table flashed onto the previously blank screen.

"Oh," he replied equally as casually, "I'm just messing around with that code-breaking program I started last spring. You remember, the one that's supposed to be the answer to that multilevel encryption system that everyone's starting to use now to keep the hackers out. Anyway, I've found that if I reverse the—"

Price knew a line when she heard it and closed her ears to Kurtzman's cybernetic technobabble, listening instead to the tone of his voice and the other nonverbal clues that told her he was lying through his teeth. It wasn't unknown for him to try to keep things from her, but this time she didn't have a clue as to what he was trying to hide. Since she didn't have a clue, she would have to go looking for one.

"What have you heard from Mack?" she asked when he finally concluded his long-winded explanation.

Kurtzman didn't jump at the mention of Bolan's name, but she saw the muscles of his neck tighten. Bingo, she thought. But she still didn't know what Bolan was up to, or what he had the Bear checking into for him. Whatever it was, though, she had obviously been cut out of the loop and that angered her. Bolan knew better than to try something stupid like that, and so did Kurtzman. You'd think that after all this time, they would get it straight. They weren't going to put anything over on her.

"He said that he's going to stay in California."

"What's he doing?"

"He said that he's just going to hang around with Lyons for a while."

Not too bloody likely, as McCarter was so fond of saying. Bolan and Lyons weren't the kind of men to "hang around," not even in California. If he was staying on there, it meant that he was after something, and, more than likely, that something was a fugitive named Benson Rondell.

"Did you figure out where Rondell's chopper went yet?" she asked on a hunch.

"Yeah," he said. "I tracked it and—"

He spun his chair to face her. "Dammit, Barb!" he said when he saw the big grin on her face, "that's not fair. You're not supposed to know about that."

She shrugged. "If you'll check the organizational chart, Aaron, I'm still the mission controller around this place. And I like to keep up-to-date on what's going on with the people I'm paid to keep track of. So, do you mind telling me what you've been doing lately on company time?" She paused. "Or should I guess?"

When his answer wasn't immediately forthcoming, she said, "You're helping Mack and Gadgets track down our missing politician so Schwarz can bring him to account for that woman getting wounded at Diablo Canyon, among other pending criminal charges."

She smiled sweetly. "How am I doing so far, Aaron? Have I got it figured out?"

When Kurtzman only grunted, she continued. "To date, you were able to track his chopper to a refueling point, but you lost it after that, right?"

"Okay, okay." He threw up his hands. "I'm helping them find Rondell."

"Why didn't you simply say so in the first place? You know that Mack has free rein with what he does with his time, and you know that we've often been authorized to help him if we can. What's the big deal this time? What are you trying to keep hidden from me?"

"They don't want Hal to get mixed up in this," Kurtzman admitted. "They're afraid that if he learns what they're doing he'll try to shut them down because of the political angle."

Price could only agree with them on that assessment, but that wasn't the way the game was supposed to be played at Stony Man Farm. They were an arm of the government, albeit an arm that very few people, even in Washington, had ever heard of. But they were a government agency nonetheless. And while even fewer had ever heard of their operations, all of their missions had been undertaken on the orders of the President.

Operating on a whim or from personal motives wasn't to be done. Only Bolan could get away with that and, even then, he could do it only as long as he disassociated himself from the organization. As he himself had said at the mission briefing with Brognola, taking Rondell out smacked a little too much of political assassination. But the argument could be made that since Rondell hadn't been elected to any public office, he wasn't yet a politician, still only a candidate, and candidates were fair game.

"Give me the details," she ordered, "and don't leave anything out. If I find out later that you held something back on me, I'm going to start kicking ass."

"Okay," he said, sighing, "here it is. You're right. I tracked the helicopter to a dirt landing strip in Barstow, California, where it took on a full load of JP-2, paid for in cash, and took off. Beyond that one refueling point, I don't have the slightest idea where he went.''

"Which means that it probably landed again somewhere within its range radius.''

"That's what I'm trying to run down now. I have Akira working on that angle with a phony FAA alert, but we haven't come up with another sighting of it yet.''

"So, what have the boys come up with on their own to get a lead on him?''

"Not much," he admitted. "The main thing they're working is that there seems to be a fire sale on cocaine going on in Santa Barbara. Someone is moving a lot of high-grade powder at cut-rate prices. They think that Gilmore's getting out of business before taking off for parts unknown.''

"And that's it?''

Kurtzman nodded.

"That's not much. Keep digging, and keep me apprised. I mean it, Aaron.''

Santa Barbara, California

SCHWARZ WASN'T the only one who had learned of the cocaine sale and had linked it to Gilmore. Rico had followed Gilmore to his last-known address in Santa Barbara and picked up on it almost the moment that he hit town. And since he had a good idea where the powder had come from, he intended to get it back under cartel control ASAP.

It was bad enough that Benson Rondell and Hector Garcia had fallen from favor, but it was much more serious that Derek Gilmore had also crossed the line and was apparently stealing from the cartel.

Even though he was going to have to kill him, Rico had always liked Gilmore. For an Anglo, the mercenary had a fine sense of honor and knew how things should be done. For him to do what it looked like he was doing wasn't easy for the Colombian to understand. Apparently, as with so many gringos, the lure of the money had finally gotten too much for him. That was a shame; he had been a good specialist and would be difficult to replace.

Nonetheless, he had dishonored his contract with the cartel and would have to pay the price for that mistake. Contracts were sacred in Cali because they were the heart of the business. These weren't paper contracts like the ones businessmen used to cheat one another. These were man-to-man agreements and they obligated a man's trust and honor. A man who violated that trust or who went back on his honor wasn't worthy of being called a man.

And a man who had given up being a man didn't deserve to live.

UNLIKE SCHWARZ, though, Rico didn't need to get into his drug dealer outfit; he wore it every day. It was easy for Rico to get his first lead on the cocaine sale. All he did was have his driver stop the car by the first street dealer he found and open the rear door.

"Hey, man," the street dealer said as he stuck his head inside the car. "What you need? I got crack, I got a little China white. I got—"

The dealer shut his mouth abruptly at the sight of the muzzle of a Glock semiautomatic pistol aimed between his eyes.

"If you try to run, you die," Rico told him.

"Hey, man," the dealer said, making sure that he kept both his hands in plain sight, "take it easy, I'm cool."

"Get in the car and shut the door behind you."

The dealer did as he was ordered.

"Fasten your seat belt."

He did that as well.

"Now," Rico said, "we're going to go for a little ride so we can talk without being interrupted. If you tell me what I want to know, you get to live. You give me any jive, as I think you call it, and you die."

"Anything you say, man." The dealer tried hard to keep the fear out of his voice.

"Who's selling the coke?"

"I really don't know his name," he answered honestly, "but he's an Anglo, you know, a big blond dude, blue eyes, the whole thing."

"Does he have other men working with him?"

"Yeah, man. And they're all Anglos, too."

"Where's he dealing from?"

The man quickly gave him the address. "It's a warehouse," he added.

"Is it guarded?"

"The guys hanging around there, they have guns, yes."

"Stop the car," Rico told the driver.

The dealer looked relieved when the car pulled over. "I hope you find him, mister."

"I will. Thank you for the information."

"No problem, man." Now that it looked like he was going to live, the dealer tried to sound upbeat. "I'm glad I could help, you know."

As the dealer turned to get out of the car, Rico whipped his hand inside his jacket and came out with a shiv. With a single movement, he slammed the needle point of the narrow-bladed knife into the base of the dealer's skull and drove it into his brain. The man shuddered once as he died and pitched forward, facefirst, into the gutter.

When the dealer's body cleared the door, Rico closed it behind him. "Drive on."

Now Jose Simon understood what the other men in Cali had told him about Rico; he had struck like a mean snake.

BOLAN AND SCHWARZ took the same approach to the problem of finding Derek Gilmore as Rico had. They also talked to a street dealer about his source, but they didn't leave him dead. They made him think that he was going to die, however.

Schwarz made initial contact, acting like an aging yuppie who still thought that snorting cocaine was a harmless pastime. The dealer was used to selling drugs to yuppies and didn't suspect a thing when Schwarz lured him around the corner to where he said he had left his car. When Bolan stepped out, though, and invited him into the car, he realized that he had made a serious mistake.

"Ah...guys," the dealer started to say when Schwarz slid behind the wheel and put the key into the ignition switch. He shut his mouth quickly when Bolan put his finger to his lips and shook his head.

"Out," Bolan ordered. "But if you try to run, you're dead. I only want to talk to you."

"Yes, sir."

Schwarz kept watch at the head of the alley while Bolan backed the dealer against the wall and patted him down for weapons. When he found that he was clean, he backed off and leveled his cold blue eyes at him. There was no need for him to show a weapon; his eyes were enough.

"There's only one thing I want to know," the Executioner said, "and if you give it up to me, you'll be free to go. If, however, we have a failure to communicate, where do you want me to leave your body?"

"I'll tell you anything you want to know, mister." The dealer was having a difficult time making his legs support the weight of his body. "Believe me."

"So tell me, who's holding this reduced price cocaine sale?"

Faced with what seemed to be certain death, the street dealer was more than willing to give up the name of his supplier and exactly where he could be found. As a rule of thumb, he liked to keep his business contacts confidential. It ensured that he could stay in this very competitive business. Business was one thing, but dying was entirely another. There was no doubt that the big, blue-eyed guy would kill him in a heartbeat if he didn't produce.

Bolan memorized the directions to the warehouse the dealer swore was the place he went to make his buys. He claimed not to know the seller's name, but he gave a good description of Derek

Gilmore, right down to the BDU pants and combat boots.

The Executioner allowed his face to relax. "That's what I wanted to hear, so you can go.

"But," he added as the dealer poised himself to run, "I advise you to take up another line of work. If I ever see you dealing again, I won't let you go."

"Yes, sir."

"I don't know how you do it," Schwarz said admiringly as he watched the dealer sprint down the alley and barrel around the corner. "I would have had to slap him around awhile before he talked."

Bolan let a faint smile cross his face. "It's all in the attitude."

CHAPTER TWENTY-SIX

After getting the information they wanted from the dealer, Bolan followed Schwarz back to his apartment to get ready for the raid. They intended to initiate a snatch and grab, but considering what Lyons and Blancanales had had to go through to get Schwarz back from the same people, it could easily turn into another bloody brawl. They had to be ready for any eventuality.

So they got into their full kit—combat blacksuits, face paint, rubber-soled boots, assault harnesses and comm links. Schwarz readied his CAR-15 and Beretta backup, while Bolan checked over his H&K MP-5 and his Beretta 93-R. A pair of flash-bang grenades and night-vision goggles completed their equipment. Now they were ready for war.

THE TWO MEN DROVE IN through the rear gate of the warehouse area in their rented van. Parking the vehicle in an unlighted area two buildings from their objective, they silently stepped out. Taking cover against the side of the building, they locked and loaded their weapons as they checked out the immediate area.

"Comm check," Schwarz whispered over the throat mike of his comm link.

"Lima Charlie," Bolan whispered back.

"Let's get it," Schwarz said.

The approach to the building was clear. When they reached the end of the warehouse next to their target, Schwarz stayed in the shadows to provide covering fire while Bolan went ahead to clear the rear of their objective.

Moving like a black cat, the Executioner made no sound as he slipped from one shadow to the next. Even though their target was blacked out, with the number of lights shining throughout the area he could see well enough that he didn't need to use his night-vision goggles. He was making his move to the rear of the building when he spotted the first of the opposition.

"Gadgets," he whispered over his comm link, "they've got security out. I've got a guy halfway up the rear fire escape, and he's packing an AK."

"Can you take him out quietly?" Schwarz asked.

"I'm moving now."

The problem with Bolan's target was that he was ten feet above him and there was no way he could go up the fire escape without attracting attention. He freed the silenced Beretta 93-R from shoulder leather. Once more old reliable would do the trick. All he would have to do would be to catch the guy when he fell so the men inside wouldn't hear the sodden thud of a body hitting the ground.

The man was leaning back against the side of the building, his head partially obscured by the iron framework of the fire escape. To get a clear shot, Bolan would need to attract his attention without making him sound the alarm. Activating the red-dot laser sight on the Beretta pistol, he aimed it at the railing in front of the target. As Bolan had thought he would do, the hardman didn't recognize the red light as a danger and moved forward to see what it was. When he did, his head came into the Executioner's line of fire.

Smoothly moving the red dot from the railing to the man's temple, he triggered one round, which cored the gunner's brain, killing him instantly. He stiffened and staggered forward, the AK falling from his hands. The sling over his shoulder kept the weapon from falling to the steel platform of the fire escape as he toppled over the edge.

Bracing himself, Bolan broke the body's fall and eased it to the ground. "I've got him," he reported. "And he was also packing a small radio, so look for another guard out front."

"Roger," Schwarz sent back. "I'm moving up to the front now."

Schwarz made a more straightforward kill when he discovered the guard Gilmore had placed to watch the front of the warehouse. He simply walked up behind his man with his Cold Steel Tanto fighting knife in his right hand. With one smooth move, he clamped his left hand over the man's mouth and jerked his head back and to the side. When his neck was exposed, the broad razor-sharp blade whipped across his neck from one side to the other, severing his carotid, jugular and windpipe in one swipe.

When the man's feet stopped kicking, he lowered the body to the ground and rolled it against the wall. "I'm clear," he transmitted. "And I've got an open entry."

"I'm inside on the second level," Bolan whispered.

"Wait a minute," Schwarz said as he ducked back into the shadows, "we've got visitors."

INSIDE THE BUILDING, Derek Gilmore and his team of Green Shirts were busy breaking cocaine into wholesale quarter-kilo lots. His earlier run-in with Able Team hadn't cured him of his habit of using out-of-the-way warehouses as his business addresses.

Business had been good the past two days, and they were working hard to keep up with the demand. There was a danger in selling coke this way; too many people knew about it. But Gilmore was willing to take the risk to move the stuff quickly. The way he figured it, he'd be done and gone before anyone picked up on where he was. Gilmore was fairly good at what he did, but he sometimes had a deficit in his logical-thinking circuits.

He had taken more precautions this time, though. He had brought in several more of his trusted Green Shirt cadre to beef up his security and had posted lookouts at both ends of the building. Having the extra men outside should give him ample warning of potential trouble. And he was screening his customers, as well, selling only to people he had dealt with in the past. Because of that, he was surprised when he heard a car drive up to the front of the warehouse. He wasn't expecting customers at this late hour.

"Jason?" he called out over the radio. "What's going on out there?"

When there was no answer, he knew something was wrong and didn't even try to call Erik on the fire escape. "Kill the lights," he hissed as he reached for his AK.

JOSE SIMON, Rico's number two, checked the front of the warehouse as his driver drove up to the structure. Taking the briefcase from the back seat, he stepped out and walked over to the partially opened door in the front of the building. "Hey! It's Slick Jimmy!" he called out, using the name of the dealer Rico had killed. "Is anyone in there?"

"Come on in," a voice called.

Simon didn't like the sound of the voice, but Rico had said that they had to go through with this. After motioning for the driver to join him, he held the briefcase in front of him to cover the silenced Uzi slung under his jacket as he walked into the dimly lit interior of the building. His partner followed close behind him.

In the dim light from the single bulb high on the ceiling, he saw an older blond Anglo standing by a stack of wooden crates, holding an AK-47.

"I've got money," Simon said, holding out the briefcase. "And I need to get—"

Without saying a word, Gilmore raised the assault rifle and the Colombians threw themselves facefirst onto the floor, sliding for cover behind the nearest pillar. A burst of 7.62 mm gunfire chipped the concrete floor behind them.

"MACK!" SCHWARZ SHOUTED over his comm link. "I'm going in!"

"Flash-bang!" Bolan radioed to warn Schwarz to guard his eyes. From his position high inside the warehouse, he pitched a grenade toward the center of the floor before dropping from his perch. The flash of the grenade threw sharp shadows that hid his movement.

One gunner fled, and another, blinded by the grenade, started firing long bursts from an Uzi, spraying silenced 9 mm slugs in front of him. One of the bursts connected with a Green Shirt, and the man went down. So Schwarz and Bolan had company—and Gilmore had another visitor.

Schwarz kept to the inside wall by the door as he made his way through the stacked crates for the center of the building. The silencers on the newcomers' subguns kept him from spotting them by sound, but the Uzis still showed a small muzzle-flash when they were aimed at him. And that small flash was all he needed.

When a spray of bullets splashed to his left, he saw a twinkle of muzzle-flashes. Carefully sighting in his CAR-15, Schwarz triggered a quick burst of 5.56 mm rounds. He was rewarded by a sharp cry of pain and the clatter of a weapon falling to the concrete. That sound was quickly followed by the thud of a body hitting the floor.

When the shadowy figure staggered out into his view, he put him down with a single shot to the head.

"I got one," he transmitted.

Bolan had dropped to the main floor when the grenade went off. Seeing a single man standing in the light, blazing away with his AK, he triggered a 3-round burst from his H&K. The man staggered under the impact of the rounds and went down. Bolan ducked under cover to look for his next target.

"Two down," he transmitted.

The next two, both Green Shirts, went almost as quickly. One of them tried to flank Bolan and simply got blown away for his efforts. The second one stepped out in front of Schwarz, his AK wildly blazing fire. Schwarz figured him for one of the Green Shirt amateurs, but that didn't keep him from putting a bullet in his head.

Bolan had slung his H&K subgun and had his Beretta out, exchanging fire with a man crouched behind a roof pillar. Neither one could get a clear shot at the other. When the Executioner stopped to change magazines in his pistol, the gunman made a dash for the front door and ran right into a burst from Schwarz. He skidded to a heap, his subgun clattering to the floor.

Gilmore had pulled himself completely behind a pillar to change magazines in his assault rifle. "Get out of here!" he yelled out to any of the Green Shirts who might still be alive. Spraying half a magazine of 7.62 mm rounds to clear his way, he sprinted for the rear door.

Bolan caught Gilmore's streaking shadow, and he sprinted after him. The mercenary brushed against a pile of empty boxes as he ran and they crashed to the floor, then he spun, bringing his weapon to bear.

The soldier dived for cover as the man sprayed a long burst in his direction. Before Bolan could answer with a 3-round burst from his Beretta, Gilmore took a hit from someone else, gave a cry and went down.

Bolan then spun to his right to drill the guy who had tagged the runner. Bringing the pistol back up, he looked, but didn't seen any more targets. Silence descended.

"You okay?" Bolan asked.

"Roger," Schwarz sent back.

"Take a look to see if we left anybody alive to talk to."

DEREK GILMORE WASN'T fatally wounded, but he was bleeding badly. He had taken a bullet that had torn up the inside of his thigh and had both hands clamped around the wound. "Help me," he called out when he heard Bolan and Schwarz moving through the warehouse. "Over here. I've been hit."

"Keep your hands open and in sight, mister," Bolan ordered as he walked up to him and kicked the fallen AK out of his reach. "You move, you're dead."

"I won't do anything stupid."

"You already did."

Keeping the muzzle of his H&K trained on him, Bolan keyed his comm link. "I think I've found Gilmore, and he's alive."

"Outstanding!"

Bolan knelt beside the mercenary. "Put your hands out in front of you, slowly," he cautioned, "and put your wrists together."

When Gilmore's bloody hands were in the proper position, Bolan secured them with a set of plastic riot cuffs. Only then did he take his fighting knife out of its sheath and cut his pant leg away to expose the wound. To Bolan's experienced eye, the wound wasn't as bad as it looked. Taking a pressure bandage from one of his side pockets, he tied it over the bullet holes to slow the bleeding.

"That's him, all right," Schwarz said after having checked all the other bodies. "Let's get him out of here before the cops show up."

"He's ready to go," Bolan answered as he stood.

"Where are you taking me?" Gilmore asked through clenched teeth as Schwarz hauled him to his feet.

Bolan motioned with the muzzle of his subgun. "Shut up and move out."

Gilmore did as he was told and let Schwarz lead him away. With Gadgets in a blacksuit, and with combat cosmetics smeared across his face, he hadn't recognized him.

HIDING IN THE SHADOWS in a second car parked across the road next to a building, Rico knew that he didn't have to wait to see if his two associates were going to return. From the sounds of the battle, they weren't. There had been too much gunplay for it to have gone well. Plus, he had spotted a man dressed in black slipping in through the front door right behind his men after the firing broke out.

Even when the gunfire died down, he continued watching, not about to go to the warehouse there until he knew who had won. When he saw two black-clad men step out carrying a blond man between them with his hands bound, he immediately recognized Gilmore as their captive. The mercenary was limping, but didn't seem to be too badly wounded.

The men with him didn't look like any policemen he had ever seen, so they had to be gunmen from a rival gang. Gilmore had been stupid to upset the price structure on the streets by offering cocaine at cut-rate prices. It made people nervous, and nervous people acted rashly. They did things, like try to take you out so you wouldn't ruin their business.

He was split between following the men who had taken Gilmore and going into the warehouse to see if he could recover any of the cartel's stolen property. After quickly weighing his options, he decided to go after the cocaine. He could always report that Gilmore had been killed in the shootout and, after the losses they had suffered in Baja, the board would be very happy to get their goods back.

CHAPTER TWENTY-SEVEN

Schwarz's rented van had just cleared the rear gate of the warehouse complex when a caravan of police cars and two SWAT-team vehicles roared in through the front gate. Apparently the local cops had finally learned to respond to reports of gun battles in their industrial areas. Gravel flying, they slammed to a halt in front of the warehouse and poured out of their vans, their weapons at the ready. When no one shot at them, the SWAT teams leapfrogged forward to the partially opened front door. Hugging the wall, they tossed flash-bang grenades through the door. When the grenades went off, they stormed inside.

"That's cutting it a little too close for my tastes," Schwarz muttered as he restrained himself from standing on the gas as he merged into the traffic of the freeway. The last thing they needed right now was to get popped for a speeding ticket.

"We got what we came for, though," Bolan said as he turned around to look at his bound and gagged prisoner. "Now we can find out where Rondell is."

"Who do you think those two party crashers were?" Schwarz asked.

"Probably cartel men," Bolan said. "But I don't mind that they showed up. They did help us out by cutting the odds down a bit. They took out a couple of Gilmore's men for us."

"They damn near got me, as well," Schwarz growled.

DEREK GILMORE'S interrogation was short and to the point. Back at Schwarz's place, Bolan checked the field dressing on the man's wound before taking the tape off his mouth. He didn't, however, remove the plastic restraints from his wrists and ankles.

Gilmore was a real pro; he didn't waste time asking stupid questions like who they were and where he was. He also didn't demand that he be taken to a hospital. He knew that if he lived through this, there would be time enough to take care of that later.

"I'm not with the cartel," Bolan started out, "and I'm not with the government. I represent a private interest, and I want to know where Benson Rondell is."

"What happens to me if I tell you?"

Bolan shrugged. "If you tell me what I want to know, you get to surrender to the authorities and take your chances with them. If you don't tell me, you die."

There was something in Bolan's matter-of-fact, simple presentation of the situation that convinced Gilmore that he had no options. In a situation like this the only thing he had to bargain with was information, and he didn't owe Rondell anything.

At that moment Schwarz came out of the bathroom, where he had washed the combat cosmetics from his face and hands. "You're the P.I.," Gilmore said when he recognized him. "The guy who said that he was checking in on the Jordan case for the family."

"That's what I said, yes."

Gilmore's eyes flashed back to Bolan and looked past the face paint he still wore. He also saw for the first time the military-style comm link and state-of-the-art weapons and assault equipment the two men were wearing. Over the years he had heard stories about a private strike team, some kind of supersecret force that took care of gangs and terrorists that the authorities couldn't get to for whatever reason. He hadn't believed the stories before, but he did now.

"I haven't heard from Rondell since the Baja complex went up," the mercenary said honestly. "But my guess is that he and Garcia made it to the

Green Earth forest camp by Crescent City and are holed up there till things calm down."

"Who's Garcia?"

"Hector Garcia," Gilmore explained, "his cartel controller. He's the one who signed Rondell on with them, and he's been calling the shots since then. He's a Mexican national and fronts as a businessman."

"Tell me about this camp."

After a half hour's discussion, Bolan slapped a piece of tape over Gilmore's mouth.

"What are we going to really do with him?" Schwarz looked over at their prisoner.

Bolan shrugged. "Just what I told him. We leave him here and call the local DEA office to come and get him."

"He set Sylvia up to be shot," Schwarz said coldly.

"I know that. But he did it on Rondell's orders. He's not getting away clean, I can promise you that. He'll never see the light of day again."

"It doesn't seem enough," Schwarz said, shaking his head.

"This time, it'll have to do."

The Green Shirt Training Camp

BENSON RONDELL DIDN'T like being stuck in the California woods northeast of Crescent City one bit. The Green Earth Movement's camp hidden in the towering ancient fir trees was oppressive, to say the least. His idea of showing his concern for the environment was limited to black-tie functions with the press in attendance or carefully staged appearances in a sunlit forest clearing. Hiding in a cold, damp cabin in the woods like a common fugitive wasn't his way of celebrating Mother Earth.

The weekly supply runs into town brought the newspapers, and he saw that the media was having a field day with his apparent death in the Baja explosion. The American government had been blamed at first, until a joint Mexican and American investigation team discovered the remnants of the liquid-propane tank shell embedded in the bedrock of the mountain. Then it was realized that a propane-gas explosion had destroyed the Sunflash facility. Nothing had been reported about any evidence having been found that indicated commandos had attacked the complex.

He knew, though, that he had been attacked, and whoever the commandos had been, they had set the propane tank off with some kind of explosive charge. He had known that propane was an explosive gas, but he had no idea just how destructive it could be. He wanted to go public, to prove that he was alive and had survived the blast. He thought that if he could take up his campaign again, he would be able to use the attack to his advantage.

When he mentioned this idea to Garcia, the Mexican had gone ballistic. "Are you out of your mind, man? Did you hit yourself on the head? What in the hell is wrong with you? You show your face out there, and you've signed your death warrant."

The Mexican then went on to graphically explain that as soon as the cartel discovered where he was, he would be as good as dead and he would be lucky if his body was thrown in a ditch for the rats to eat.

He had also gotten another chewing out from Garcia when he had mentioned wanting to have the money in his Pasadena accounts transferred to a bank in Crescent City.

"Why don't you just send up a balloon saying 'Here I am, come and get me,'" Garcia said, sneering. "Jesus, man, how many times do I have to tell you? You've got to lay low for a while. In a month or so, when this has blown over, we can see about getting our finances together so we can take off. All we can do now is relax and enjoy the scenery."

It wasn't like he was stuck in a remote cabin with only Hector Garcia for company. This was the Green Earth Movement's secret training camp, and a couple dozen of Gilmore's handpicked Green Shirts, both men and women, were undergoing paramilitary and sabotage training in the forest far from prying eyes. Later they would take the destructive skills they had learned and apply them to their so-called demonstrations and protests.

If the Green Earth camp had been located in a Middle Eastern country, it would have been described as a terrorist training base. Only in California would it be considered getting back to nature. He had to admit, though, that Gilmore had done a good job putting the training program together. From what he had seen, the Green Shirts were being turned into good little environmental storm troopers. And, thinking of Derek Gilmore, he wondered where the man had gotten to. He had never really liked being around the mercenary, but Garcia had insisted on his becoming involved with the movement.

The worst thing, though, was that since his role in the movement was all but unknown, none of these people had any idea that he was their founder and primary benefactor. To them he was just a liberal political candidate who had fallen on hard times and was hiding out from the authorities. That was both good and bad. Good because the Green Shirts viewed the establishment as the enemy, and an enemy of their enemy had to be a friend. At least he didn't have to worry about one of them turning him in.

The flip side of that coin, however, was that since he was a "guest" he didn't have the authority to get them to do anything for him. Anything he wanted to have done had to be requested as a "favor," and all he could do was hope that the favor would be granted. That included everything from getting enough blankets to getting something to drink. There was plenty of pot—the Green Shirts grew their own—but alcohol was on their list of proscribed items in the camp.

Garcia was even worse off; he was only the friend of a guest. Even though he was the man who had signed all of the checks for the organization, no one had any idea who he was. The orders for the Green Shirts had always come from Gilmore, and now that he was nowhere to be found, his lieutenants were giving the orders in his name.

It was a fine irony that the man who made the movement what it was and the man who had financed its operations for so long were completely unknown. But that was the problem with secret organizations. When the thin chain of command was broken, communications and the ability to act were broken, as well. When he got out of this place, the first thing he was going to do was burn his Green Earth Movement membership card and cut the bastards loose. They could save the earth with someone else's money.

Washington, D.C.

IN HIS JUSTICE Department office, Hal Brognola smiled as he read the fax from the DEA unit he had ordered to Santa Barbara. The night raid on the warehouse had all the earmarks of a Bolan move; the cocaine had been left where it was, along with the bodies and the weapons. That was sure as hell not the act of a rival drug gang.

Two of the bodies, listed in the report as Latino, had been carrying fake Green Cards, and silenced Uzis had been found with them. That added another dimension to the equation, but one that wasn't completely unexpected. His bet was that they were Cali hit men who had been sent to extract cartel vengeance for Rondell's men having hijacked a rather large amount of their product. If that was the case, it was further evidence that Rondell had been financed by the Cali bosses.

He wished that he could simply ring up the Farm and have Kurtzman download the latest information and reports he had accumulated. But, the way he was forced to run this one, he didn't dare. For whatever reason, the President had said hands off Benson Rondell, so hands off it had to be. He had to be cleaner than clean so that if the operation blew up, he could honestly say that he had no idea what had been going on behind his back. And, more importantly, he would be able to produce his fax and phone logs to show that he hadn't been involved in any way.

This was a gutless way to do business, but while he wanted to see Rondell zeroed for sure, he had much bigger fish to fry. He was more concerned about finding the rest of the cartel informants in the Intelligence and Armed Forces committees.

Flushing out a congresswoman had been a complete fluke. If she hadn't been such a knee-jerk liberal amateur, she wouldn't have panicked when she learned about the Farm's investigation of Rondell and warned him. But if she hadn't done that, she would still be sitting on the committee, passing their secrets on to the cartel and anyone else she was in contact with.

The President was having a difficult time buying the fact that the congresswoman had been on the cartel payroll, but the investigation of her death had proved conclusively that it had been a carefully staged hit, and as far as he was concerned, a cartel hit.

The forensic medical examination of the bodies had shown that the young woman who had been found with Woodburn had died well before the congresswoman. It had also shown that Woodburn had been raped before being fatally injected. The use of forensic lasers had also detected several fingerprints on the bodies that hadn't come from either of the women. Other people had been in the room with them that night—men, judging from the size of the prints.

The Cali cartel had several ways of dealing with those who they felt had betrayed them. The spectacular murder and display of a mutilated corpse was a well-known tactic, as were car-bomb assassinations and kidnappings. A shameful death that ruined the reputation of the deceased was also a cartel specialty.

None of the forensic information about Woodburn's death had been released to the press, nor would it ever be. Brognola had insisted on that. The media had labeled Woodburn a drug-using sexual libertine. But if it became known that she had been a spy for the drug lords, it would cause a major scandal on the Hill, and the other cartel informants would go into hiding. The overriding concern was to find them and stop them.

After they were identified, the Farm might be called in again to deal with them. But he would have to wait and see what the Man wanted to do first.

CHAPTER TWENTY-EIGHT

The Green Shirt Training Camp

Even though Benson Rondell had assured Hector Garcia that he would lay low, the thought of being a fugitive for the rest of his life didn't sit well. No matter how much money he would have later, running and hiding, always having to look over his shoulder, wasn't any kind of a life to lead. Regardless of what he had promised Garcia, he decided to get back in touch with the Cali cartel bosses and see if things were really as bad as the Mexican had made them out to be.

He still couldn't believe that men who controlled so much money and power wouldn't listen to reason. Their plan to put him in the statehouse was still sound, and he could still get back into the race. He could make up a story to account for his disappearance from the Sunflash facility and tie it into the government investigation of his campaign. The press and voters would love it, and it might even put him over the top in the polls.

Or, if all else failed, he could simply set up a new solar-power facility somewhere in Latin America and continue working for them. It wouldn't take that much money to set up something simple that would let him manufacture the units. The stage had been set to replace nuclear power throughout the world, and they could make untold millions selling his solar-power equipment. They would be able to recover their losses and then some in no time at all.

He simply refused to believe that all was lost. Rational men, and the board had to be rational or they would never have been as successful as they had been, wouldn't kill him because of something that he'd had absolutely no control over. It wasn't as if he had invited those men, whoever they were, to attack him. He had done nothing wrong and shouldn't be punished. And Garcia had been in control of the security, not him. If they were angry at anyone, it should be Garcia.

Once he had made up his mind, Rondell ran into a major problem—there were no phones anywhere in the camp. All communications were handled by radio, so there was no way for him personally to get in touch with his contact man in Pasadena. And there was no one that he could trust with a message.

Then the helicopter flew in with some supplies Garcia had ordered. Seeing the pilot gave Rondell an idea. Quickly jotting down a phone number, he waited until Garcia was gone and gave it to the pilot. After reassuring him that it was okay, he told him to call the number and let the man on the other end know where he was and that he wanted to talk.

When he walked back into the cabin he shared with Garcia, Rondell tried to keep his face from showing his delight. Now he could get the hell out of here and back to civilization.

ONE OF GILMORE'S Green Shirts had survived Bolan and Schwarz's raid on the warehouse solely by virtue of not having been there when it went down. He had been making a delivery to a customer, and when he returned he found the Santa Barbara cops already at the warehouse. He stayed undercover and watched long enough to see the body bags being carried out before he got out of there. He couldn't tell whether his leader was in one of those bags, but as one of Gilmore's most trusted lieutenants, he fled straight for the forest camp to warn the other members of the inner circle.

Being more than a little paranoid, and not very analytical, he had no idea who could have hit the warehouse. But it didn't matter. They had to be prepared to defend themselves. Gilmore had warned that it might come down to this and had made contingency plans. Within an hour of his arrival, the forest camp had been turned into a fortress.

When Gilmore had set up the place, being of a military mind, he had directed that fortified positions be built in a 360-degree perimeter like a hidden VC basecamp. He knew that the chances were good that they would never be needed, but it never hurt to be prepared. Also, the digging had been a good exercise in teamwork for the trainees.

There wasn't much in the line of heavy weapons in the camp, but everyone was issued a full-auto AK-47 and a Chinese-army-style chest-pack ammo magazine carrier. It was enough firepower to take care of anything short of a major federal raid.

BENSON RONDELL'S ATTEMPT to contact the Cali bosses worked only too well, but not in the way he had intended. The chopper pilot got through to Rondell's contact in Pasadena and delivered his message. The contact immediately passed it on to the Cali board of directors, who sent the information back to Rico with instructions to move on the camp immediately and kill Rondell.

The board had also ordered half a dozen soldiers from Colombia onto the next plane, and Rico met them outside the immigration and customs area at San Francisco International Airport. From there, he drove them to his safehouse and outfitted them with the weapons and equipment they would need for the mission. Within an hour they were on the freeway headed north to Crescent City. Rondell had said that he wanted to come back to the cartel, and he would be allowed to do that. But he wasn't going to like what that would mean.

Stony Man Farm

BARBARA PRICE WAS WAITING when Mack Bolan called from Santa Barbara with the results of their interrogation of Derek Gilmore.

"We've located Rondell," Bolan said. "He's hiding at the Green Earth Movement's forest camp northeast of Crescent City, California."

"I know. We just found him, too. Aaron finally located the Sunflash chopper. It's had its tail number and paint scheme changed, but the turbine serial number is the same. It was spotted in a hangar at an airfield in southern Oregon, being serviced. He put two and two together and came up with a reference to the Green Earth's forest training camp not too far away by chopper."

"What does Aaron have on that camp?"

"Not much. The forest in the area is too dense for the cameras to pick up anything, and the sensor run was inconclusive. It could be anything from a fire base to a resort getaway under all those trees."

"Fax me the photos and a map."

"Will do. By the way," she asked, "how did you dispose of Derek Gilmore?"

"We left him in the motel room and phoned in an anonymous tip to the police that he was there. He's in custody by now and, if he's smart, he's telling them everything they want to know about Rondell and the cartel. Gilmore gave us the name of another player in all this."

"Who's that?"

"A Mexican national named Hector Garcia. He's been Rondell's cartel controller. You might want to have Aaron put him in the data bank and see if he comes up with anything."

"Can do. Anything else?"

"No, that's it. As soon as I get the faxes, I'm terminating the comm link. Get in touch with Carl and tell him to meet me as we planned."

"Good luck."

"Thanks."

As soon as Bolan hung up, Price reached for her phone to alert Carl Lyons. He and Blancanales were scheduled to go in for the grand finale. It was okay for Mack and Gadgets to run the initial phase of the operation, but when they closed in on the camp, the rest of Able Team would be right there with them.

Washington, D.C.

HAL BROGNOLA immediately spotted the arrival of the six Colombians on the San Francisco INS report and took it as an ominous sign. He had put the word out to all of the West Coast ports of entry to photograph all male arrivals from Colombia between the ages of fifteen and sixty and to fax them to him immediately.

The surveillance-camera photos of this latest group of six Colombians traveling together showed that they were all young, fit men who had the look of soldiers, or cartel hit men, not businessmen or tourists. This was something that Bolan and Schwarz needed to know about, and he had figured out a way to get the information to Kurtzman without drawing attention to a connection between the report and Price's secret operation.

Two days before, he had made out a routine request for Stony Man to start a data-base program on all incoming Colombian males as part of a joint DEA, INS pilot project to try to spot drug runners. There were dozens of these types of projects already in existence, but the powers-that-be were always cooking up new twists to them. This would be seen as just another unnecessary redundancy. But if Kurtzman was as good as he thought he was, he should be able to pick up on this report and pass the word on.

He knew Rondell was as good as finished, and it was a race to see if the cartel or Bolan would be the first to reach him. But it was frustrating to have to sit in Washington and not be in on the operation. This time, though, like it or not, he had to forgo the pleasure. The other investigation was coming to a head and was taking all of his attention.

A detailed investigation of Woodburn's background had turned up a relationship with the single female member of the Armed Forces Committee. That congresswoman had been put under twenty-four-hour surveillance and, along with being a casual cocaine user, it had been discovered that she had more assets than her congressional paycheck or her campaign contributions could account for.

As far as Brognola was concerned, she was the number-one suspect, but that didn't mean that he was satisfied. If there were two bad apples in the barrel, there could well be more.

Northern California

"WHY ARE WE stopping here?" Hermann Schwarz turned to look at Mack Bolan as the big man pulled the Dodge Ram pickup to the side of the muddy service road half an hour northeast of the coastal town of Crescent City. The trip from Santa Barbara had been boring, even in the fancy four-wheel-drive pickup Bolan had rented. An Alaskan cold front had moved into the northwest, and the steady rain had cut the visibility to almost nothing.

When two men in combat blacksuits stepped out from the trees, Schwarz dived for his CAR-15, but

Bolan held a hand out to restrain him. "It's Iron-man and Pol."

Schwarz looked past the rain-spattered wind-shield, saw that it really was his two partners and rolled down his window. "What are you guys doing here?"

Blancanales grinned as he approached the truck. "We thought we'd give you a hand with this mob. We didn't want you going in there alone. You might get captured and forced to eat spotted-owl stew and dandelion salad or something environmental like that."

Schwarz cocked an inquiring eyebrow at Bolan.

"When I told them what we had going down, they asked if they could come along."

"But won't Barb be suspicious when she can't get hold of any of us?"

"She knows too. But Hal's still on the outside on this one."

"Geez!" Schwarz said. "Why didn't you call in the National Guard while you were at it?"

"I did. They'll be coming in to clean up after we leave here."

Now Schwarz was completely stunned. "How did you manage that one?"

"Friends in high places. All I had to do was tell them that I expected to run into a large pot farm up here, and they said that they'd be right out."

"What about the rest of what they're going to find up there? Dead bodies and stuff like that?"

Schwarz was completely baffled at the arrangements Bolan had apparently made behind his back. Bringing the authorities in on an unsanctioned raid could very well land them all in jail.

Bolan shrugged. "They'll just think that it was another drug-gang shootout, Gadgets. They happen all the time up here in the woods."

"Judas priest! I don't believe that you're doing this."

"Remember," Bolan said, only halfway joking, "you're the guy who got this thing rolling. This was your idea, and I just went along with it."

"Yeah," Schwarz said, shaking his head, "but I wasn't planning on starting a full-fledged war. I was just going to go after Gilmore and Rondell. I figured on sneaking in after dark or something like that."

"Remember the old saying about being careful what you wish for because you might get it?"

"If you two are done bullshitting," Lyons growled. "I'd like to get in out of the goddamned rain."

Stony Man Farm

BARBARA PRICE WAS on board, as Bolan had told Schwarz, but she was beginning to wonder if she had gotten in over her head. When she had figured out what Kurtzman was doing, she had jumped right in with both feet. But she hadn't figured on this unsanctioned operation getting as complicated as it had. Raiding the forest camp of an environmentalist group was pushing the limit. The problem now was that Kurtzman had come up with a group of six Colombians flying into San Francisco who looked like cartel heavies. She didn't know if they were connected, but she had no way to warn Bolan about them. All communications had been cut off to reduce the chance of something leaking.

The situation was starting to look a little too much like something out of the bad old days of Iran–Contra and the CIA, a cowboy operation with a John Wayne movie plot. If a single word of this ever got out to the press, the best they could hope for would be a plush cell in a federal prison.

That was why she had to ensure that she did everything she could to make certain that this thing worked as Bolan had planned. And, when it was all over, everything that even hinted at the operation would immediately be destroyed. Beyond the sanctioned Baja raid on Sunflash, not a trace of any operation against Rondell could remain in any form—electronic or hard copy.

CHAPTER TWENTY-NINE

Northern California

Rico ordered his driver to park the van on the graveled turnout halfway up the mountain. Beyond this point, the road was bare dirt turned to mud by the rain, and he didn't want to risk getting the van stuck. It was worth having to walk an extra thousand meters, even up the side of a mountain, to make sure that they could drive back out as soon as the job was done.

After the hardmen had donned their combat gear, Rico gave them their marching orders. He didn't have aerial photos of the camp, but he had a map with its location marked that Gilmore had sent to Cali right after it had been set up. According to the map, there was a gradual draw that would bring them up to the northern edge of the camp on the side closest to the cluster of buildings in the center. That's where Rondell and Garcia were sure to be. Both of them were big-city men, and he couldn't picture either one living in a tent in the deep woods.

After showing the soldiers' leader the route he had planned, they picked up their weapons and moved out into the wet brush. It didn't take long before they discovered that it wasn't going to be as easy as it had looked on the map. The six Colombians were experienced soldiers, but they were used to operating in the jungles of Latin America, not crashing around in the ancient forests of North America.

Their U.S. Army-surplus BDU camouflage uniforms worked well to conceal them in the vegetation, and the full-auto AK-47s Rico had supplied for them were familiar. What wasn't familiar was the cold rain and the high altitude. They were used to operating in the warm lowlands of Colombia and the thin, cold air of the mountains was getting to them. At least the rain had slacked off, but they were still cold and wet.

Rico held back in the drag position at the end of the small column and let the others break the trail for him. Even so, it was still tough going for him. Although he carried only his Uzi with a couple of spare magazines and not a full combat load like the others, they were younger men and were fit. He knew, however, that it would be over soon and he could go back to his comfortable life in Cali. He had been to North America many times, but had never found it to his liking, even when the weather was good.

He still didn't know if Gilmore had died in the Santa Barbara warehouse raid or if he had somehow escaped. If he had made it out, though, this was where he would be, and where he would remain alongside of Rondell and Garcia in shallow graves. He had decided against trying to take the Mexican back to Cali for a cartel trial. The job had become a little more complicated than he had planned, and he didn't want to risk it.

A color photograph of Garcia's decapitated head placed next to Rondell's would do to placate the board. Gilmore wasn't important enough to warrant a photograph of his corpse, but he might take one anyway for his personal collection. After going to all this trouble, he at least wanted that.

RICO'S HARDMEN WERE the first to make contact with the Green Earthers' outer defenses. The two Green Shirt ecowarriors in the well-camouflaged bunker between two towering firs weren't fully trained fighters, but they had eyes and knew the woods better than the Colombians. The sight of the camouflaged men moving through the ferns toward them put them on alert. Had they been better trained, they might have held their fire until the Colombians got closer.

As it was, as soon as they called in the sighting to the command bunker in the middle of the camp, one of them stuck the barrel of his AK through the firing port in the front of the bunker and ripped off a short burst of 7.62 mm rounds on full auto. But due to the fact that he was firing downhill and hadn't compensated for the extra gravity drop, he completely missed his target. He wouldn't get another chance for that good a shot.

At the sound of the first shots, the Colombians dived for cover. Even though he was carrying his Uzi, Rico held back as they broke up into two three-man teams. This part of the operation wasn't his fight. After the soldiers had fought their way into the main camp and captured Rondell and Garcia, then he would do what he had come to do—kill his quarry. Until then, he wasn't going to risk his life in a firefight. He was much too valuable to the cartel.

"WHAT'S THAT?" Rondell jumped as the first shots rang out in the woods.

"Oh, sweet Jesus," Garcia moaned. "They found us."

"Who found us?"

Garcia's eyes narrowed when he looked at his former boss. "Jesus, Mary and Joseph, you contacted them, didn't you? You found a way to tell the board that you were hiding here, didn't you?''

"I had to," Rondell tried to explain. "Don't you see? My whole life was tied up in Sunflash. I thought they would take me back and I could continue working for them."

Garcia was beyond words. He started cursing in Spanish and turned to get his few personal belongings together in a small bag.

"You can explain it to them, can't you?"

"If you think that I am going to stick around here for some Cali foot soldier to come and put a bullet in my brain, you are crazier than you look. I'm getting out of here so I can live to enjoy my enforced exile."

"You can't leave me here, Hector." Rondell reached out to grab his arm. "I don't speak Spanish. How can I talk to them when they come?"

"You still don't get it, do you?" Garcia pulled away from him in disgust. "They are going to kill you as soon as they see you. They are not coming to talk. Do you hear that gunfire out there, you stupid bastard? Do you?"

"Yes."

"If they had wanted to talk to you, they wouldn't have come in shooting." By now Garcia was almost shouting. "Get it in your head, Rondell, they are coming to kill us. They are going to take us outside, make us kneel on the ground and then they are going to shoot us in the head.''

"Take me with you.''

Garcia spun on him. "You got yourself into this, now get yourself out.''

Rondell backed off quickly. "But where are you going?''

"As far from you as I can," he snapped. "You have a sickness called terminal stupidity, and I don't want to catch my death from it.''

Grabbing his bag, the Mexican pushed past Rondell and left the man standing there with a horror-stricken look on his face.

BOLAN AND THE ABLE TEAM warriors also heard the beginning of the firefight. They had taken a different road to the camp and were moving in to the south of the Colombians.

"It looks like we're not the only ones visiting the Green Shirts today," Blancanales commented.

"Either that or they're having a little marksmanship training in the rain," Schwarz said.

"No way they're training." Lyons flicked the safety of his H&K to the fire position. "They aren't that hard-core. The cartel gunmen got here before us.''

"It's nice of them to let us know that they're here," Blancanales said.

"Okay," Bolan stated. "We'll head in that direction, but let's allow the cartel troops to draw fire for us and cut the odds down."

"Suits me," Schwarz told him, grinning.

AFTER THE SURPRISE of the opening encounter, Rico's men recovered quickly and went to work. The two Green Shirts in the bunker in front of them were quite willing to fight, but they didn't last long against professional hardmen. Pushing through the wet brush, one of the Colombian fire teams kept them pinned down while the other one outflanked them. Once they were in position, they rushed the rear of the bunker and simply blew them away.

Their radio call, though, had alerted the camp's command bunker, and more eager Green Shirts rushed to that part of the perimeter to repel the invaders of their mountain sanctuary. For the first few minutes the Colombians simply took cover where they were and returned fire. Then, as soon as they had located all of the Green Shirt positions, they started taking them out one by one.

HECTOR GARCIA WASN'T a trained woodsman, nor was he a trained fighter. He was, however, an experienced survivor and now was the time for him to put all of his survival skills to work. His only chance was to get as far away from the camp as fast as he could. If Rondell wanted to die, that was fine with him, but he had no reason to want to be a martyr to the Cali cartel's paranoia.

Outside the cabin, the camp was in a panic. A man with a wound to the arm stumbled toward him. "Help me," he cried.

Garcia didn't want to get involved, but he also didn't want to be seen as an enemy. Throwing the man's arm over his shoulder, he put his own arm around the guy's waist to support him and walked him over to the building that served as the group's headquarters. After helping the man through the door, he went back outside. Heading away from the firing, he slipped from one towering fir tree to the next. Most of the brush had been cleared from the center of the camp, so he had to use the trees for cover.

Another Green Shirt ran past him, his AK in his hand. "Hey!" he shouted. "Where are you going?"

"They told me to take this," Garcia replied, holding up his small bag, "over to the bunker."

Seeing the blood on Garcia's jacket, the man didn't answer, but ran on toward the sounds of the gunfire.

By now most of the fighting positions on this side of the perimeter were empty. The Green Shirts had left their bunkers to go to the aid of their embattled comrades. Even Garcia knew that that was a bad move tactically, but it made his escape that much easier. Racing past the perimeter, he plunged into the deep brush and headed uphill.

AFTER GARCIA SO QUICKLY decamped, Benson Rondell didn't know what to do. It was crazy for the Green Shirts to fight the cartel, but there was no way he could get it stopped and he wasn't even going to try. He didn't have any military training, and if he went out there, he could get killed. And if he was seen to be involved in any way, the cartel men could take it wrong and think that he was against them.

His only chance was to stay in the cabin and wait until the fighting was over. Then he would go out, contact the Colombians and explain what had happened.

BY THE TIME Bolan and Able Team reached the main camp, it was apparent that the cartel gunmen had cut into the Green Earthers' numbers. They had come across several bodies on their way in, both men and women. Most importantly, though, the Colombians had sucked all of the Green Earthers over to their side of the perimeter. All they had to do now was come in behind them and break them up.

Though it had been some time since Bolan and Able Team had worked together in the woods, some things were never forgotten. They broke up into two fire teams, Bolan with Schwarz and Lyons teamed with Blancanales. Then it was simply fire and maneuver, move and shoot.

Caught between the Colombians on the north and Able Team hitting them from the west, most of the Green Shirts soon realized that getting killed was a very real possibly. All of them had made a carefully staged, ceremonial blood oath to defend the ancient forest to the death. But no one had told them anything about having to defend it from people who had guns. Their idea of defending the trees was to shoot at unarmed loggers and blow up road working equipment. No one had mentioned anything about being shot at themselves.

Faced with death from two directions, the Green Shirts dropped their weapons and ran for cover in their beloved trees. Others saw their comrades fleeing and did the same. Bolan called for Able Team to let them go.

Outside of their bunkers on the open ground, the Green Shirts posed no real problem and Bolan didn't want to massacre them. Even though he knew that there were many who would disagree with him, he didn't think that being a freaked-out, fanatical environmentalist should necessarily be a capital offense. Regardless, if they were packing AKs and got in the way, they'd be taken out.

Not all of the ecowarriors went back on their
blood oaths. A young woman screamed her war cry
as she charged Schwarz, her AK blazing. He
snapped up his CAR-15 to drop her, but thinking
of Sylvia Bowes, held his fire.

Reaching down to his assault harness, he grabbed
a flash-bang grenade, pulled the pin and threw the
bomb directly at her. It hit her hip and bounced off
to land at her feet before detonating. There was no
killing shrapnel from a flash-bang, but the concus-
sion knocked her to the ground, stunned.

Schwarz rushed forward, kicked the AK away
from her hands and then rapped her smartly on the
jaw with his fist. Hopefully, when she recovered,
she'd understand that she could get killed screwing
around with guns and would flee with her comrades.

The woman had been the last of the Green Shirts
who wanted to risk death. Now the problem was the
Colombians. They, too, had been whittled down.
One had been killed and another wounded, but the
fight wasn't out of them yet.

Bolan and the Able Team warriors weren't about
to give those guys the benefit of the doubt, as they
had with the Green Shirts. They would surrender
instantly or they would die just as quickly.

CHAPTER THIRTY

In the Green Earth Camp

Rico's surviving Colombians were startled when they came under fire again. They had thought that that part of the operation was over. They were even more surprised when they realized that their opponents weren't environmentalists this time, but experienced warriors.

Bolan and Schwarz laid down a base of fire while Lyons and Blancanales moved forward under their cover. A blaze of return fire echoed through the woods and was answered by short, accurate bursts from the commandos' H&K assault rifles. Two of the camouflage-clad Colombians burst from behind a large clump of fern and rushed them from the flank, their AKs chattering.

Ignoring the storm of fire whipping through the brush, Schwarz spun to face them, his CAR-15 spitting death. The first man fell instantly, and before the other one could find cover, Bolan put him down with a well-aimed 3-round burst to the upper chest.

Lyons and Blancanales had worked their way around to the side where the last three Colombians were holed up in one of the bunkers. Lyons didn't have any fragmentation grenades, but he had a flash-bang, and it would do just fine. Pulling the grenade, he nodded to Blancanales who shot him a thumbs-up.

"Now!"

Blancanales laid down on his trigger and emptied a full magazine into the bunker's aperture as Lyons rose to his knees and hurled the flash-bang in. The instant the grenade detonated, he rushed forward, his H&K assault rifle spitting flame. Jamming the muzzle through the aperture, he emptied the magazine.

Blancanales had followed right behind him, changing magazines as he ran to the rear of the bunker. Not bothering to check if anyone was still alive, he emptied the new clip into the fighting position.

When he and Lyons checked their handiwork, there was no need for mercy shots.

LIKE THE GREEN SHIRTS, Rico wasn't afraid to cut his losses and run. He was hanging back, well out of the line of fire, when he saw the last two of his soldiers fall to the black-clad commandos. Not wanting to share their fate, he turned and started to run back down the mountain. This wasn't the first time he had ever had to run, and he was confident that he would be able to find a place to hole up until he could make it back to the van.

The problem was that he wasn't in downtown Bogotá or Cartagena or anywhere else that had a warren of back streets and alleys for him to duck into and hide. He was in an ancient forest of North America, and this was definitely not his element.

BOLAN CAUGHT a flash of movement from the corner of his eye and saw a chubby Colombian trying to make his break. He didn't know who the man was, but from his civilian clothes, he knew *what* he was. He was a cartel killer, and the Executioner wanted him. The others had only been foot soldiers. This guy was their brain.

"Their leader is bugging out," he radioed to Lyons. "I'm going after him."

"We'll finish cleaning up here," the Able Team leader sent back, "and find Rondell."

RICO DIDN'T HEAR the man behind him because he was making too much noise crashing through the brush himself, and his mind was on more than just making his escape. He didn't know who those black-clad fighters were, but he had a feeling they were the same men he had seen at the Santa Barbara warehouse. Back then, he had thought that they were a rival drug gang, but he no longer was so sure of that. From the way they had operated, they had to be some kind of special strike force, probably federal agents.

Whoever they were, they weren't men to be underestimated. Once more he had lost his gunmen to them, but he knew that he could explain that to the board and still keep his head. After all, he was Cali's most famous shooter. What he would have a more difficult time explaining was that he had failed to carry out his assignment.

Rico was so busy making up his excuse for not having killed Rondell that he thought he had tripped when he stumbled and fell. An instant later, he heard the shot and felt the pain in his right leg.

The Uzi had fallen out of his reach, but when he started crawling for it, a black-clad man stepped between him and the subgun. The assault rifle in the man's hands was aimed at his head.

"Where do you think you're going?" Bolan asked casually.

Rico looked up and saw his death. He scrambled for the Uzi, but it was no contest.

A single 5.56 mm round drilled him between the eyes, went on to explode his brain, then blew half of it out the back of his skull.

Bolan reached down and pulled Rico's wallet and papers out of his inside jacket pocket. The name in the Panamanian passport didn't mean anything to him, but Kurtzman could possibly use the information for his data bank.

Flicking his assault rifle back on safe, Bolan started back up the mountain.

LYONS AND THE REST of Able Team quickly searched the camp for Benson Rondell. They didn't expect he'd be on the firing line with a weapon in his hand—that wasn't his style—but they checked each of the bodies anyway. When they came up with a blank, they started to search the cluster of buildings under the trees.

The fourth building they checked was the small cabin the two fugitives had been hiding in. When Lyons thought he saw movement inside, he kicked the door open and stood back to the side. "Come out with your hands up!" he shouted.

A man slowly walked out, his arms held high. "Don't shoot," he pleaded. "I'm not armed."

Lyons held his H&K on his prisoner and reached out to frisk him, but pulled back. "Well, look what we have here," he said when he recognized his captive. "It's Mr. Benson Rondell himself. How about that?"

"But you're not from Colombia!" Rondell said when he heard Lyons's pure California accent.

Lyons raised one eyebrow. "They're all dead. We're from the—"

His face showing horror, Rondell spun and took off running.

When Lyons started after him, Schwarz yelled. "No, Ironman! He's mine!"

Lyons backed off and let his partner have him.

Slinging his rifle behind his back, Schwarz sprinted after the fugitive, carried along on a red-hot tide of rage that seemed to lift him above ordinary life. A diving tackle drove Schwarz's shoulder into the small of Rondell's back and slammed the man facefirst into the wet ground.

Keeping his face pressed into the dirt, Schwarz repeatedly slammed stunning blows to his ribs and kidneys. The sound of Rondell grunting from the blows was soothing to his enraged senses. He had waited a long time to hear it. A final twist of the neck rendered the businessman silent and immobile.

Picking up his CAR-15, he turned and went to rejoin the others. His work was done here. Sylvia Bowes would still be in a wheelchair for the rest of her life, but he was powerless to change that. However, Benson Rondell had been taken down.

"DO YOU FEEL satisfied now, Gadgets?" Bolan asked as he approached him.

Schwarz looked up. "Yes," he said, "the bastard deserved it."

That was one thing that separated Able Team and the rest of the Stony Man warriors from the other men who did the dirty work of protecting civilization from the barbarians within. The police, federal authorities and courts all did their very best, but they were hampered by the constraints of law. The Stony Man team was a law unto itself, and the men had been at their business for so long that they had no more illusions about the sanctity of life and all the other liberal, legal mumbo jumbo that had little application in the real world.

There was sanctity of life, true. But one had to earn it by being a good human and a good citizen. When you crossed the line into barbarous behavior, you forfeited your right to basic human respect and deserved whatever justice came your way. Benson Rondell had crossed over that line and then some. From the minute he had gotten into bed with the Cali cartel, his life had ceased being sacred and he had become just another predator.

"What are you going to tell Sylvia Bowes about this?" Bolan asked.

"Nothing," Schwarz said after a moment's pause. "I'll just let her read about it in the papers. It'll be better that way." He nodded his head. "I don't think that she's ever going to want to hear from me again. Particularly not now that I've taken her icon down big time."

"I think there may be something we can do for her, though," Bolan said. "Lyons found a stash of cash in the cabin—several hundred thousand dollars. I can see that she gets it to take care of her medical expenses."

"That would help," Schwarz said. "I don't know a lot about her financial situation—insurance and all that. But I do know that she didn't have a hell of a lot of money, and she has a daughter to raise."

"Shall we get it on the road?" Lyons asked. "Unless we want to try to explain all this to various state and federal authorities." His hand swept out to include the carnage of the forest camp behind him. "We really ought to be as far from here as we can before the National Guard sweep starts."

"I'm ready," Schwarz said. "I've had enough of this place."

DEEP IN THE WOODS, Hector Garcia was still putting as much distance between himself and the camp as he could before any search parties were sent out to look for him. In his haste he had eyes only for the well-traveled game trail he was following, with time for an occasional glance back behind him.

The cougar watching him approach was a young female, and her body was telling her to feed the two cubs growing in her belly. The smell of hot blood on the cool mountain air was fueling her hunger, but the gunshots had agitated her. She knew what gunshots meant, but her fear only sharpened her hunger.

Suddenly the smell of fresh blood was closer. A human was coming down the trail directly under the tree she crouched in. Over the smell of blood on the man, she could also smell his fear. That fear would make him careless.

Garcia never saw the cougar as she dropped from the tree onto his back. He staggered under her weight and fell on his face, too stunned to understand what had happened until he felt her razor sharp teeth scrape along the bones of his skull before finding a purchase at his nape. Her jaws snapped tight, and he felt no more.

After giving the limp corpse a final shake to break its neck, the cougar crouched to feed. Her deep, raspy purr sounded to warn other predators to stay away as her teeth ripped through Garcia's clothing to get to his warm flesh. After she had assuaged her raging hunger, she would carry what was left into her tree to eat later.

CHAPTER THIRTY-ONE

Stony Man Farm

Barbara Price arched her back sharply to relieve the tension, then let her head go forward. She had just gotten off the phone to Mack Bolan, and it was over. Now she could relax. A quick call to the computer center would instruct Kurtzman to key in the dump program, and everything could return to what passed for normal around the Farm. A few keystrokes and all the evidence of a very successful mission would be gone. Benson Rondell had paid for his crimes, and several cartel gunmen had been thrown in as a bonus.

Not bad for a mission that never happened.

She smiled as she stood. Rather than call, she would take the good news down to the team herself. Good news needed to be shared.

Washington, D.C.

HAL BROGNOLA SMILED as he quickly read through the report that had just been faxed from the

Northern California office of the DEA. The sun was shining outside his Justice Department office, and it was a beautiful day. The report was about a joint DEA and National Guard marijuana sweep of the woods north east of Crescent City, which revealed the aftermath of a big drug-gang shootout in the forest camp of the Green Earth Movement.

For a drug-war battle, the body count had been high and included both Green Earthers and as yet unidentified men in camouflaged uniforms who were thought to be members of a Colombian drug gang. Some of the surviving environmentalists spoke of a third group of men who had appeared in the middle of the battle, four or five of them dressed in black combat suits who had killed everyone they came across. But since none of the bodies left behind were clothed in black, the DEA was discounting that story as being a case of mistaken identity in the heat of battle.

The biggest discovery, though, was that the body of the missing, and believed dead, Sunflash CEO and would-be California governor, Benson Rondell. He had sustained a beating, and had apparently died of his injuries.

The DEA interpretation of the carnage they had found was that the Green Earthers and Rondell had had a falling out and that they were the ones who had beaten him. The press would go crazy when they got their hands on this information, and Brognola would see to it that it was released immediately. Benson Rondell, the darling of the radical tree huggers and antinuke freaks, had survived the mysterious explosion of his Baja Sunflash facility only to turn up dead in the aftermath of a drug-gang battle, apparently killed by the Green Earthers he had so fervently supported.

All told, it had been a good raid even if few drugs had been found beyond a small pot farm of a hundred or so plants. And, of course, Brognola thought, Bolan and Able Team hadn't left any trace of their presence behind. He hadn't known that Schwarz had it in him to beat a man to death, but that wasn't to say that Benson Rondell hadn't deserved it.

For the time being, all was well. There was absolutely no connection between this incident and the Stony Man team. And with any luck, it would stay that way.

Gold Eagle Presents
a special three-book in-line continuity

Beginning in June 1996, Gold Eagle brings you another action-packed three-book in-line continuity, The Red Dragon Trilogy.

In THE EXECUTIONER #210—FIRE LASH, book 1 of The Red Dragon Trilogy, The Triads and the Red Chinese have struck a bargain sealed in hell—with a quick payoff in escalating terrorism, murder and heroin traffic. But long-range plans include a conspiracy of terrifying global consequence.

Don't miss the first book of this new trilogy, available in June at your favorite retail outlet.

Or order your copy now by sending your name, address, zip or postal code, along with a check or money order (please do not send cash) for $3.75 for each book ordered ($4.25 in Canada), plus 75¢ postage and handling ($1.00 in Canada), payable to Gold Eagle Books, to:

In the U.S.	In Canada
Gold Eagle Books	Gold Eagle Books
3010 Walden Ave.	P.O. Box 636
P.O. Box 9077	Fort Erie, Ontario
Buffalo, NY 14269-9077	L2A 5X3

Please specify book title with your order.
Canadian residents add applicable federal and provincial taxes.

DT96-1

Bolan's war against an old enemy is dogged by strange alliances—and even the Vatican is not exempt

DON PENDLETON's

MACK BOLAN.

DEAD CENTER

An old-line mafioso's death and the abduction of the capo's young great-grandson launches a turf war that reaches all the way to Romania's most powerful crime boss. Mack Bolan steps in, and his baptism by hellfire won't stop until he's exacted the highest price from those who wage war against the innocent. Justice is coming, and it will be relentless....

Available in June at your favorite retail outlet or order your copy now by sending your name, address, zip or postal code, along with a check or money order (please do not send cash) for $5.99 ($6.50 in Canada) for each book ordered, plus 75¢ postage and handling ($1.00 in Canada), payable to Gold Eagle Books, to:

In the U.S.	In Canada
Gold Eagle Books	Gold Eagle Books
3010 Walden Avenue	P.O. Box 636
P.O. Box 9077	Fort Erie, Ontario
Buffalo, NY 14269-9077	L2A 5X3

Please specify book title with your order.
Canadian residents add applicable federal and provincial taxes.

SB48

An old enemy develops a deadly
new train of thought...

THE Destroyer

#103 Engines of Destruction

Created by
WARREN MURPHY
and RICHARD SAPIR

The railways have become the fastest—and surest—way
to get from here to eternity. Could the repeated sightings
of a ghostly samurai swordsman be linked to the
high-speed derailments that are strewing the rails with
headless victims? Suspecting the train terror is merely a
decoy, Remo Williams and Master Chiun become
involved, only to find they may literally lose their heads
over an old enemy.

Available in July at your favorite retail outlet or order your copy now by sending your
name, address, zip or postal code, along with a check or money order (please do not
send cash) for $5.50 ($6.50 in Canada) for each book ordered, plus 75¢ postage and
handling ($1.00 in Canada), payable to Gold Eagle Books, to:

In the U.S.

Gold Eagle Books
3010 Walden Ave.
P.O. Box 9077
Buffalo, NY 14269-9077

In Canada

Gold Eagle Books
P.O. Box 636
Fort Erie, Ontario
L2A 5X3

GOLD EAGLE®

DEST103

Please specify book title with your order.
Canadian residents add applicable federal and provincial taxes.

Don't miss out on the action in these titles featuring THE EXECUTIONER®, ABLE TEAM® and PHOENIX FORCE®!

SuperBolan

#61444	SHOCK TACTIC	$4.99 U.S.	☐
		$5.50 CAN.	☐
#61445	SHOWDOWN	$4.99 U.S.	☐
		$5.50 CAN.	☐
#61446	PRECISSION KILL	$4.99 U.S.	☐
		$5.50 CAN.	☐
#61447	JUNGLE LAW	$4.99 U.S.	☐
		$5.50 CAN.	☐

Stony Man™

#61901	VORTEX	$4.99 U.S.	☐
		$5.50 CAN.	☐
#61903	NUCLEAR NIGHTMAR	$4.99 U.S.	☐
		$5.50 CAN.	☐
#61904	TERMS OF SURVIVAL	$4.99 U.S.	☐
		$5.50 CAN.	☐
#61905	SATAN'S THRUST	$4.99 U.S.	☐
		$5.50 CAN.	☐

(limited quantities available on certain titles)

TOTAL AMOUNT	$
POSTAGE & HANDLING	$
($1.00 for one book, 50¢ for each additional)	
APPLICABLE TAXES*	$_____
TOTAL PAYABLE	$_____
(check or money order—please do not send cash)	

To order, complete this form and send it, along with a check or money order for the total above, payable to Gold Eagle Books, to: **In the U.S.:** 3010 Walden Avenue, P.O. Box 9077, Buffalo, NY 14269-9077; **In Canada:** P.O. Box 636, Fort Erie, Ontario, L2A 5X3.

Name:_____

Address:_____ City:_____

State/Prov.:_____ Zip/Postal Code:_____

*New York residents remit applicable sales taxes.
 Canadian residents remit applicable GST and provincial taxes.

GEBACK14A